FIREFIGHTER GRIFFIN

FIRE & RESCUE SHIFTERS 3

ZOE CHANT

Copyright Zoe Chant 2016
All Rights Reserved

✾ Created with Vellum

The Fire & Rescue Shifters series

Firefighter Dragon
Firefighter Pegasus
Firefighter Griffin
Firefighter Sea Dragon
The Master Shark's Mate
Firefighter Unicorn

Fire & Rescue Shifters Collection 1
(contains Firefighter Dragon, Firefighter Pegasus, and Firefighter Griffin)

All books in the Fire & Rescue Shifters series are standalone romances, each focusing on a new couple, with no cliff-hangers. They can be read in any order. However, characters from previous books reappear in later stories, so reading in series order is recommended for maximum enjoyment!

CHAPTER 1

"Ma'am, is it your son or your cat who's stuck up the tree?"

The words snagged Griffin MacCormick's attention as he finished handling another grueling emergency call. Pulling his headset off his ears, he cocked an eyebrow at his colleague at the opposite desk. Kevin caught his eye, and rolled his own, mouthing "time waster" as he pointed at his own headset.

"Let me see if I understand you, ma'am," Kevin said to the caller, his tone leaden with jaded weariness. "Your cat, who is like a son to you, is stuck up a tree. And you would like the fire services to send a very expensive emergency vehicle, which is meant for *emergencies*, to attend to your…pussy."

Having just spent an heart-pounding thirty minutes on the phone with a traumatized caller who was pinned under two tons of smashed, burning car, Griff could sympathize with his colleague's irritation with the nuisance call, if not his unprofessionalism in letting sarcasm seep into his tone. The East Sussex Fire and Rescue Service was stretched thin just handling the major crises. The seaside city of Brighton might not be particularly large—especially not compared to London—but it was one of the most vibrant cities in England, attracting millions of visitors with its quirky, alternative culture. And lots of drunk, excited tourists looking for a wild night out meant a *lot* of work for fire dispatchers like Griff.

Especially when quite a few of those drunk, excited tourists were dragons.

Not that Kevin, or indeed any of Griff's other colleagues in the control room, knew *that* little secret about their city.

Kevin raised his eyes to the heavens—or at least, to the control room ceiling—as if praying for the strength to deal with the idiot in his earpiece. "I'm sorry, ma'am, I'm not sure I'm following you. Are you trying to tell me that your son turned *into* a cat and shot up a tree?"

Now *that* got Griff's full attention. Bringing up the office chat utility on his PC, he typed to Kevin, *Want me to take over?*

Kevin shook his head at him across the desk. *Nah,* he typed back, one handed. *Nearly got rid of her.*

"Yes, ma'am, that does sound unbelievable," Kevin said into his headset. "I see. Yes, ma'am, this *was* a bad idea. You do that. In future, please don't call the fire department unless you actually have an emergency. Goodbye." Pushing his headset down around his neck, he stretched with a groan. "Goddamn bored housewives. I swear that one must have been high on her kid's meds or something."

"Sounded like an interesting call," Griff observed mildly.

"Nah, just another time waster." With a push of one foot, Kevin propelled his office chair backwards to the whiteboard in the corner, where the dispatch team kept a highly unofficial tally of handled calls. Picking up the blue pen, he added another tick to his row with a sarcastic flourish. "At this rate, I may beat even your record for prank callers this week. I swear you're some sort of magnet for the weirdos."

Griff smiled, privately amused. *You have no idea.*

"Hey, what was your call just now? Another crazy?" Kevin waved the blue pen. "Or a real one?"

"Big traffic pile-up," Griff said. "I sent Alpha Team to sort it out. They've got it under control."

"Alpha Team's the one you used to work with, right?" Kevin said idly, swapping the blue pen for a red one in order to put a tick next to Griff's name. "Back when you were a firefighter, I mean."

All Griff's muscles tensed, sending a jolt of pain through his bad leg.

"Yes," he said, in a flat tone that he hoped made it clear he didn't want to discuss his previous profession.

Unfortunately, Kevin's career as a dispatcher had given him the sensitivity of a rhinoceros. "Must have been interesting. Is Alpha Team really as good as people say they are?"

"No." The corner of Griff's mouth twisted wryly. "They're better."

A little pang went through his chest as he thought of how Alpha Team would be working together right now, saving lives with their unique combination of shifter skills. Fire Commander Ash calmly controlling the flames while John Doe called down the rain to quench them…Chase sensing where victims were trapped, fireproof Dai charging headlong into the blaze to pull people out to where Hugh would be waiting to heal them…

Griff shook his head, forcibly dispelling the memories. *I did my part*, he tried to tell himself. *I took the call. I got them there, told them what to expect. I'm still part of the team.*

His inner eagle stretched its wings proudly. *We watch and guide. We fly high, scouting out the way. Our role is essential.*

His lion snarled in bitter denial, baring its fangs at the eagle. *We cower in the den when we should be defending our pride! And it is all your fault!*

Griff mentally thrust his two inner animals apart before they could start fighting yet again. He could still feel the eagle's fury and the lion's rage as he wrestled them down to the back of his mind. The effort of keeping the two beasts separated and subdued gave him a splitting headache…but that was better than the alternative.

He became aware that Kevin was giving him an odd look. "I'm sorry, what were you saying?"

"Just that you must have some good tales to tell." Kevin eyed him for a second. "You know, you really should see a doctor about the way you keep spacing out, Griff. What if it happens on a call?"

"It won't." Griff said firmly. "And actually, I am."

For all the good it does me.

"I'm just saying, you have to be fit for the job," Kevin blundered on, displaying his usual tact and compassion. "We dispatchers may not need muscles like the front line meatheads, but that doesn't mean we have room for cripples. If your condition interferes-"

"I *said*, it won't." Holding Kevin's stare, Griff let him see just a hint of the lion behind his own golden eyes.

Kevin flinched back in his chair, and Griff immediately felt ashamed of himself for letting his temper get the better of him. Unleashing his dominance on a regular human—not to mention a colleague—was not only rude, but unsporting. Even another shifter would have a hard time standing up to an alpha lion's commanding nature.

He called his lion back, allowing his eagle to rise again. His vision sharpened, letting him see Kevin's slight nervous sweat and increased pulse rate.

"I can do my job," Griff said, more gently. "You have my word on that. Speaking of the job…did that caller just now really say that her son had turned into a cat?"

"Uh, yeah." Kevin scooted his chair back to the desk, though Griff noticed he stayed a few inches further away from him than previously. "That was a new one on me. You'd think she'd pick something more plausible, if she was hoping to score a hot firefighter booty call."

Before Griff could quiz him further, a light on Kevin's phone started to flash. "Damn it, I was just about to grab a fresh coffee…" Kevin let out a heart-felt, long-suffering sigh, pulling his headset back into place and jabbing a button. "East Sussex Fire and Rescue Service. Where is your emergency?"

Griff took a sip of his own stone-cold coffee, thinking. With a swift glance around to make sure no one else in the control room was watching, he pulled up the record for the call Kevin had just handled. He wasn't technically supposed to be able to do that, but there was no hiding passwords from his shifter senses. When his eagle was ascendent, he could tell what someone was typing from ten feet away, just from the sound of their fingers hitting the keys.

Kevin might have the compassion of a rock when it came to callers who he thought were time wasters, but he did at least follow proper procedures. He'd dutifully logged the woman's name and address, before starting to ask questions about the nature of her "emergency."

Griff logged out of Kevin's account and sat back, frowning at the screen. A few more clicks showed him that Alpha Team was still fully occupied with the car crash he'd sent them to. Just as well, really. He could just picture Fire Commander Ash's expression if Griff tried to send him—the one and only Phoenix, and quite possibly the most powerful shifter in Europe—to go rescue a cat from a tree.

Even if the cat is really just a scared little boy...

Problem was, all the shifters in the East Sussex Fire and Rescue Service were in Alpha Team. And while Griff knew a lot of the other shifters in Brighton, it would be a gross breach of confidentiality to share a caller's address with someone not in the service.

We must go, his eagle said, unexpectedly. *She called. We must answer.*

The bird is right, his lion rumbled. *Go, now, quickly!*

Griff blinked. He could count on the fingers of one hand the number of times in his life that his two inner beasts had ever been in agreement on *anything*.

"And another 'dumb kids setting fire to leaves in the park' for me," Kevin grumbled, flipping up his headset's microphone. "Only six more bloody hours to go. Griff, not that I'm complaining about the amount of unpaid overtime you put in, but you do realize your shift ended over an hour ago, right? Isn't it time you went home?"

Letting out his breath, Griff pushed himself to his feet. "Apparently not," he murmured.

CHAPTER 2

As a single mom, Hayley Parker was used to having to handle every parenting challenge on her own. With no one else to back her up, she'd always tried to make sure she was prepared for anything. She'd borrowed and read every child development book in the library. She'd scoured the internet for tips on raising a son without a father figure present. She'd even spent uncounted hours plowing through her old college textbooks, making sure she was up-to-date on Early Years literacy and numeracy educational strategies.

None of these, however, had given her any hint on what to do when your five-year-old unexpectedly turns into a lion cub and shoots up a tree.

"Okay, Danny," she said, fighting to keep her voice calm and steady. It was important to always give the appearance of being in control, she knew, so that your child could feel safe and secure. No doubt that was doubly important if your child happened to be a lion. Animals could smell weakness, couldn't they?

Oh God, this can't be happening.

"The fire trucks are a little busy right now," she continued, clasping her hands together so that he wouldn't be able to see how they were shaking. "So we're just gonna get you down ourselves, okay? Now, do you think you could scoot back a little? Just move one foot...um, one paw at a time. Nice and slow."

She could just make out Danny's round, fuzzy face, peering down at her through the leaves. He let out another tiny, desperate mew, and her heart broke. She knew, just *knew*, that he was calling for her. Calling for Mommy to rescue him.

"Don't worry, baby," she forced out past the tightness in her throat. Her heart hammered at every slight sway of the branch. "You just keep your, your nice sharp claws locked tight in that tree, okay? That's my big, brave boy."

Hayley fought down a hysterical giggle. *Big brave lion.*

My boy turned into a lion.

Please, I'd really like to wake up now.

She looked wildly around their small backyard, hoping against hope that some inspiration would strike. Her gaze snagged on her discarded cellphone, and she flinched. Her ears still burned from the blistering sarcasm of the emergency call handler.

How was I supposed to know that the fire services in England don't deal with cats stuck in trees?

To be fair, Hayley wasn't sure they did back home in California, either, but with her baby thirty feet off the ground and squalling in panic, her first reflex had been to dial emergency. Thank Heaven the dispatcher *hadn't* believed her. Halfway through the call, she'd had a sudden horrific vision of what could happen if firefighters turned up and discovered that she really did have a lion cub in her backyard. Her little boy could have ended up in the local pound. Or the zoo.

Or some secret government lab, being sliced apart to discover how he transforms...

Hayley jammed a fist in her mouth, stifling the whimper that wanted to rise in her throat. She hadn't had the luxury of weakness since Danny's father had left, in the early days of her pregnancy. She definitely couldn't afford to fall apart now.

Taking a deep breath, she straightened her spine. *Just another unexpected crisis,* she told herself firmly. *Pull it together, Hayley. Danny needs you. It's not like anyone else is going to come to the rescue.*

"Hello?" called a strange male voice, and Hayley nearly leapt out of her skin. Someone knocked on the side gate, which led from the backyard to the narrow alleyway that ran alongside her house. "Ms. Parker? Sorry, didn't mean to scare you, but you weren't answering the doorbell."

Of all the times for a door-to-door salesman or charity collector to come round!

"Th-this isn't a good time!" Hayley yelled over her shoulder.

"I know it isn't," the unseen man said. His warm, rolling Scottish accent wrapped round her like a comforter on a cold night. "That's why I'm here. My name's Griffin MacCormick, and I work for the East Sussex Fire and Rescue Service. May I come in?"

Oh no, they sent a firefighter after all!

Visions of secret labs and gleaming scalpels flashed through Hayley's mind. "No! I...it was just a prank call. I'm really sorry. I swear I'll never do it again."

Danny had gone very still and quiet up in the tree, his small round ears pricked toward the sound of the man's voice. She prayed he wouldn't meow again.

"It wasn't a prank call," the man said, his voice a deep, reassuring rumble. "Your son turned into a lion cub, and now he's up a tree and can't get down."

He knows Danny's a lion? But he can't see the tree from the alleyway. And I said 'cat' to the fire dispatcher.

"How...?" Hayley whispered to herself.

"I can smell him," the man added, as if he'd heard her.

...He can smell him?

"Please let me help you," the man said gently. "I know what's happening. I promise you, everything will be fine."

Biting her lip, Hayley sidled over to the gate. She hesitated a moment with her hand on the latch, but somehow she had an instinctive, gut feeling that she could trust this stranger. Before she could have second thoughts, she opened the gate.

"That's it," he said as the gate swung open. "Now-"

The man stopped dead as his eyes met hers.

"Oh," he breathed, very softly. *"Oh."*

Hayley found herself equally stunned, mesmerized by his astonishing eyes. They were gold—not just a pale hazel or light brown, but a deep, rich, true gold. They glowed like fall sunlight through yellow maple leaves. Caught by those eyes, she felt as if she'd turned to glass, as if that penetrating gaze could see straight through to the secret, innermost center of her heart.

The man blinked, breaking the moment. "Well now," he said, his voice a little rougher than before, as if he too had been shaken to the core. "That explains a few things. But I think we ought to see to the wee lad first, aye?"

Hayley pulled herself together, worry swamping the odd moment of recognition. "He's- he's up in the chestnut tree. This way, Mr... MacCormick, was it?"

"Call me Griff." The man brushed past her, and Hayley's pulse thudded at the momentary touch of his arm against hers. "Ah, I see him, the poor brave lad. We'll have him down in a tick, just you see."

Okay, maybe I am *still dreaming. Even firefighters don't look like that. At least, not outside of Vegas shows.*

Griff must have stood at least six foot two, and gave the impression of being at least that wide across the shoulders as well. His stocky, muscular build made Hayley feel dwarfed in comparison, even though she was hardly tiny herself. He moved with the easy confidence of a powerful man comfortable in his own skin, but there was the slightest hint of a limp to his stride as he headed for the chestnut tree. Hayley couldn't help staring at his broad back as she followed, hypnotized by the sheer strength he exuded. She wondered if she would even be able to span his chest with her arms...

How can I even be noticing his chest at a time like this? Danny's in danger! Hayley mentally slapped herself. *I'm a mom, I shouldn't be thinking of anything other than my baby!*

Stopping under the tree, Griff tilted his head up, his thick mane of blond hair brushing his broad shoulders. "Well, you've certainly got yourself good and stuck there, hey laddie?"

Danny had cowered low to the branch, leaving only a dangling, tufted tail visible. A faint, scared mew drifted down.

Griff put his hands in his pockets, looking completely unperturbed by the situation. "Funny thing," he said conversationally to Hayley. "My littlest sister did exactly the same, first time *she* shifted."

"Your...*sister?*" Hayley echoed faintly. A pair of wide yellow eyes appeared over the edge of the branch, thirty feet up.

"Aye." Griff chuckled fondly. "Near panicked the rest of us, see, 'cause Da had told us all to take good care of the baby while he was out. My other sisters shifted in reflex to climb up after her, and then *they* got stuck too. So there they were, four little lions in a tree, all too scared to shift back. And only me left with human hands and wits, trying to figure out how to get them all down before our da came home." Laughter lines creased around his amber eyes as he smiled at her. "At least there's only one cub to rescue this time."

His sisters...can turn into lions too? It's not just Danny?

The thought echoed around Hayley's stunned mind as Griff pulled off his shoes and socks. Planting his bare feet in the grass, he looked consideringly up at the overhanging tree branches for a second. Then, he leapt.

Hayley gasped as Griff caught hold of a branch at least twelve feet above the ground. His biceps strained against his shirt sleeves as he pulled himself up.

He can't be a regular human being, she thought, watching in amazement as Griff climbed the tree, using his arms more than his legs. *Does he turn into a lion too?*

"Ah, and that's as high as I can go," Griff said, edging out along a branch that dipped and creaked under his weight. Danny was still out of reach, on a thinner branch higher up. "So the next bit has to be up to you, laddie. What's your name?"

"He's-" Hayley started, but Griff waved her to silence. He kept his head cocked, his eyes fixed calmly on Danny's.

Hayley didn't hear Danny make even the faintest meow, but Griff nodded in satisfaction. "Pleased to meet you, Danny," he said. "Now,

I'm going to use human words to talk to you, but you can talk back just like that, aye?"

A pause, then Griff laughed. "I suppose I do talk funny to you. 'Aye' means 'yes,' or 'okay,' where I come from." He laughed again. "No, not Africa. We have lions in Scotland too, believe it or no. Now, Danny, I can't come to you, so you're going to have to come to me. Your claws can't grip so well going backwards, so I need you to turn yourself around."

Hayley's heart leapt into her mouth as the leaves rustled. "*Be careful*, Danny!" she called out.

"No, don't look at your ma down there, Danny. You keep your eyes on me," Griff said, a hint of steel entering his warm voice. "Hayley, we're doing just fine up here. Could do without any distractions, please."

Hayley bit her knuckles, in agony as Danny gingerly edged around until he was facing Griff. Under Griff's patient coaching, he inched along the swaying branch toward the firefighter. Bits of bark pattered around Hayley like fine rain, dislodged by Danny's scrabbling claws.

Danny stopped directly above Griff, but even from the ground Hayley could tell that he was still a couple of feet out of the firefighter's reach. She wanted to call up to ask what Griff was going to do, but didn't dare distract them again.

"That's good, Danny," Griff said. Carefully, he drew up himself up to a crouching position on the branch. His bare toes gripped the bark.

He can't possibly be considering standing up *on that twig?*

If he had been, he thought better of it. With a grimace, Griff dropped back down to straddle the branch again, rubbing absently at his left knee. "Danny," he said, very calmly. "In a moment, I'm going to ask you to do one more thing. But you're going to have to trust me."

Danny made a small, suspicious noise, half-mew and half-growl.

"No, I'm not going to tell you yet. When I do, I need you to let your lion instincts take over, without your human mind getting in the way. I promise you, I won't ask anything you can't do. But for this to work, you need to trust me as your alpha. Your lion will understand what that means."

"What are you doing?" Hayley called, unable to help herself. She couldn't control the tremble in her voice.

Griff made a short, quelling gesture at her with one hand, never taking his eyes off Danny's. "In return, I'll give you this promise. I will keep you safe. I will protect you. I will never, ever let anything harm you, not while I have breath in my lungs and blood in my body. That's what an alpha lion does for his pride, and that's my promise to you. So. Will you trust me?"

Danny had gone absolutely motionless, not even the tip of his tail twitching. Hayley couldn't move herself, every muscle frozen rigid by a combination of terror and Griff's magnetic, compelling charisma.

"Good," Griff said softly. He locked his legs around the tree branch, freeing his hands. "Then as your alpha, I tell you...*jump.*"

Hayley shrieked, her hands flying to her mouth—but Danny was already in mid-air. Without a second of hesitation, he leaped straight into Griff's outstretched arms.

"There now!" Griff hugged the cub close, rubbing his cheek against the side of Danny's muzzle in an oddly feline gesture. "Well done, laddie, well done."

Hayley rushed forward, hands stretching futilely upward. "Danny!"

"Let's get you down to your ma," Griff said to Danny, tucking him under one arm. The little cub snuggled against him, leaning trustingly against Griff's broad chest.

Hayley hopped impatiently on tiptoe as Griff descended, a little more awkwardly than he'd gone up. Danny leaped for her before Griff had even reached the ground, claws tearing the firefighter's shirt in his desperate haste to get to her. Hayley staggered as he barreled into her, nearly knocked off-balance by his surprising weight. She clung to him, tears finally spilling down her face at the feel of his little heartbeat hammering against her chest.

"Steady now, lass." Griff's strong hands grabbed her shoulders, supporting her as her knees threatened to give way. "It's all right. Everything's fine now."

"No, it's not! My baby's a lion!" Hayley's relief gave way to a familiar sense of parental outrage at her offspring for having made her worry in the first place. She thrust Danny out at arm's length, glaring at him sternly. "Daniel Jamie Parker, you turn back human right this instant!"

Danny scrunched up his face, his little lion nose wrinkling. He let out a plaintive, distressed squeak.

Behind her, Griff chuckled ruefully. "It'll be easier if you aren't shaking him like a wee rag doll, Hayley." Gently but firmly, he pushed down on her shoulders, guiding her to sit on the grass. "Let's all just catch our breaths for a moment, hey?"

Hayley cuddled Danny on her lap, stroking his soft, spotted fur. "He *will* go back to normal, won't he?" she asked anxiously.

"Oh, aye," Griff said, and the tightness in Hayley's chest eased at the utter certainty in his tone. "Just needs a little prompting, that's all." He knelt down next to her, the slightest hint of a wince flickering across his rugged face as he bent his left knee.

"Are you okay?" Hayley asked. She'd noticed him favoring that leg earlier.

"Ah, just been a while since I climbed a tree," Griff said lightly, though she was oddly certain that he was in a lot more pain than he was letting on. "What about you? How are you feeling?"

"Me?" Hayley said blankly. It had been so long since anyone had been concerned about how *she* was doing, she almost couldn't process the question. "That doesn't matter. What-"

"Yes, it does," Griff interrupted, with a hint of that strange, commanding tone he'd used on Danny. "You've had quite a shock. I have a friend who's a paramedic. Would you like me to call him? Don't worry, he's a shifter too."

"Shifter?" Hayley latched onto the strange word. "Is that what…" She gestured helplessly at both him and Danny.

"Yes, we're called shifters. There are quite a few of us, all different kinds, even just here in Brighton. And you still haven't answered my question."

Hayley shook her head, trying to grasp the idea of a whole secret world of people who turned into animals. "What question?"

"How. Are. *You?*" Griff spaced out each word clearly, poking her shoulder lightly in emphasis.

His touch burned on her skin even through two layers of clothing. She was abruptly, acutely aware of how close he was. His intense eyes were focused on her with absolute attention. She could lose herself in those molten, golden depths...

He's concerned about me because it's his job. And here I am staring at him slack-jawed like some hormonal teenager.

"Fine. I'm fine," she stammered, her cheeks heating with embarrassment. Under the pretext of moving Danny to a more comfortable position in her lap, she scooted a little further away from Griff. "I don't need any help. Thank you."

Fortunately, the firefighter hadn't seemed to notice her inappropriate reaction to his proximity. Then again, looking the way he did, he was probably used to women losing their train of thought in his presence. "You just let me know if you change your mind about that, all right? In the meantime, let's see about getting Danny back into his usual shape. Come here, laddie."

Danny was normally very shy with everyone except Hayley, but he climbed down from her lap without hesitation. He stumbled a little over his outsized paws as he padded over to Griff, his big yellow eyes fixed trustingly on the firefighter's deep gold ones.

The corner of Griff's mouth quirked upward in amusement. "Still a wee bit stuck, hey?"

Plopping his fuzzy hindquarters down on the grass, Danny let out a woeful yowl of agreement.

Griff cocked his head to one side, looking down at Danny thoughtfully for a moment. "You must be hungry after your adventure. My sisters always told me that shifting takes a lot of energy, usually while stealing food off my plate. Bet you could do with a snack."

Danny's ears perked up. He let out a hopeful whine.

"That sounds perfect," Griff agreed. He turned to Hayley. "Danny seems to think there might be a few chocolate chip cookies lurking in your kitchen. Mind if we have some?"

"How do you do that?" Hayley asked as she got to her feet. "Know what he's saying, I mean."

"Most shifters of the same general type can talk to each other telepathically," Griff said, following her into the house. Danny bounced along at his heels. "Wolves to wolves, bears to bears, cats to cats, mythic to mythic…you get the idea. Makes it easier to communicate."

So he is a lion shifter.

And there are wolves, and bears, and…what did he say?

"Mythic?" she repeated, frowning. "What on earth is a mythic?"

"Oh, you know, uncanny beasties," Griff said casually, as if there was anything *normal* about people turning into lions and bears and whatnot. "Dragons, pegasi, wyverns, that sort of thing."

Hayley stopped dead in the doorway of the kitchen, turning to stare at him. "*Dragons?!*"

"Don't worry. They aren't like the fiery monsters from stories." Griff hesitated for a fraction of a second. "Mostly. But two of my best friends are dragon shifters, and they're some of the kindest, bravest, most honorable men I've ever known. I'll introduce you to them, and you'll soon see that there's nothing to be afraid of."

Danny let out an impressed squeak, staring up at Griff in wide-eyed amazement.

"Aye, real dragons just like in Mike the Knight," Griff said with a laugh. "One of them *is* a knight, actually. A proper one, on a quest and all. I'm sure he'd love to tell you all about it."

Hayley wasn't sure *she* was quite so excited at the prospect of meeting an honest-to-God dragon, but her heart did give an odd little skip at Griff's casual assumption that she'd be meeting his friends.

Don't read too much into it, she told herself sternly as she stretched on tiptoe to fetch the cookie jar down from its hiding place on top of the fridge. *He probably just wants us to meet other shifters so that Danny can learn to control his powers from them. Griff can't possibly want to spend his free time tutoring a stranger's kid.*

"Mm, these do smell good," Griff said, taking a cookie from the jar. "Homemade, too. My favorite." He took a big, appreciative bite.

Danny jumped up, dancing on his hind legs as he pawed at the cookie jar.

Griff shot him a stern look that made the cub instantly sink back against the floor. "Time for a lesson in lion manners. Alpha always tastes first, then mothers, then other grown-ups, and finally cubs. That's how you show respect for other members of the pride. You want one, Hayley?"

Hayley was dying to ask him what he was up to, but held her tongue, trusting that he knew what he was doing. She shook her head.

Danny whined, his rump wiggling in barely-restrained anticipation.

"Good lad. Yes, it's your turn." Griff flipped a cookie to him.

Danny leaped to catch it, his jaws closing with a *crunch*. Then he froze, a comical look of dismay spreading across his face. He went cross-eyed as if trying to see into his own muzzle.

"Eh? No, don't think so." Griff ate the rest of his cookie with every sign of enjoyment. "Tastes fine to me."

Danny's jaws worked a few times. He spat out the soggy cookie, glaring at it with an air of wounded betrayal.

"Of course, lion tongues do work a bit different to human ones," Griff added casually, as though this thought had only just occurred to him. "Can't taste sweet things. Now, real lions don't know what they're missing out on. But you know how that cookie *should* taste…"

Griff trailed off, a broad grin spreading across his face as the air around Danny shimmered.

"*Danny!*" Hayley snatched her son up, overcome with joy. She anxiously patted him, searching for any remaining hint of whiskers or fur, but he was entirely back to normal.

And also, stark naked.

He wriggled impatiently out of her embrace. "Can I have a cookie now, Mommy?"

"You can have a cookie." Nearly faint with relief, Hayley shoved the whole jar into his hands. "You can have *all* the cookies." Leaving Danny to his feast, she threw her arms around Griff. "Oh, thank you, thank you, *thank you!*"

She felt his hard chest rise with a sharp intake of breath. His strong heartbeat thudded against her cheek, his pulse as fast as if he was running a marathon, though he was absolutely motionless under her hands.

"Oh!" Hayley jerked back as if he was literally rather than just metaphorically hot. She was certain she was blushing from throat to forehead. "I-I'm so sorry, I just-"

"My pleasure," he interrupted her, his voice a deep, rough rumble. He cleared his throat, glancing down at Danny. "Lad, where'd you leave your clothes?"

"Out in the yard," Danny mumbled, spraying crumbs.

"Are you clever enough to get dressed all by yourself?" Danny nodded in response. "Off you go then, before you have any more of those. I need to have a word with your ma here."

Griff waited until Danny's bare backside had scampered out of sight before he spoke again. "Dad not around, I take it?" he murmured, very quietly.

Hayley couldn't help flinching a little at the old wound. "No," she said, trying to sound casual. "He left before Danny was born. He… wasn't ready for kids. Why?"

"Shifting is hereditary. You get the occasional surprise quirk of genetics, but as a rule, shifter kids have at least one shifter parent." He cocked an eyebrow at her in unspoken query.

"Well, he certainly didn't get it from my side of the family! But Reiner never said anything…" Hayley gasped, one hand creeping up to cover her mouth. "Oh. *Ljonsson.*"

"Dad's last name, I take it?" Griff grimaced. "I'd say that's pretty conclusive, then. Reiner Ljonsson. Hmm. He never told you what he really was? Not even after you became pregnant?"

Hayley shook her head. "He didn't want anything to do with it."

A low, savage growl ripped from Griff's throat, making Hayley jump. "Sorry," he said, looking a little embarrassed. "Lion got the better of me. We're rather big on family. Or at least, we're *supposed* to be. Do you have a way of getting in contact with him?"

"I can try," Hayley said dubiously. "But I don't think-"

"Mr. Griff, Mr. Griff!" Hayley cut herself off as Danny ran back into the room, his face aglow with triumph. He had his T-shirt on inside-out and his pants back-to-front, but he proudly presented himself for Griff's inspection. "I did it all on my own!"

Griff's eyes gleamed with suppressed laughter, but his face was solemn as he looked the boy up and down. "So you did, Danny. Well done."

"Mr. Griff?" Danny sidled closer, his expression turning a little shy as he peered up at the towering firefighter. "Can…can I see *your* lion?"

Something flashed across Griff's face, too quickly for Hayley to read. "I'm afraid not, lad," he said, ruffling Danny's blond hair. "I have to go, unfortunately. No doubt it's nearly your teatime, and I'm expected back home for my supper too."

Danny's hopeful face fell. Hayley felt just as disappointed, which was completely silly of her. She couldn't help glancing at Griff's left hand. He wasn't wearing a wedding band, but lots of men didn't.

Of course a man like him would already have a partner. It's no business of mine, anyway. Why should it make any difference to me whether or not Griff has someone waiting for him at home?

The corner of Griff's mouth twitched up. "Just a friend who needed a place to stay," he said, as if her entire embarrassing train of thought had been printed on her forehead. "He's still a bit new to the entire concept of cooking, so it's best if I'm home before he can get into too much trouble. It's unfortunate for a firefighter to set his own kitchen alight, after all. But I'd like to come and see you both again soon, if that's all right with you?"

"O-of course," Hayley stuttered, trying not to let her expression betray the ridiculous leap of her heart at the prospect. "I'd love that. I, I mean, I have a lot of questions I'd love to ask you."

"Here's my number," Griff said, handing her a card. "If Danny shifts again, or you're worried about anything—anything *at all*—give me a call. I promise I'll come straight away."

"Can you come back tomorrow?" Danny asked eagerly, bouncing along in their wake as she led Griff toward the front door. "Mommy, can he? *Pleeeeeease?* Can he stay for dinner? Can we-"

"Danny!" Hayley covered his mouth before he could propose that 'Mr. Griff' stayed for a sleepover. "I'm sure Mr. Griff is very busy."

"Actually, I'd love to come round tomorrow," Griff said, crooking a smile at her that made her go weak at the knees. "If it wouldn't be too much of an imposition."

"Oh, no!" Hayley bit her lip. "I mean, after everything you've done, the least I can do is cook you dinner. We didn't have any plans for tomorrow, anyway."

"In that case, why don't I come by around four?" Griff winked at Danny. "That gives us plenty of time to play before supper, eh lad?" He looked back at Hayley, his expression turning more serious. "And maybe after Danny's in bed, you and me could have a wee chat about…a few things."

Was she imagining the heat burning in the depths of those golden eyes?

Don't be a fool. Of course you are. You're a tired, stressed single mom wearing no makeup and a sweater with spaghetti sauce stains. No man—especially not one like him—*is going to look at you* that *way.*

Hayley tore herself away from Griff's charismatic gaze, feeling the blush creep up her cheeks again. "Yes," she said faintly. "I'd…like that."

"Bye Mr. Griff!" Danny waved vigorously after the firefighter's retreating back. "See you tomorrow!" He heaved a great, heartfelt sigh. "Mommy, I wish he could stay *now*."

Hayley smoothed his hair. "I know, baby. I know."

So do I.

CHAPTER 3

Not even the deep, throbbing pain in Griff's overstrained knee could dim his elation as he drove home.

My mate! I've found my mate!

He'd never dared to hope that he even had one true mate, like a normal shifter. He'd lain awake many nights, worrying that his two inner animals would mean that he had two separate mates—one for the lion, and one for the eagle. What would happen if his lion fiercely pulled him towards one woman, while his eagle equally fiercely pulled him away…?

In his darkest moments, he'd even hoped that he didn't have a mate at all. A lifetime alone would be better than having his mind torn apart by his bitterly jealous beasts.

But as it turned out, his fears had been groundless. For once, his lion and his eagle were in perfect agreement. Hayley was their mate.

Hayley was *his* mate.

And what a mate! Griff sighed in longing at the thought of her sweet round face and glorious curves. With her son in her arms, she'd made a perfect picture of lush, fertile womanhood, the sort that stirred a man's deepest, most primal urges to claim and protect. Soft yet strong, tender yet fierce...so fearless in defense of her child, yet so sweetly shy when it came to herself.

Griff had tried his best to stay professional, but a man would have to be deaf, blind, and dead not to react to her plump hips and full breasts. Yet she'd blushed and looked away when she'd noticed his appreciation of her stunning body. Not in the manner of a woman who didn't want such attention, but in the way of one who didn't believe anyone could possibly look at *her* with desire. She'd reacted like someone who'd become so used to thinking of herself as a mother, she'd forgotten that she was a woman as well.

Griff burned to show Hayley that side of herself again. To trace slow, lingering kisses across her softly rounded shoulders, to cup those bounteous breasts, his thumbs teasing their erect tips, while–

Griff shook his head, forcing such thoughts away as the ache in his groin threatened to rival the pain in his bad leg. He made himself concentrate on the road until his cock grudgingly subsided. Much as he wanted with every fiber of his being to sweep Hayley off her feet and into his bed, he couldn't.

We can, corrected his eagle, impatiently. *She desires us, as much as we desire her. It is obvious from the way she looked at us. Simply clasp her close, and–*

Stupid bird! interrupted his lion. *She is a mother! Her first thought must always be for her cub. We must approach her slowly, carefully, in order to win her trust. We must show her that we mean him no harm.*

His eagle clicked its beak in irritation. *Of course we will treasure her fledgling as our own. She would never even doubt that, were it not for you, accursed cat. She is only wary because she can sense your savage, feline nature–*

ENOUGH! Griff roared inwardly, shoving between his two inner beasts as they went for each other's throats. Searing pain split his skull, the lion's claws and the eagle's talons raking across his soul.

Gritting his teeth, he swerved to the side of the road, ignoring the annoyed honks of the cars behind at the abrupt maneuver. Safely parked, he focused on his breathing, trying to subdue the feral energy racing through his veins. His hands clenched on the steering wheel. His skin felt hot and tight, stretched wrongly over his bones...

Not here! Not now!

In desperation, he focused on the memory of Hayley's shy smile and warm brown eyes. He concentrated on how she made him feel, the things his inner beasts agreed on—the bone-deep need to protect her, the fire she sparked in his blood, the hunger for her touch and the all-consuming longing to be with her.

It worked. Griff scarcely dared to believe it, but his inner beasts subsided, drawn back into disgruntled alignment by the overpowering instincts inspired by their mate. His lion still paced and snarled, and his eagle still mantled its wings and stared at the cat balefully, but at least he was no longer being tugged apart by them.

Griff let out a shaky breath, painfully straightening his cramped fingers. He rolled his shoulders and neck, loosening his knotted muscles before he restarted the car. He pulled back onto the road, relieved and astonished that he'd managed to avoid a full-blown fight between his inner beasts.

If this is the effect Hayley has on them, maybe I should tell her what she means to me. Sooner rather than later.

You won't, though, growled his lion, right at the back of his mind. *You agree with me.*

Griff made a noncommittal noise, unwilling to provoke his eagle by siding too clearly with his lion. But it was true. Regardless of his own personal situation, he had to think of what was best for Hayley. And what was best for Danny.

From Danny's endearing, heartbreaking eagerness to win his approval, Griff was certain that the little boy had never had any sort of father figure at all. Hayley and Danny had been alone together, just the two of them, for a very long time. But for all their obvious devotion to each other, there was still a secret, hungry hole in Danny's soul. Griff longed to fill that gap, nearly as much as he ached to heal the matching wound in Hayley's heart.

But if he did...he'd just be setting them up for future pain.

Griff set his shoulders, pushing his impossible longings into a small, sealed box in the back of his mind. He refused to let the bleak reality of the future spoil the joy of meeting his mate. He made himself concentrate on what he *could* do for his mate and her son, rather than what he wanted to do.

I can be Hayley's friend. I can be Danny's alpha. I can help them, support them, take care of them...at least for now. That's more than I ever thought I'd have. It'll have to be enough.

His eagle and his lion both bristled in protest, but he overruled their objections. Hayley and Danny had already been abandoned once. He was not going to break both their hearts again.

That would make him no better than Hayley's ex.

If we ever meet this Reiner Ljonsson, his lion and his eagle snarled as one, *we shall make him suffer for what he did to our mate and her son.*

"At least we all agree on something," Griff said under his breath as he pulled into his driveway.

His house was just a small semi-detached—*a duplex, Hayley would call it* he thought with a small smile, remembering her American accent—but it was still *his*. His nest, his den. Both his lion and his eagle relaxed at being back in their own territory again.

He could tell immediately that John was already home, both from the enormous pair of muddy boots neatly lined up on the doormat and the sound of humming emanating from the kitchen. Not that most people would have recognized the peculiar sound as "humming." It sounded more like a couple of bassoons having a relaxed, friendly conversation, with occasional comments from a passing humpback whale.

Griff grinned, recognizing the melody. John was cleaning.

A lot of people hummed as they did chores. With John, you could tell exactly which chores he was doing...though not what *else* he was doing at the same time.

Griff poked his head round the door of the kitchen. Sure enough, John was washing the dishes. This meant that he was standing at the stove, stirring a pan and humming, while six feet behind him a floating sphere of water industriously rinsed off a stack of plates in the sink.

Living with a sea dragon certainly had its moments.

"You know," Griff observed, leaning on the door frame, "we *do* have a dishwasher."

The dishwasher barks. John's deep mental voice echoed in Griff's head. The enormous shifter didn't pause in his humming, maintaining his control over the water washing the plates. *Its tone of voice is too abrupt. I prefer to ask the water politely.*

Griff had never worked out why his two inner animals meant mythic shifters like John could communicate with him telepathically, but it came in handy. Of course, it would be even handier if he could actually talk back that way, but he couldn't even send to fellow lions or eagles. If he tried, his own mental voice just came out as a doubled, incoherent jumble, rather like two people screaming in an echoing cavern.

"Well, I guess I should be grateful you at least approve of the shower's manners," he said out loud. "Not to mention the toilet. Sorry I'm late, I got delayed. Everything under control?"

I believe I have correctly burned the fish this time. John's telepathic tone radiated pleased accomplishment. *It is now black on the outside, but the machine in the ceiling has not yet screeched at me. This is the way humans like it, yes?*

"Smells done to me." Well past done, actually, but at least John hadn't set off the smoke detector. By John's standards, that counted as a culinary triumph. Griff clapped him on the shoulder, having to reach up to do so. "Good job. It all looks delicious."

This was a *slight* exaggeration, but Griff liked to be encouraging. And John *had* come on amazingly, considering he'd only a year ago he'd been new to the entire idea of "cooking." Or indeed, "fire." Most of John's people spent their entire life in sea dragon form, at the bottom of the ocean. Much of life on land was utterly foreign to them.

Like the difference between "fruit" and "vegetables," Griff thought to himself, eying a simmering pot of what smelled suspiciously like a mixture of diced carrot and apple. *Oh well, at least it has to be more edible than that banana-tuna casserole last week.*

"Did you have a good day?" he asked John, starting to set the table.

"What happened with that car crash I sent you all to?"

The water churning in the sink fell still as John stopped humming. His broad forehead creased thoughtfully. "I had an argument with a cloud," he said out loud in his deep, oddly-accented voice. "The water had travelled unusually far, and wished to continue its journey. But I managed to persuade it to taste English soil in the end."

Griff suppressed a wry chuckle. Even though John had lived with him for almost a year now, the sea dragon's unique perspective could still surprise him. "I meant, what happened with the trapped people," he said patiently.

"Oh." John shook his head, the golden charms braided into his long, indigo hair chiming against each other with the motion. "Yes, we saved them all. There were no serious injuries. We vanquished the flames easily, without great challenge to our skills."

John sounded mildly disappointed. Then again, he'd once told Griff that the literal translation of "have a nice day" in his own language was "may you be sorely tested by worthy opponents," which said an awful lot about sea dragons.

"And you?" John asked, a little hesitantly. "Did you too have a… productive day?"

John's stoic, controlled face was hard to read for most people, but to Griff's eagle eyes the sea dragon was an open book. John was worrying about making him feel inferior. After all, John's job involved charging into infernos and saving lives. Griff, on the other hand, got to answer telephones.

Griff appreciated John's tact, but for once it wasn't a sore point to compare their respective days. "Fairly good," Griff said casually. "Handled calls. Dispatched fire teams. Found my mate."

John's spatula clattered to the ground as the sea dragon spun round to stare at him.

"Funny story, actually." Griff dropped his pretend-casual tone, unable to contain his broad grin. "She called the fire department, and–"

That was as far as he got, before all the air whooshed out of his lungs as John seized him in a bone-cracking hug. An excited torrent of sound like an entire woodwind section having a party burst from the sea dragon shifter's mouth.

"Language, John!" Griff managed to gasp out. He was hardly a small man himself, but John had still managed to lift him clean off the ground. "I don't speak sea dragon, remember?"

John reluctantly switched back to English, though he still half-sang his words with excitement. "But this is wonderful news, oath-brother! Where is she? Why have you not brought her back with you? Oh!" He abruptly set Griff back on his feet, a slight shadow crossing his overjoyed expression. "Of course, I understand. I will pack my hoard immediately."

"Whoa!" Griff caught John's arm as the sea dragon turned for the door. "Hang on, what do you mean, pack? You don't have to go anywhere."

John cocked his head to one side. "Surely you wish privacy for you and your mate?"

Griff's blood heated at the thought of Hayley in his house. In his *bed*. "Oh, you have no idea how much I *do* wish that." He couldn't help letting out a wistful sigh. "Unfortunately, it's not likely to be necessary."

John blinked at him. "But...she is your mate. Will she not be moving into your territory immediately?"

"I'm flattered that you think I work that fast. But no, of course not. I only met her this afternoon, John!"

"But she is your mate," John repeated, sounding utterly baffled. "You have met each other. How can you not have mated already?"

It was Griff's turn to blink. "Is that how it works for your people? You meet your mate and immediately, ah, mate?"

"Of course," John said, looking just as dumbfounded as Griff felt. "This is *not* how it works for you land shifters?"

"Alas, no. Though I have to admit, your way sounds rather appealing." Griff shook his head, a little envious of John. It must be nice, living in a culture where everyone knew about shifters and their mates, and understood the overwhelming power of that instant bond. "It's more complicated for us."

John shook his head too. "Humans. I shall never understand you. Are you certain you are not over-thinking this, my oath-brother? As I recall, Dai and Chase consummated their respective unions with appropriate speed when they met *their* mates."

Griff shot him a level look. "Are you seriously suggesting I take *Chase* as a role model in matters of romance? Or even Dai?" The two other firefighters were still the subject of much good-natured teasing down at the pub for the ridiculous problems they had caused themselves in the course of pursuing their mates.

The corner of John's mouth curled up. "Hmm. Perhaps not. But still-"

"There are complications," Griff interrupted him. His overworked knee was threatening to give way at last. He sat down in one of the kitchen chairs, stretching his bad leg out with a wince. "Not all of them on my side, too. She has a wee son, you see."

"So she is fertile," John said approvingly as he turned to retrieve the forgotten plates of food. Sliding one in front of Griff, he sat down too, having some difficulty fitting his seven-foot tall bulk behind the table. "Why would that be a complication? Unless—*oh*." His expression changed abruptly to understanding sorrow. "Oh, oath-brother. The father still lives? She is still joined?"

"Married, you mean? No, he's not in the picture." Griff suppressed a growl at the thought of Danny's worthless so-called father. *If I ever get my hands on him...*

John was back to looking lost again. "Then…is she still in mourning for her former partner? A noble sentiment, of course, but surely joining with her one true mate would ease that grief?"

Griff leaned his elbows on the table, contemplating the sea dragon shifter across it. "This is one of those times when we're having two entirely separate conversations, isn't it?"

John let out a rich, rueful laugh. "It would indeed appear we have swum into a cultural misunderstanding." He picked up his fork. "Perhaps you should explain how human women can apparently have children without fathers."

"Do you really not have absent fathers, among your people?" At

John's blank look, Griff clarified, "When a man doesn't want to take responsibility for his child, so refuses to have anything to do with them."

John spat out a brief, low phrase in his own language, a rippling arpeggio of shock and disgust. "No," he said, switching back to English. "We do not have that."

"Huh. Wish I could breathe underwater. Your people sound increasingly appealing the more I learn about them. In any case, that's what's happened to Hayley. The bastard got her pregnant and then abandoned her. He was a shifter, too. So's the boy, as it turns out."

John shook his head, slowly. "I begin to see what you mean by complications. So your mate is now wary of men, having been cruelly betrayed by this, this…" He made a noise somewhat like an angry tuba, apparently not finding an insult strong enough in English. "Well. Do not be disheartened, oath-brother. I shall compose a great ballad of your noble deeds! When she hears it, her heart will swim straight into your hands."

Good God, he's actually serious. "Ah, that's a…very generous offer. But unnecessary. I'm not going to mate with her. Not now. Not ever."

John stared at him as if he'd announced his intention to give up breathing. "You cannot possibly mean that, oath-brother. You will rip your soul into pieces if you try to deny your mate."

"Better me than her." He gestured at his leg. "Think about it, John. What have I got to offer?"

John's blue eyes darkened as he took Griff's meaning. "I think that you can offer her the same that any man can offer his mate," he said forcefully, each word ringing out like the clarion call of a hunting horn. "All of you, unstintingly, for as long as your heart still beats."

"You great soft numpty," Griff said affectionately. "No wonder you can charm the very rain down out of the sky. But I'm not a cloud, and you can't sway me with pretty words. I'm not going to mate her." He held up a hand as John opened his mouth, forestalling him. "And that's final."

We shall see, whispered his eagle…and Griff shivered at the cold threat in its voice.

CHAPTER 4

To: <u>reiner.ljonsson@nordindustri.dk</u>
From: lionmom192@gmail.com
Subject: Hereditary medical condition

Reiner,

I've just discovered that Danny has a rare condition which I think he must have got from you. I don't want to say too much in an email, but let's just say it's a big shift in our lives. If you know what I'm talking about, then please get in touch.

I promise, I don't want money or anything. I just want information.

Hayley paused with her fingers on the keyboard of her laptop, uncertain how to sign off. "Regards" seemed rather impersonal, considering that Reiner was the father of her child. On the other hand, "Best wishes" would be a flat-out lie. She couldn't wish him well, not when Danny always stared wistfully at other kids playing with their dads in the park.

With a sigh, she just typed "Hayley," and hit Send. The message whooshed cheerfully off into the ether, leaving her staring at her empty inbox. She'd thought it best to create a throwaway account, just in case he had her regular email address blocked.

He'll probably just delete it as soon as he realizes who it's from, anyway.

When Danny had been a newborn, she'd bombarded every phone number and email address she had for Reiner with cute baby photos. She couldn't understand how anyone—let alone his own father—could look at those big brown eyes and adorable chubby cheeks and remain stone-hearted. But Reiner had never responded, not even to demand that she stop bothering him.

She still sent Reiner a photo and update every month, but it was more out of habit than any real hope that he would finally get in contact. Hayley had a sinking feeling that this time wouldn't be any different.

At least Danny has Griff to help him.

Hayley bit her lip, glancing across the living room to where Danny was sprawled belly-down on the carpet, hypnotized by the TV. It was the first time all day he stopped chattering about "Mr. Griff," asking if it was four o'clock yet and whether they could go to the playground and if they could be lions together for Halloween. He was clearly completely star-struck by the firefighter.

Not that Hayley could blame him...

I can't let him get too attached. Griff seems nice, but he won't be around forever. I have to make sure Danny understands that. Better a little disappointment now than heartbreak later.

She knew *that* from experience.

"Mommy?" Danny said thoughtfully, his bare feet kicking in the air. On the TV screen, Mike the Knight and his dragon friends were puzzling over how to clear a giant tree trunk that had fallen across a path. "How big do you think Mr. Griff's lion is?"

"I don't know, honey." She had a sudden mortifying image of Danny innocently asking Griff how big he was, and she hastily added, "It probably wouldn't be polite to ask."

"I bet he's *real* big," Danny said in deep satisfaction. "I bet he could just knock that tree trunk away with his paw, bam! I bet he's big enough to beat anything. Even Darth Vader. Mommy, do you think Mr. Griff could beat the Hulk?"

Oh dear. "Baby, turn off the TV and come here a second, okay?"

Danny made a *what-have-I-done-now* face, but dutifully climbed onto her lap. Hayley hugged him tight, still treasuring the feel of his human-shaped little body. "I know you like Mr. Griff a lot, and I'm sure he likes you too, but you need to remember that he's a big, grown-up man. He won't want you clinging to him and following him everywhere. He needs to spend time with his own grown-up friends."

Danny squirmed a little in her arms. "But I'm going to play with his dragon friends too. Mr. Griff said so."

"Yes, but…sometimes people make promises that it turns out they can't keep. You mustn't be disappointed if it doesn't work out."

"Mr. Griff won't break a promise to me," Danny said matter-of-factly, with perfect confidence. "Never ever. He's my alpha."

Where on earth had he learned *that*? Now that she thought back, she remembered Griff using the same word. She knew that wolf packs had alphas, but lions? "What do you mean, honey? What's an alpha?"

"Mr. Griff is," Danny said, with the serene circular logic of a five-year-old. "When will he be here, Mommy?"

All thoughts of mysterious alphas fled from Hayley's mind as she glanced at the time. "Oh, fudge! In ten minutes!"

Danny yelped with excitement, bouncing off her lap as she hastily stood. "Is that now?"

"It might as well be now!" Hayley cursed herself for spending too long agonizing over the email to Reiner. She'd meant to have a shower, she'd meant to change-! "Honey, can you be a good boy and sit quietly watching TV while Mommy tries to make herself pretty?"

"Silly Mommy." Danny rolled his eyes at her as plopped down in front of the TV again. "You're always pretty."

Hayley wasted precious seconds scooping him up for another hug —he squawked in protest, wriggling to keep the screen in sight— before dashing upstairs to her bedroom. She struggled out of the torn jeans and old, comfy sweatshirt she'd been wearing, flinging them carelessly across the bed. She'd worked hard all day to try to get the rest of the house cleaner than its usual state of child-induced chaos, but at least this was one room she didn't have to worry about keeping tidy. It wasn't like Griff was going to be seeing it.

More's the pity.

Squashing the stray, ridiculous thought, she rifled through her clothes in the vain hope of finding something that was both respectable and attractive. Unfortunately, the only things she owned that weren't stained and tired were her work clothes, and as an elementary school teacher she didn't exactly dress to impress.

I'm being silly, Hayley told herself firmly as she grabbed a pair of black leggings that weren't too badly bobbled. *It's not a date. Griff isn't going to care what I'm wearing. He's coming to see Danny, not me.*

Nonetheless, she pulled on a low-cut floral tunic that she normally wore over a vest. She hesitated for a second, trying to decide whether it was *too* revealing, but it was too late to change her mind. She barely had enough time to drag a brush through her limp, mousy-brown hair and dab a bit of concealer on the dark circles under her eyes before—on the stroke of four o'clock—the doorbell rang.

"Mommymommymommymommy!" Danny shrieked at the top of his lungs. So much for not getting too attached. His feet thundered toward the front door. "He's here, Mr. Griff is here!"

Hayley charged for the stairs. "Danny, don't open the-!"

Too late. She got to the landing just in time to see an overenthusiastic lion cub hit Griff squarely in the chest.

"Whoa!" Griff hastily stepped inside, making sure his broad bulk shielded Danny from view of the road. He kicked the front door shut behind him. "Good thing I wasn't the mailman. Oof! I hope you haven't been pouncing on your ma like this."

"Danny!" Mortified, Hayley ran down the stairs. "Get down off Mr. Griff this second!"

"Ah, it's fine." Still hugging Danny in one powerful arm, Griff handed her a stunning bouquet of soft pink roses, smiling. "Just glad I didn't drop these."

Hayley stared at the bouquet in her hands, momentarily speechless. No one had *ever* given her flowers before. Not even Reiner. "What- why-?"

It's just a hostess present. British people are very strict on good manners, remember?

"I mean, th-thank you!" Hayley stuttered, certain that her cheeks were as pink as the roses. How had he known that exact shade was her favorite color? Just co-incidence? "Please, come in. Um, come in more, that is. Danny, get *down!* And, and human!"

Danny reluctantly dropped to the ground, but seemed a bit lost as to how to obey the latter command. He shuffled his paws, then mewed plaintively at Griff.

The firefighter shook his head. "You got yourself into that shape, you can get yourself out of it, laddie. Think about it." He looked back at Hayley. "This the first time he's shifted since yesterday?"

Hayley nodded. "Thankfully. How often is he likely to do this?"

"Let's just say you may want to keep the lad in big old T-shirts and the like for a while," Griff said ruefully, tilting his head to indicate the abandoned, shredded remnants of Danny's best—and only—dress shirt and pants. As I recall, most of my sisters spent the best part of a year running around in the cheapest, baggiest shifts my da and ma could find."

"He's going to shift every time he gets too excited?" Hayley gasped, her hand flying to her mouth as a horrible thought struck her. "Oh God, he's got kindergarten tomorrow. And I'm a teacher, I can't just phone in sick and keep him at home."

"Ah now, don't fret." Griff put one hand on her shoulder, his golden eyes warm and understanding. His strong fingers squeezed lightly, reassuringly, before letting go again. "That's one of the reasons I'm here. I can make sure he doesn't go lion in public." He hesitated, his expression turning more serious. "I need to ask your permission, though. I should really have done so earlier, up in the tree, but things were…a mite hectic."

She could still feel the brief touch of Griff's hand, a heat that raced through her blood. It ignited a long-forgotten fire deep in her belly, so distracting that she very nearly lost track of what he was saying. "Um…what?"

The man must think I'm an absolute idiot. *Pull it together, Hayley!*

Griff absently flexed his hand, and Hayley had the sudden mad thought that maybe the brief contact had made *his* skin tingle too. "I'm an alpha lion, ye ken." His accent had thickened, the Scottish brogue becoming more pronounced. He cleared his throat. "That means I can influence Danny's lion. With your permission."

"Oh." She scrabbled to try to appear like a competent, functioning adult and not a hormone-addled woman who hadn't had sex for five years. "So…an alpha's like an authority figure? You can set a rule he has to follow?"

Danny put his ears back. He hissed.

"Only with *your* permission too, lad," Griff told him. His tone turned deadly serious, with an odd undertone of compelling power that made chills run down Hayley's spine. "A true alpha never forces anyone. You remember that, always."

Danny seemed a little overcome by Griff's sudden intensity. He hunkered down a little, his body language reminding Hayley of a worried dog, and whined.

"Baby, this is real important," Hayley said, crouching down so she could look Danny straight in the eyes. "If someone saw you turn into a lion, they might get scared and want to lock you up in a zoo. You wouldn't like that, would you?"

Danny's eyes widened. He cuddled up against her, pressing his broad fuzzy head against her side as if trying to hide.

"I'd never let anyone take you away," Hayley said hastily, worried that she'd scared him *too* much. "But it would be best if no one finds out what you are. Like…like you're a superhero, okay? And you have to protect your secret identity."

He peeped out from under her arm, and Griff chuckled as if at something Danny had just said. "Aye, just like Spiderman. Danny, all I want to do is to make sure your lion has to check with you before taking over. You'll still be able to shift when you want. I'll just make sure you don't shift when you *don't* want. That sound okay to you and your lion?"

Danny's ears flicked back and forth a few times, as if he was considering it. Then he padded trustingly over to Griff and bumped his forehead against the firefighter's legs.

Griff's golden eyes went very soft as he looked down at the cub. "Aye," he said, a catch in his voice. "And I'll try to be worthy of that." A little stiffly, he knelt. "Now, we're going to do some practicing today to improve your control, and I'm going to get my lion to give yours a little nudge sometimes to help. But first, I want to see if you can shift back all by yourself. You remember how we did it yesterday?"

"I made more cookies," Hayley volunteered. Unable to sleep, she'd spent hours last night baking after Danny was in bed. "Just in case."

"That was good thinking," Griff said, and she felt ridiculously pleased at having won his approval. "But let's see if he can do it without one actually in front of him first. Danny? Just focus on the memory of the cookie."

The lion cub's nose wrinkled up in concentration…and a moment later, a stark naked Danny leaped into Griff's arms again. "I did it Mr. Griff! I did it all by myself!"

"*Danny!*" Hayley could have died of embarrassment. She seized Danny round the waist, whirling around to try to hide him from sight. "Get your clothes back on right this second!"

Behind her, Griff burst out laughing. "Ah, don't fash yourself, Hayley. We shifters are pretty relaxed when it comes to nudity."

Nonetheless, he politely looked away as Hayley wrestled the protesting Danny back into underwear. "But *Mommy*, I don't wanna get dressed! I wanna be lions with Mr. Griff!"

"He does have a point," Griff said to Hayley, apologetically. "Some types of shifter can include their clothes in their transformations, but lions can't. And I do need to work on his shifting with him. If you want, I could wear a blindfold?"

"No, no!" Griff didn't set off any of Hayley's finely-honed protective mama bear instincts. "I don't think you're a pervert or anything like that. I mean, you've already done more in one day to help than-"

Hayley cut herself off. She never, ever disparaged Reiner in front of Danny. Even though Danny had never met him, he was still his father. "Anyway. If you're fine with the, um, lack of clothes thing, then so am I."

If Griff was going to teach Danny about shifting, would *he* have to...? Hayley blushed furiously, unable to suppress a tantalizing mental image of the firefighter stripping off.

Griff cast her a rather amused look, a sly gleam in his golden eyes. "Don't worry. I'll keep my clothes on."

Hayley wanted to sink through the floor. Was she *that* easy to read?

"But Mr. Griff!" Danny tugged on Griff's hand, looking worried. "If you keep your clothes on, you'll rip them up and then *your* mommy will be mad."

An oddly wistful half-smile tugged at Griff's mouth. "Quite the reverse, actually." He raked his hand through his blond hair as if he was debating something with himself, then sighed. "Might as well get this out of the way. Hayley, do you mind if we all go out into the garden?"

"Um, okay." Hayley's heartbeat sped up a little, with a mixture of curiosity and apprehension. It was one thing having Danny turn into a cute little cub, but Griff would be a full-size male lion...

She led the way through the house and out the back. One of the reasons Hayley had picked this house in the first place was because it was right at the end of the street, with a secure backyard that wasn't overlooked by any of the neighbors. One thing she still hadn't gotten used to about England compared to California was how *small* everything was. Brits might have mastered the art of pretending they couldn't see straight into each other's properties, but Hayley preferred actual privacy.

Not that she'd ever imagined she'd be using it for *this*.

Griff cast a swift, appraising look around at the high fences, nodding in approval. "This is good. We're safe to practice here. But... Danny, I'm afraid I can't show you my lion."

Danny's bottom lip stuck out. "Why not?"

"Danny," Hayley said warningly, though she too couldn't help feeling a bit disappointed. "It's not polite to pry. I'm sure Mr. Griff has his reasons."

"I do." Griff sat down on the grass, his left leg stretched out awkwardly. "And the reason is that I can't." He tapped the center of his chest. "My lion's stuck in here, Danny. He can't get out, not the way that yours can."

"But I thought you were a shifter," Hayley blurted out.

Griff's eyes flashed a brilliant, animal yellow. "I *am* a shifter," he said, and the hairs on the back of Hayley's neck rose at the deep, primal growl in his voice. "I am more of a shifter than most. I am descended from generations of shifters, on both sides of my family. I have inner beasts, I can touch minds with the beasts of others, I have a m—" He paused fractionally, as if thinking better of whatever he'd been about to say. "I have all the instincts of a shifter. In every way that matters, *I am a shifter.*"

"I know you're a shifter," Danny said, sounding more puzzled than alarmed by Griff's sudden outburst. "Who says you aren't? They're mean. And stupid."

The barely-leashed savagery vanished from Griff's eyes. "Ah, you're a kind wee soul," he said gruffly. "Kinder than most." He glanced up at Hayley, looking a little ashamed of himself. "Sorry. Sore spot. I'm sure you can imagine what other shifters think of one of their own who can't actually shift."

Her heart went out to him—even if it *was* still beating hard at the shock of the sudden reveal of the raw, feral strength hidden behind Griff's amiable exterior. "I'm so sorry. I didn't know. That must be…very hard."

"But *why* can't you shift?" Danny demanded, with a little kid's unabashed rudeness. "You've got a lion, just like me. I know you have."

Griff beckoned to him. "Come here, lad. Let's see if I can show you." He cupped the back of Danny's neck, drawing him close until their faces were only inches apart.

Danny stared deep into Griff's eyes for a long moment. Then he jerked back, his own widening. "*That's* not a lion."

"No, it isn't." Griff released him, letting out a long breath. "That's my eagle. My father's a lion shifter. But my mother's an eagle shifter. That's why they named me Griffin—that's a pretend beastie that's half-lion, half-eagle, ye ken." His mouth quirked wryly. "My ma and da don't have a lot in common, but they do share the same *terrible* sense of humor."

"So if your father's a lion and your mother's an eagle, that makes you...both?" Hayley asked.

"And neither." Griff grimaced. "My eagle and my lion don't get along. Shifters aren't supposed to have two animals. Neither one of mine will let the other one fully take control. If I try to shift, I end up tugged back and forth between lion and eagle."

That sounds awful. And painful. From the way both Griff and Danny talked, Hayley had the impression that a shifter's animal was like some sort of alter-ego in their minds. The idea of having *two* of them, at odds with each other...it was amazing Griff wasn't completely schizophrenic.

"But you said your sisters are lions," Danny said, his forehead wrinkling. "How come they only got one animal, but you got two?"

"Because...ah, just unlucky, I suppose," Griff said. Hayley wondered what he'd decided not to say. "Four of my sisters are lions, and three are eagles, and I'm neither fish nor fowl nor good red herring."

Danny frowned. "If you can't shift, how're you gonna teach me?"

"Lad, I've studied more theory than most shifters even know exists. I taught all seven of my sisters how to control their animals." Griff poked Danny playfully in the ribs, making him giggle. "And *they* taught me how to wrestle a lion. Come on. Shift back, and I'll show you."

CHAPTER 5

Griff hummed to himself as he put the last few plates in Hayley's dishwasher. He smiled a little, thinking of John as he started the machine. He hoped the sea dragon shifter was having a good time at the pub right now.

On a Sunday evening, they always went down to the Full Moon together to meet up with the other firefighters on Alpha Team. It was usually both the high point of Griff's week, and a kick in the teeth. Alpha Team were his closest friends...but also a reminder of everything he'd lost.

The afternoon with Danny and Hayley had been similarly bittersweet. Romping with the cub should have been pure joy, but even as they chased and wrestled and pounced, Griff had kept being stabbed by pangs of wistful longing. Much as he tried to just enjoy the moment and be content with what he could have, he couldn't help wanting more. He couldn't help wanting to *be* more.

Danny should be *his* cub.

He is our cub, his lion said matter-of-factly. *He is the son of our mate. That makes him ours.*

Griff shook his head, muzzling the lion again. No matter what his inner beasts whispered, he had to remember that he had no claim to Danny.

Or to Hayley.

He heard her close Danny's bedroom door upstairs, and the soft tread of her feet down the stairs. Realizing she was heading toward the front room, he quietly called out, "I'm in here, Hayley."

She retraced her steps, coming into the kitchen. "Oh!" she exclaimed, her jaw dropping as she took in the tidy work surfaces and sparkling floor. "You cleaned?"

"I could hardly sit on my backside while you were busy putting the bairn to bed, now could I?" Griff dried his hands on a tea towel, smiling at her.

He was simultaneously pleased by her evident astonishment…and infuriated. Not at Hayley, but at the previous men in her life. If they'd treated her right, she wouldn't have looked so flabbergasted that a man might do a few chores.

Reiner Ljonsson, you have a lot *to answer for.*

He nodded at the two glasses he'd placed on the kitchen table, an inch of deep amber liquid from his hip flask at the bottom of each. "Do you drink whisky? It's from my clan's distillery. I'll warn you now, though, my ma's spirits aren't for the faint-hearted. It's a bit like swallowing the sun."

"I could do with that," Hayley said ruefully, seating herself and picking up one of the glasses. "I don't think I've been warm since we came to this country." She took an incautious sip. "Hey, this is act-"

She stopped mid-word. Her eyes went very wide.

Griff laughed out loud as she struggled valiantly not to cough. "I did warn you. It's bloody freezing in the Highlands. Especially at fifteen thousand feet. Eagle shifters need a bit of fire in their bellies."

He took the other glass, and sat down as well, surreptitiously stretching out his aching leg. "So how does a warm-blooded Californian lass end up in this cold, wet land, anyway?"

"Work," Hayley replied succinctly, taking a second, rather more respectful sip of her whisky. "I'm from SoCal. School funding there is slashed to the bone. I happened across an article about teacher shortages in England, and, well, it seemed like a good idea."

Griff took a tiny sip of his own whisky, savoring the sweet burn. It was a taste of home—and one he couldn't indulge in very much any more. Alcohol didn't interact well with his pain meds. "Long way to come for a job."

She went a little pink. "Well...this is going to sound stupid, but I thought coming to Europe might help with Reiner. I hoped that if Danny was closer, easier to visit, he might finally get in touch."

Griff's lion snarled, and his eagle's wings spread. *Not now*, he told them, not letting his beasts' anger show on his face. "He lives over here?"

"Yes. Well, not England. Denmark, or rather a little island near it. He was always kind of evasive about exactly where."

"Hmm." Griff furrowed his brow. *An island near Denmark...?* "Was it Valtyra, by any chance?"

Hayley's eyebrows rose. "I think so. You know it?"

"It's actually a shifter country. There are a couple of them in Europe. Tiny wee places, out of the way, keeping themselves to themselves. Hard to get into, generally."

"Oh. I was hoping to at least take Danny to see his dad's homeland someday, but it sounds like that's going to be harder than I thought." Hayley pursed her lips a little. Griff firmly repressed a fantasy of how that full, enticing mouth would feel under his. "Griff, if there are entire shifter countries...does the government know about you, then?"

"Aye. Well, some of the government. Our existence is a state secret, but we're quietly interwoven through most of society here in the UK. Our own Parliament, our own courts, our own additional laws."

Hayley sighed with relief. "So does that mean I don't have to worry about Danny being dragged off to some Black Ops secret lab?"

"Not in this country." He flashed a grin at her. "The Queen looks out for our interests. The entire British royal family have been dragon shifters ever since the War of the Roses."

"Wow," Hayley breathed. He loved the way her face lit up with delighted curiosity. "Now I *really* want to read a shifter-written history book. What about America? Is there a, a secret shifter President or something?"

"Ah, no. Shifters in America have to be more careful. There are rumors...well, let's just say that shifters who go to ERs over there don't tend to come out again. If you're thinking of going back..." His heart lurched at the thought. He realized his knuckles were going white, and made himself relax his hand before he broke the glass. "Talk to me first. I can put you in contact with some good people, who can watch out for you and Danny. Shifters in the States have to stick together."

Hayley had gone a little pale. "Okay. Though I don't actually have plans to return. There's nothing for me in California."

Thank God. "No family?"

Hayley's shoulders tensed fractionally, betraying an old, deep pain. "No. My mom died when I was at college, and I never knew my dad." She attempted a smile. "You have no idea how envious I am of your family. Seven sisters! I would have killed to have grown up in a big pack like that."

Griff turned his glass absently, watching the amber liquid catch the light. "Ah, well, it wasn't quite such a horde as you're imagining. We were never all in the same place at once. Technically they're my half-sisters, you see."

"Oh." Griff could see Hayley's mind working as she put two and two together. "*Oh.* So that's why you're the only one who's both a lion and an eagle."

"Aye. I've got the same da as my lion sisters, and the same ma as my eagle sisters." Griff grimaced a little. "I'm not ashamed of it or anything, but...I wasn't sure how much you'd want me to tell Danny. It's a bit complicated to explain to a wee bairn, especially one who doesn't know about shifter customs."

He read a hint of sudden wariness in the way she eyed him. "Um, is it usual for shifters to be..." She appeared to be groping for a word. "That is, to have kids by lots of different partners?"

Griff choked on his whisky. "Good God! No!" That was one misapprehension he *really* didn't want her to have. "Quite the opposite, in fact."

Hayley looked rather relieved, but also confused. "What do you mean?"

Oh, we're flying into dangerous winds now...

Griff hesitated, wondering whether it was safest to just deflect her line of questioning. But clan loyalty meant he was reluctant to leave her with an erroneous bad impression of his kinfolk. Or, indeed, shifters in general.

"My ma and da met in their late twenties," he said slowly, picking his words with care. "They both knew that they weren't the love of each other's lives. But they got on well enough, and they both wanted the same sorts of things, especially when it came to kids. So they settled."

Hayley looked down at her hands. "A lot of people do."

"Aye. Shifters are just like regular people in that respect. So they got married, and had me, and were happy enough." Griff tapped his chest. "This was before it became obvious there was something wrong with me, ye ken. For a few years, everything was fine."

Hayley's round, pretty face was filled with compassion. "And then?"

"Then my da *did* meet the love of his life," Griff said, simply. "So he left."

Hayley's mouth dropped open. "Just like that? Abandoning his wife?" She was suddenly as fierce as a lioness, outrage flooding her features. "Abandoning his *child*?"

"No, no, it wasnae like that! He didnae shirk his duty to me or my ma." He took a deep breath, getting his emotions back under control. "Not like Reiner and you and poor wee Danny. My da would have stayed with my ma, if she hadn't released him. But she knew that he would have been miserable. So she let him go. Though…she was sad, for a while. Very sad."

Griff tossed back the rest of his whisky. He welcomed its searing fire, a distraction from the painful memories of that black time. Hayley said nothing, watching him.

"Anyway, a year or two later my ma met *her* mate," Griff said thickly, when he could speak again. "So it all worked out for the best in the end. For everyone."

"Except you," Hayley said, very softly.

"Ah, well, I did all right. Got a passel of sisters and two loving homes out of it. Not many are so lucky." Griff was painfully aware that his light-hearted tone was not fooling Hayley in the slightest.

She frowned, putting her empty glass down on the table. "So your mother let your father go just because of shifter custom? I'm sorry, I don't mean to offend you, but that sounds…kind of awful. I get that your dad fell in love elsewhere, but I'm afraid I don't think much of a married guy who lets his eye wander like that."

"He didn't," Griff said, struggling to keep his voice even. It took all of his control to pretend that all of this was just of academic interest. "That's where we *are* different from regular humans. Every shifter has one true mate. Many are never lucky enough to meet them. But those who do…well, that's it. My da didn't want to leave my ma. But he *had* to. He'd met his mate, and from that moment on, there was no one else he could want, no one else he could be with, ever again."

"But how did he know?" Hayley pressed.

I shouldn't be doing this.

Griff dropped his gaze, afraid that she would see the truth in his face. "He just did," he said roughly. "From the moment he saw his mate, he knew. From her scent, from her glance, from the fire of her barest touch. He just *knew*."

Even without looking at her, he could tell that Hayley had gone very still. He kept his eyes fixed on his empty glass. Her hand rested on the table a little way from his own.

Slowly, tentatively, Hayley moved her hand, until the very tip of her little finger just brushed his knuckle. So quietly that even his shifter senses could barely catch her words, she breathed, "Like this?"

He closed his eyes, fighting to control the surge of his blood at even that tiny contact. He should move away, he should draw back, he should stop this before it went too far…

Without his own volition, his hand turned, capturing her small soft fingers under his broad calloused ones. "Aye," he said, still with his eyes closed. "Just like that."

Yes! roared his lion, and *yes!* called his eagle. His two animals were in such accord, it almost sounded like they spoke with one voice. They beat against the bars of his mind, fighting to break the iron chains of his control. *YES!*

He could feel her fast pulse thrilling through her fingertips, hear the tiny catch of her breath. "Griff-"

"Wait," he interrupted. Steeling himself, he opened his eyes, although he didn't release her hand. "There's something you need to know, before you decide if you want to take this any further."

"*If* I want to take this any further?" Hayley's face was flushed with disbelief and astonishment and slowly rising joy. She let out a short, giddy laugh. "Why on earth wouldn't I?"

He forced himself to meet her shining eyes. "Because I'm dying."

CHAPTER 6

For a moment, Hayley was convinced that she had to have heard him wrong.

Griff, dying?

That can't be right. Just look at him!

Surely sick people couldn't possibly radiate strength and power like Griff did. He could have appeared on the cover of GQ, or in an ad for protein supplements. How could he be dying?

Sure, she'd noticed he limped a little, but she'd thought he must have just sprained his knee or something. Nobody died of a bad leg, after all.

Unless...

Hayley couldn't help flinching a little, horrible images of her mother's final weeks slicing through her mind. She knew that he'd noticed her reaction from the way he instantly released her, drawing his hand back.

"Aye, well." Griff's voice was rough, betraying the depth of feeling walled off behind his suddenly closed, impassive expression. He looked away from her. "So now you know."

"No, I don't! I don't understand—I mean, you can't be-" The words burst out of her of their own accord, tearing themselves free from the depths of her heart. She drew in a deep, shaky breath. "I'm sorry, it's just that this is a lot to take in. And you need to know, if, if what you've got is bone cancer…that's what my mom had. It wasn't treatable for her, either."

Griff winced, his face softening back into its usual open, compassionate lines. "I'm sorry for bringing up bad memories. If it helps at all, I don't have cancer." He shook his head, looking rather rueful. "Is it terrible if I say that sometimes I wish I did? At least doctors believe in cancer."

"But not in shifters, I'm guessing." The pieces were falling into place in Hayley's head. "What's wrong with you…it's to do with your two animals, isn't it? You're-" The word *dying* stuck on her tongue. Saying it would make it too real. She substituted, "sick because you can't shift."

"Exactly. We shifters are *supposed* to shift. We have to. If we don't do it of our own volition, eventually our animal takes over and forces the issue." Griff's mouth tightened. "I'm better than most at controlling my inner animals. But I can't keep them chained all the time. And when they get free…well. It isn't pretty. So you see, I'm in no position to think about a mate. I don't have anything to offer you. I don't have a future."

Something about his resigned tone made her irrationally angry. "But you said that you've never been able to shift," she said, as if she could somehow *argue* him better. "And you've survived this long, haven't you? Who's to say you can't survive just as long again? I mean, you seem fit, healthy…you climbed that tree as if you were just strolling down the sidewalk. For Heaven's sake, you're a *firefighter!*"

His head jerked upward, surprise flashing across his expression. Then he let out a brief bark of humorless laughter. "It really is my day for disappointing people, it seems. I *was* a firefighter, Hayley." He gestured at his left leg. "Not anymore. About a year ago, I had one of my seizures, a bad one. I came back to human eventually, but not quite in the same shape I started. It ended my career."

Hayley blinked at him, taken aback. "But I thought you said you worked for the fire service."

"I do. As a dispatcher. That's how I knew to come to you. I overheard your call." He fell silent for a moment, head bowing. "Hayley, my condition…the episodes are getting more frequent. And worse. At some point, it's going to be more than just a leg that goes wrong. Probably sooner rather than later."

The weary slump to the set of his shoulders stabbed her to the heart. Hayley desperately wanted to touch him again, but he'd retreated back out of her reach. The few feet of space between them seemed like an impassable chasm, impossible to bridge.

Griff let out a long, slow sigh. "Maybe it would have been better for you if I'd sent someone else. If we'd never met. You've already been through this kind of thing once, with your mother. I can't ask you to do that again. I *won't*. But…"

He raised his head, meeting her gaze at last. Hayley's breath caught. His eyes had gone that intense, feral yellow again…but this time they burned with something other than anger.

"I'm not sorry," he growled, low and forceful. "I don't regret coming myself. No matter what happens, I won't ever regret meeting you."

The naked desire in his gaze ignited an answering heat in her core. Hayley found that she was leaning forward, every part of her drawn towards him like a moth to a flame. If he touched her, if he moved toward her, even just a little…

But he didn't.

Griff closed his eyes for a moment, and when he re-opened them they'd gone back to their usual deep, warm gold. "It's enough," he said, very softly. "Enough just to have known you. Thank you."

It's not enough for me!

But her rational mind overruled her yearning body. She pressed her thighs together, trying to cool the throbbing need between her legs with cold logic.

He's right. This can't go further. What about Danny? How can I let Griff into our lives, knowing that we're going to lose him? How can I expose Danny to that sort of pain? What kind of a mother would I be? Think of Danny!

Grief filled her chest, heavy and leaden. It was more than just mourning for what-might-have-been. The thought of Griff's kind, generous soul being snuffed out, lost to the world forever...it was intolerable.

Desperate for any glimmer of hope, she asked, "Is there really no treatment? Nothing that might help you?"

He hesitated, and her heart leapt into her mouth—but then he said, firmly, "No. Nothing."

And she knew, *knew*, that he was lying.

"There is!" She jumped to her feet, crossing the distance between them in a single stride. "There is something, and you don't want to tell me what it is. Why? What are you trying to hide?"

Griff was shaking his head with increasing vehemence. "No. No!" It sounded more like he was shouting at himself than at her. He knotted his fists, his face contorting in sudden pain. "I. Will. Not! *No!*"

"Griff!" Frightened, Hayley grabbed his head between her palms, forcing him to look at her. "Is it your beasts? Is it one of your episodes? What am I supposed to do?"

His breath hissed between his clenched teeth. With a jolt, Hayley noticed that they'd visibly sharpened, the canines extending down into leonine fangs. His skin prickled under her palms, as if fur or feathers were trying to break through. "My eagle wants—me to tell you—*no*."

"Whatever it is, just tell me!" Hayley yelled at him, terrified he was about to start shifting uncontrollably right there in her kitchen. "Do what it wants! *Please*, Griff!"

Griff grabbed hold of her hands, clinging onto them as if he was lost in a howling storm. His blazing golden eyes locked onto hers. Hayley couldn't move, couldn't even breathe, as he focused on her as if she was the only thing in existence, the only thing in the entire world.

Griff drew in a deep, shuddering breath—and relaxed. The spasms shaking his muscles slowed, stopped. "All right," he said hoarsely. He let go of her hands, scrubbing his palms across his face. "I didn't want to tell you this. I didn't want it to influence...bloody hell, this is going to sound like the worst line ever. But there *is* something that helps."

"Well, why didn't you *say* so?" Overcome with a mixture of relief and anger, Hayley jabbed him in the shoulder, glaring. "Spit it out! What is it?"

He dropped his hands, tilting his head up to meet her eyes. "You," he said, simply.

Caught off-guard, Hayley gaped at him.

"You...bring me and my beasts into harmony," Griff continued reluctantly, every word sounding like it was being forced out of him. "It's like you're the missing part of us. Just now...you stopped me from starting to shift. And yesterday, I was on the brink of a seizure, but the memory of you brought me back. I've never been able to do that before."

If just the memory of me did that...what else could I do?

"This doesn't put any sort of obligation on you," he said forcefully, before she could speak. His expression was fierce, determined. "You mustn't feel that this means you have to—that is, just the thought of you helps. That's enough. More than enough. You don't-"

Hayley gently put a finger on his lips, silencing him. "Does it help more when I'm close to you?"

Griff held very still, as if her touch had frozen him in place. "Aye," he whispered, his lips barely moving against her hand.

"And this?" Hayley traced a path over his chin and up the strong line of his jaw. The slight, rough drag of stubble caught at her fingertips. She laid her whole palm flat against the side of his face. "Does this help even more?"

Very slightly, never taking his eyes off hers, he nodded.

Hayley leaned in closer, closer, until those golden eyes filled her world, until his warm breath caressed her parted, eager lips. "What about this?"

Fire raced through her blood at the first touch of his mouth against hers. The kiss stayed soft and gentle for barely a moment before Griff's strong hands seized her upper arms. Hayley gasped against his mouth as he yanked her down to straddle him, her wet, eager core pressing tantalizingly against the hard bulge in his jeans. She rubbed shamelessly against him, unable to help herself, every touch sparking lightning bolts of pleasure through her body.

Once they'd started, there was no question of stopping. Desire swept them both up, as all-consuming as an inferno. His tongue plundered hers, seeking and claiming. His hands roved up over her shoulders, pulling down the soft fabric of her top and exposing her breasts. His mouth still hard on hers, Griff growled deep in his throat, the vibration thrilling through Hayley's bones. He broke the kiss, ducking his head down, licking and nipping.

Hayley arched against him, her fingers twining through his hair as his mouth found her taut nipple. Even through the fabric of her bra, the sensation was almost more than she could bear. A hot, powerful ache built between her legs. She writhed against him, desperate for release, tormented by the layers of clothing separating them. "Griff—please, I need—"

His mouth captured hers again, silencing her plea. His large hands scooped under her butt, effortlessly lifting her. With one powerful motion, he flipped her up onto the kitchen table, carelessly knocking the empty glasses aside. Before she even knew what was happening, he'd stripped away her leggings and panties.

He spread her legs wide, kneeling down between them. Hayley had a brief, fleeting moment of concern for his bad knee—and then his mouth closed over her, and she was lost to everything except him.

"Griff!" she cried out, as powerful waves of pleasure shook her. He didn't stop, his tongue still circling and teasing as her thighs shuddered and her breath came in helpless gasps. He entered her with two strong fingers, and she clenched around him, throwing back her head. "*Griff!*"

He straightened at last, bracing himself against the tabletop, one hand on each side of her hips. His own breath came in ragged pants, but a devilish, satisfied smile curved his lips. He kissed her again, long and slow and lingering.

"You were right," he said, pulling back a little. "That *does* help."

Hayley hooked her fingers through his belt loops as he started to push away. "Don't you dare. You haven't taken all of your medicine yet."

Even despite the lingering flutters of pleasure, she was still wet and eager, needing more. She fumbled with his fly, releasing his cock. She caught her breath at the sight—so thick and full, the broad, glistening head straining toward her.

Griff groaned as she ran her fingers over him, thrusting forward a little with his hips in an involuntary, jerking motion. "Hayley...are you sure?"

"Yes. *God*, yes." She needed him inside her, *now*—

She stopped abruptly. "*Fudge*." Long habit made her substitute the swearword, even at a moment like this. "I don't have condoms."

Griff shot her a sideways, gleaming look. "Will you think terribly of me if I happen to pull one out of my wallet?"

In answer, she grabbed his head, drawing him down for a deep, devouring kiss. Releasing him again, she leaned back on her elbows, waiting impatiently as he efficiently sheathed himself.

"Ah..." Despite his rock-hard, eager cock and the animal hunger in his eyes, Griff hesitated. He sheepishly gestured at his left leg, then at a chair. "Do you mind if we...?"

"Any way you want," Hayley gasped, wiggling off the table. "Seated. Backwards. Upside down. Just *now*, Griff!"

Griff laughed, a deep, delighted growl at her eagerness. Seizing her hips, he guided her down with him as he sat, once more pulling her onto his lap...but this time, there were no clothes between them.

Hayley arched her back as at last, *at last* he slid into her. His thick girth stretched her deliciously wide. Her inner walls clenched, the friction of his cock along her most sensitive areas nearly pushing her over the edge with his first thrust.

He snarled, arching up against her for a moment as though fighting for control—then his fingers dug into her hips as he surrendered himself to her, pounding into her with unrestrained need.

Hayley wrapped her legs around his torso, grinding to match every thrust. His powerful arms flexed, lifting her so that she slid intoxicatingly against his full length with every stroke. A last intense wave built within her, as unstoppable as a tsunami.

She covered his mouth with hers as he arched up into her one final time, muffling both their cries of ecstasy as they came together. For a timeless moment, he filled her utterly, body and soul. Together, they were complete.

Hayley collapsed against Griff's shoulder. For a long moment, all she could do was lie there, languid and wrung-out. His chest heaved below her, gradually slowing.

It had been so long since she'd last had sex, her memory was a little hazy…but she was pretty certain it had never, ever been like *that* before.

"Well, I don't know about you," she mumbled into his neck. "But *I* certainly feel better." She felt as relaxed and glowing as if she'd just spent a week on a beach in the Bahamas.

Griff's soft, low chuckle rumbled in her ear like a cat purring. He traced a lingering, gentle caress down her spine. "I've never felt so well in my entire life."

"Good." Reluctantly, Hayley pushed herself up off him, sitting upright. Suddenly a little self-conscious about how disheveled she must appear, she tugged her tunic back up to cover her overspilling breasts.

Harsh kitchen lighting, and I'm not even wearing my good bra! What I must look like-

"Hayley." Griff caught her wrist, bringing it up to his lips. He inhaled deeply, his eyes half-closing in rapture, then pressed a gentle kiss to the delicate skin. His other hand skimmed the curves of her waist and hips, lightly, reverently. "You look beautiful. God, you're so beautiful."

The simple sincerity in his tone chased away her insecurity. "How do you do that?" Hayley asked as she scooted off his lap so he could deal with the condom. Away from his intoxicating heat, gooseflesh rose on her bare legs. She retrieved her panties and leggings. "Always know the right thing to say. It's like you know what I'm thinking."

"I do, somewhat," Griff said absently as he zipped himself back up.

"I'm good at reading people, thanks to my eagle." He dropped the condom into the garbage. "My mother's clan are white-tailed sea eagles, renowned for our uncanny perception. *Olar sùil na grèine*, we're called in Gaelic."

Hayley's toes curled at the rolling, beautiful words. She'd always been a sucker for a gorgeous accent. "What does that mean?"

"'Eagle of the sun's eye.'" He pointed at his own bright eyes, winking at her. "When you can spot a fish swimming underwater from ten thousand feet up in the sky, noticing tiny tells in the body language of someone within arm's reach isn't hard. I can spot when people are lying, or trying to hide something. And now you're getting nervous about that. But you're also reassuring yourself that you don't have anything to hide anyway, so it doesn't matter that I can read you like this. And *now* you're starting to get just a wee bit annoyed with me-"

"Griff!" Hayley took a mock-swing at him, which he avoided easily, laughing. "Stop that!"

Her heart skipped a beat as she noticed that he'd casually put his full weight on his left leg, without a hint of a wince. There was something looser, easier about his movements. She hadn't realized before just how constantly he'd been in pain.

Until now, when that pain had finally ceased.

Did I do that? Hope rose in her soul, sparkling light and effervescent as champagne bubbles. *Is it permanent, or will it wear off? Not that I mind if we have to keep doing this...*

Griff's gaze heated, roving over her body hungrily. "Me neither."

"Okay, that really *is* unfair." Hayley pouted at him, crossing her arms. "I wish I could tell what *you're* thinking." Of course, from the growing bulge in his pants—*seriously, already?*—she actually had a pretty good idea at the moment, but still.

"Well..." Griff hesitated, the playfulness in his expression turning more serious. He shot her a sidelong, strangely shy glance. "You could, actually. If...you wanted to. Eventually. One day. You see, if we were fully mated-"

And then he collapsed.

CHAPTER 7

*T*here was no warning. One moment his inner beasts were sprawled happily in separate corners of his soul, smug and satiated—and the next, they were lunging at each other, screaming in rage.

Relaxed by pleasure, he was caught completely off guard. The eagle's claws and the lion's teeth tore into his unprepared mind as if it was the soft, unprotected underbelly of a rabbit. Griff doubled over, every nerve in his body abruptly aflame with agony.

Our mate! his lion roared at his eagle, mane bristling and teeth bared. *Ours!*

No! Our mate! His eagle folded its wings and stooped on the lion, talons outstretched and deadly. *We will kill you!*

"Griff! *Griff!*" Hayley's voice sounded as if it was coming from very far away, drowned out by the storm of snarling and shrieking in his head. Dimly, he was aware of her hands on his shoulders, shaking him. "What is it? What's happening?"

"I—don't—know!" he managed to gasp out. His bones twisted sickeningly under his skin as his body instinctively tried to shift in response to the sudden assault. The kitchen floor hit his knees, cold and hard. "They just-!"

WHY? he shouted futilely at his raging animals. *Nothing's wrong! No one's threatening our mate! WHY ARE YOU DOING THIS?*

"Look at me!" Hayley's face swam before him, through the red haze of pain. She pressed her forehead against his, her hands on each side of his skull as if trying to forcibly hold his dissolving mind together. "I'm right here. I'm here, Griff!"

Desperately, he tried to focus on her, to anchor himself in her steadfast presence. But this time, the sight of her just seemed to enrage his beasts further. They were each still filled with the drive to protect her, to worship and cherish her…but added to that was a new, fiercely burning possessiveness that could only be satisfied by the utter destruction of any rival.

Including each other.

Our mate! Not yours! His lion sank its teeth into the eagle's powerful wing. Griff convulsed, phantom fangs plunging into his shoulder. *Ours to claim!*

You will not have her! His eagle's talons gouged great gashes in the lion's tawny hide, each one slashing across Griff's own back. *We will claim her, we alone! She is ours! Die!*

"Oh God, why isn't it working?" Hayley sounded frantic. She released him, jumping to her feet. "Griff, I'm calling an ambulance."

"No!" He grabbed at her ankle, stopping her. She cried out in surprised pain, and with horror he realized that his fingernails had already sharpened into claws.

That had only ever happened once before, at the very height of his worst uncontrolled shift. *That* episode had cost him his leg. If the claws were coming *now*, right at the start of the seizure…

STOP! he roared at his animals. *Or we're all going to die!*

It was no use. They ignored him utterly, and he didn't have the strength left to separate them forcibly. His eagle and lion tugged on his body like two dogs fighting over the same bone. If he didn't do something, they'd tear him limb from limb.

There was only one thing he could do. The last, desperate resort that he'd hoped never to have to use.

"Hayley." Griff fought to keep his throat and tongue human

enough to speak. His voice came out somewhere between a lion's snarl and an eagle's shriek, monstrous and distorted. "My coat. Hallway. Now!"

Thankfully, she seemed to understand his slurred words. She dashed off, her bare feet slipping on the tiled floor in her haste. Griff locked his jaw, curling into a tight ball as another wave of pain wracked his muscles. Only the thought of waking Danny up kept him from screaming.

Let him stay asleep, he prayed desperately. *Don't let him see me like this...*

"I've got it, Griff!" Hayley flung herself back down next to him, his heavy leather jacket in her arms. "What am I looking for?"

"Inside pocket," he gasped. "Box. Hurry!"

"Where—oh! Is this it?" Hayley's eyes widened as she freed the small, slim case from his jacket. Stark yellow biohazard and poison warning stickers covered the black steel. "It's locked. Griff, what's *in* this?"

"Medicine," he lied. "Key." He scrabbled at the thin chain around his neck, his own claws cutting his skin. Breaking the chain, he dropped the small key into Hayley's waiting hand. "Open. *Carefully.*"

"Okay." Gingerly, Hayley extracted a syringe, holding it in the tips of her fingers. "You want me to inject you?"

"Yes." He screwed his eyes shut, trying to concentrate, struggling to keep his human mind intact in the maelstrom of animal instincts. There was something else she had to do first, something critically important..."No! Wait!"

Too late.

He didn't even feel the tiny pinprick of the needle through the storm of torment—but then the wyvern venom hit his veins.

The pain of uncontrolled shifting was as *nothing* compared to that.

Black ice raced through his blood, shattering every cell in his body in its wake. His lion and eagle screamed together, once, as the terrible void swallowed them all.

"Call Ash!" he said, or tried to say, with his last breath. "*Call-*"

Everything stopped.

CHAPTER 8

"Ash?" Hayley shook Griff's shoulder. "Griff! Who's Ash?"

His whole body rocked under her touch, rigid as a statue and just as unresponsive. His limbs were still twisted into impossible configurations, but at least he didn't seem to be transforming any further. Between one breath and the next, the vicious spasms ravaging his muscles had completely stopped.

That has to be a good thing...right?

Hayley had a horrible certainty that it wasn't. Something was wrong. Very, very wrong.

"Who's Ash?" she repeated futilely. It had to be important, from the way he'd suddenly yelled the name...

Struck by sudden inspiration, she pawed through Griff's jacket again. Her hand closed on the thin hard rectangle of a cellphone.

It was locked, protected by a fingerprint scanner—she glanced at Griff's twisted, half-animal hands and immediately dismissed *that* possibility—but a small button at the bottom of the screen read *Emergency Contact*. Praying, Hayley touched it.

Dialing Ash, read the screen, and Hayley's breath whooshed out of her in an explosive gust. "Please pick up, please pick up," she pleaded as the phone rang in her ear. "Oh, please-"

"Griffin?" said a calm, cool male voice.

Hayley could hear laughter and clinking glasses in the background, as if the speaker was in a restaurant or pub. "Are you Ash?"

"I am Fire Commander Ash, yes." The man seemed perfectly unperturbed to be called by a complete stranger using his friend's phone. "Who is this?"

"Griff said to call you," Hayley blurted out, too panicked to even tell him her name. "Oh please, you have to come, he's collapsed and I gave him the medicine but I don't think it's working!"

"Medicine?" Ash sounded nonplussed—and then his tone abruptly sharpened. "You gave him the syringe? The one with the warning stickers on it?"

"Yes, he-" Hayley found herself talking to a dead line.

He hung up? But I didn't even tell him where to find us!

She frantically jabbed *Redial*, but the phone just blinked *Caller Unavailable* at her. "You can't be unavailable!" she yelled at the phone. "You're supposed to be his emergency contact! Griff, what do I do now?"

He didn't respond. He was motionless.

Completely motionless.

He wasn't breathing.

Hurling the useless phone aside, Hayley flung herself to her knees next to his rigid body. She pressed her fingertips to his neck, feeling for a pulse. His skin was freezing cold. He was as stiff under her hands as if he'd been dead for hours.

Chest compressions, she thought, suddenly icy calm. Griff needed her, *now*, and there was no time for any emotion but the single-minded need to save him. The CPR procedure sprang into her mind with crystal clarity, as if the textbook was open in front of her.

She pumped his chest, hard, counting the rhythm under her breath. At the right moment, she paused to give him mouth-to-mouth, not caring that his protruding fangs cut into her lips. It didn't matter that he was twisted and stretched, half-beast. This was *Griff*, her Griff, her mate. She knew that he was still there, a spark of life hidden deep inside that still, barely human form. And she would *not* let that life slip away.

Compressions, ventilations. Compressions, ventilations. Focus, Hayley. Keep the rhythm.

Hayley cursed herself for throwing Griff's cellphone away, out of reach. She knew she needed to call an ambulance, but she didn't dare leave his side yet. He needed her to be his heart, to be the air that he breathed...

Fiery light flooded suddenly through the window. Acting on pure instinct, Hayley flung herself across Griff's body, trying to protect him as the glass imploded inward.

An eye-searingly bright shape hurtled into the kitchen, white-hot flames streaming behind it like the tail of a comet. For a split second, the vast, bird-like form spread fiery wings over them both, its eyes as fierce and lethal as the heart of the sun.

The bird-shape vanished, leaving a man standing where it had been. He looked to be in his mid-forties, but he was still muscular and broad-shouldered, military training clear in his straight-backed stance. Wisps of smoke rose from the scorched floor around his feet.

Hayley gaped at him. "Who—what-?"

"I am Ash." He was already kneeling, his calm gaze sweeping over Griff's motionless form in assessment. "When did you give him the venom?"

"Venom?" Hayley said blankly.

He glanced up at her, briefly, and she rocked back on her heels as the power behind those dark eyes struck her like a blow. "The wyvern venom. In the syringe. When?"

"I—I don't know," Hayley stammered. *Poison? He said it was medicine!* "Not more than ten minutes ago."

Ash's expression stayed completely unreadable, but his breath hissed through his teeth. He looked at the window, as if he was waiting for someone.

Or possibly, some*thing.* Hayley stared in disbelief as a horse stuck its long, black head through her kitchen window. A...*winged* horse?

The pegasus retreated a little, folding its wings. Someone scrambled off its back and through the window—another man, much younger than Ash even though his short hair was a pure, brilliant silver. He didn't spare Hayley even the most cursory of glances as he shoved her aside to get to Griff. From the unerring, expert way his long fingers swiftly assessed Griff's vital signs, Hayley guessed the newcomer had to be some sort of medic.

"You fool," the white-haired man snarled savagely, apparently to his unconscious patient. "I warned you this was an idiotic idea. If I ever get my hands on that *bloody* wyvern—!"

"Is he going to be okay?" interrupted an anxious Irish voice. Yet *another* man climbed in through the window, this one lean and agile with a shock of wild, curly black hair. "Hugh, can you heal him?"

"Who *are* all you people?" Hayley demanded.

"Get her out of here, Chase," the white-haired man snapped without looking up. "I have to work fast if I'm going to have any chance of saving this moron."

"What? No!" Hayley tried to twist away, but the Irish man—Chase, she assumed—was inhumanly fast. He seized her wrists, bundling her out of the kitchen despite her kicks and protests. "Let me go! I have to stay with Griff!"

"I'm sorry, but you can't." Chase elbowed the door shut behind them, still effortlessly restraining her. He was a *lot* stronger than his lean physique suggested. "Hugh won't shift if you're watching, and right now he's Griff's only hope."

"He's a shifter?" Hayley stared at Chase's windswept hair, suddenly making the connection. "You're *all* shifters. You were the pegasus."

"Yep." He flashed her a brief, strained grin, though the rest of his face was still set in grim, worried lines. "Chase Tiernach-West, at your service. The two back in there are Hugh Argent and Fire Commander Ash." He cocked his head to one side, as if suddenly hearing someone call his name. "And…just landing outside are the last two members of our team. We'd better let them in, or else John will kick your door down. Or possibly your wall."

"Team?" Hayley said, towed helplessly in his wake as he headed down the hallway. "Landing? What?"

"We're firefighters. Alpha Team. And Griff's still one of us." Chase opened the front door. "He'll *always* be one of us. And we look out for our own."

Hayley's breath froze in her throat.

There was a dragon in the road.

It looked exactly like an illustration from a fairytale book—horned, winged, with a long, sinuous tail and glittering crimson scales. There was a man astride its broad neck, and *he* could have stepped straight out of a fantasy novel too. His long, braided blue hair and fierce, rough-hewn features made him look like some barbarian warrior.

"They're in plain sight!" Hayley exclaimed. British people might be good at politely ignoring each other, but surely none of her neighbors were going to overlook a huge red dragon in the street. She looked wildly around at the surrounding houses, but no one's curtains had so much as twitched. "Why isn't anyone noticing?"

"It's a mythic shifter thing," Chase said. He waved at the dragon and its rider. "We have a kind of mind-trick we can do, which stops ordinary people from seeing us in our animal forms. Comes in handy."

The man jumped down from the dragon's back. The instant he was clear, the dragon's bulk shimmered, condensing into a red-headed man. Even though the dragon had been the size of a bus, in human form he barely came up to the long-haired man's shoulder. The two men strode toward the house.

That's weird, Hayley thought inanely, still half-numb with shock. *Who'd have thought a dragon shifter would be...so...little...*

Oh.

The dragon shifter wasn't little. In fact, he was even taller than Griff.

It was just that the man next to him was *motherfudging enormous.*

"Where is he?" the giant rumbled as he squeezed himself through her front door. He couldn't even stand up straight inside. Despite his bulk, there was an intelligent, noble look to his chiseled face that meant Hayley couldn't feel afraid of him.

"With Hugh and Ash. We're to stay out of the way," Chase said, shutting the door. Turning to Hayley, he pointed at the red-headed dragon shifter. "This is Daifydd Drake—but you can call him Dai, he accepts that the rest of us find Welsh names unpronounceable." His finger swung to the giant. "And *this* is John Doe, whose real name is *literally* unpronounceable if you're breathing air, so don't worry about that. Dai, John, this is…" Chase hesitated, looking down at Hayley. "Actually, I haven't the foggiest idea who you are. Sorry."

"I do," said John Doe. His voice had an odd, musical quality, and she couldn't place his accent at all. He sank gracefully to one knee in front of her, bowing his head. "My lady. I am the Walker-Above-Wave, Knight-Poet of the Order of the First Water, Guardian of the Pearl Throne, Seeker of the Emperor-in-Absence, Firefighter of the East Sussex Fire and Rescue Service, and Griffin's sworn oath-brother. If by my life or my death I can serve you, I will."

Hayley blinked at him, completely lost for words. From the startled looks on both Chase and Dai's faces, she wasn't the only one.

"Uh, John?" The red-headed dragon shifter—Dai—tapped John's massive shoulder. "Care to explain what's going on?"

John got to his feet again, keeping his head tilted to avoid hitting it on the light fitting. "She is my oath-brother's mate, kin-cousin. As he would defend me, so will I defend her."

"She's Griff's *what* now?" Chase exclaimed, staring at Hayley in astonishment.

"Mommy?" To Hayley's horror, Danny stood at the top of the stairs, rubbing sleepy eyes. "I heard noises."

"Holy sh-" Chase started. Dai elbowed him hard in the ribs, silencing him.

Danny flinched back, hiding behind the banister. "Who're they? Mommy, where's Mr. Griff?"

"It's okay, baby." Hayley twisted out of Chase's suddenly slack grip. She hurried up the stairs. "These are—these are some of Griff's friends."

Danny peeked round her at the three huge men. "Mr. Griff's dragon friends?"

"That's right." Hayley tried to block his view of the hallway, terrified that at any moment the kitchen door might open. "Mr. Griff's dragon friends. We're just talking. You go back to bed now."

"Hey," Chase protested. "*I'm* not a dr-"

This time both Dai *and* John elbowed him. He wheezed, shutting up.

"Why're they here?" Danny dragged his feet, resisting as she tried to hustle him back toward his bedroom. "Why're you all funny-looking, Mommy? Are you crying?"

"No, of course not." It was the hardest thing she'd ever done in her life, but she managed to paste a convincing smile onto her face. "Everything's fine. Come on, you've got school tomorrow and you need your sleep."

By the time she'd gotten Danny resettled in bed—which involved a trip to the bathroom, a glass of water, two lullabies and finally making him pinky-promise to *really, really* go back to sleep now—and returned downstairs, the firefighters had moved Griff from the kitchen to the couch. Her small front room seemed completely filled with broad shoulders and beefy arms, barely able to hold so many big men.

Hayley only had eyes for Griff's limp body. Although he was still deeply unconscious, he'd finally relaxed from that tormented, curled position. His chest rose and fell with his shallow breathing. All the breath rushed out of Hayley's own lungs with relief.

"Oh, thank God." She pushed her way through the wall of muscle to his side. "Is he stable? Is he going to be okay?"

"I've neutralized the poison. That was the hard part. Now I'm healing the carnage it did to his heart." Hugh was resting his bare hands on Griff's exposed chest with a look of intense concentration. He glanced up at her, his handsome, finely-drawn face pale and exhausted. "At least you did the right thing, starting CPR right away. It stopped him from getting permanent brain damage." He scowled back down at his patient. "Not that any of us would have been able to tell the difference. *Idiot.*"

"The poison did do what he hoped it would," Dai pointed out. "It paralyzed his body and knocked out his animals. It stopped him from shifting further."

"Yeah, because it practically *killed* him," Chase retorted. His fists clenched. "That psychopathic wyvern shifter is a fucking menace. We should have flung her into prison and thrown away the key when we had the chance. I am going to kick her scaly little-"

Ash cast Chase a quelling look, and the pegasus shifter subsided. "Thank you for calling us," the Fire Commander said to Hayley. His tone was still perfectly level, his face betraying no sign of the tension in the other men's expressions. "I apologize for the inconvenience, but we cannot take him away yet."

"I don't want you to take him away!" Hayley anxiously studied Griff's distorted face. His ears were still sharply pointed, his mouth almost a muzzle. "If you're healing him, why isn't he going back to human form?" she asked Hugh.

"I can only fix what's damaged." Hugh adjusted the positions of his fingertips, his jaw clenching briefly as though he was somehow drawing pain out of Griff and into himself. "Not what doesn't know it's broken. His body thinks that this is the way it's supposed to be. He has to make it shift back on his own."

Dai hissed what sounded awfully like a swear word in Welsh. "You know he can't, Hugh. There has to be something you can do."

"I'm a paramedic, not a bloody miracle worker," Hugh snapped, which seemed a bit strange coming from a man who was currently healing a damaged heart with his bare hands. "If Griff wants to be human, he's going to have to take care of it himself."

"Not entirely," John rumbled. He looked at Hayley. "Call him back to us, my lady. You are his mate. He will always come to your call, across fire, across water, across death itself. Call him back."

Hayley hesitantly started to put her hand flat against the side of Griff's face—and then snatched it back, remembering what had happened last time. "I can't. I tried to help before, when his seizure started, and I only made it worse. I don't dare touch him."

Dai and Chase exchanged uneasy glances. "Maybe she'd better not,

John," Dai said. "He's alive and stable now. It doesn't matter what he looks like."

"You think his face is messed up, you should see his pancreas," Hugh muttered. "I'm with John. The worst she can do is kill him again."

Hayley put her hands behind her back. "I'm not risking that!"

"You are his *mate*," John insisted stubbornly. "You cannot harm him, no more than he could ever harm you. You must try. You are the only one who can."

All four firefighters glanced at Ash, and Hayley found that she too had turned in his direction. The Fire Commander had such an air of quiet authority, it seemed only natural to look to him for a decision.

Ash met her eyes calmly. "Try."

Feeling self-conscious under the weight of all their stares, Hayley put her hand against Griff's cheek. She cringed a little as her palm brushed his skin, half-expecting him to cry out again in agony—but he just made a small sigh, turning fractionally into her touch.

Encouraged, Hayley bent to put her lips to his ear. "Griff?" she whispered. "It's okay now. I'm here. Your friends are here. We won't let anything happen to you. It's okay to come back now."

The drawn tightness around Griff's closed eyes eased a little. Slowly, so slowly, his face softened back into more human features.

Chase made a strangled yelp, as though he'd started to whoop with joy and then remembered that Danny was sleeping upstairs. He snatched Hayley up, spinning her round in a brief, dizzying hug. "You did it! You did it! I could kiss you!"

"You do, and Griff will punch your lights out when he wakes up." Grinning, Dai rescued her from Chase's arms, depositing her back on the ground. "But thank you. From all of us." He hesitated. "Ah, I don't think we even know your name."

"Hayley Parker," she said dazedly. "And thank *you*. All of you. How did you even know where we were?"

Chase bowed extravagantly. "Just one of my many talents. We pegasus shifters have a knack for finding people."

"I can still barely believe that there's even such a thing as pegasus shifters. Or dragons." She glanced up at John Doe. "You're a dragon too, right? Griff mentioned you. He said he had a friend who was a dragon knight."

John smiled, inclining his head in assent. "Sea dragon, and Knight-Poet, to be completely precise."

"And…" Hayley looked at Ash in awe, remembering the fiery bird that had swooped into her kitchen. "You're a phoenix, aren't you?"

"*The* Phoenix," said Ash, mildly. "Since we are being precise."

There's only one? Just like in the old myths?

Hayley felt like her entire worldview had been turned upside-down and shaken. She turned to Hugh, wondering what sort of walking legend *he* would turn out to be. "And you're…?"

"Bloody exhausted." Hugh took his hands off Griff's chest at last, flexing his fingers as if he had pins-and-needles. "There's nothing more I can do now. I want to leave him here, with you, if that's all right. He's not fully back to human yet. Maybe you can get him the rest of the way."

"I'll try." Hayley sank cross-legged to the carpet, taking Griff's hand. His fingers were still curled into claws, but they relaxed a little at her touch. "I won't leave him alone."

"And we won't leave you alone." Dai looked around at the other men. "So, who's taking first watch?"

CHAPTER 9

Griff woke up with every part of his body aching with a bone-deep, throbbing pain.

That was a pleasant surprise. He hadn't been expecting to wake up at all.

Wincing, he very cautiously pushed himself upright on the couch. All the vertebrae in his back ground against each other like granite rocks, but at least he wasn't hunched over on all fours like a beast.

His knuckles popped as he flexed his fingers, testing their movement. All his fingernails had gone back to human, but three of the fingers on his right hand were now crooked, curled into hooked claw-shapes. Grimacing, Griff tried to straighten them. The joints were locked solid.

Guess I'll be learning to write left-handed, then.

He couldn't believe he'd gotten off so lightly. Even with the wyvern venom instantly halting his uncontrolled shift, he'd expected to come back to a body that was more animal than man…if he'd come back at all.

What happened?

His eagle was still catatonic at the very back of his mind, leaving him with only human levels of perception. Griff looked around, blinking to clear his dry, strained eyes. Everything seemed dim and foggy, as if he was looking through smoked glass. He was so unused to the limitations of human sight that it took him a moment to recognize Hayley's living room.

Hayley herself was curled up on the floor next to the couch, within arm's reach of him. She was still wearing the same floral top and black leggings she'd worn yesterday. From the dark circles under her closed eyes, Griff guessed that she had to have been awake most of the night.

His eagle and lion both stirred at the sight of their mate, yearning toward her even in their poisoned, weakened state. Griff's jaw tightened. He brutally chained his beasts back down again, binding them so tightly he could barely feel them in the depths of his soul.

Got to keep a tight leash on them. This can't happen again.

Which meant other things couldn't happen again.

Griff forced himself to look away from Hayley. Moving very slowly so as not to wake her up, he levered himself to his feet. His left knee screamed in protest as he tried to put his weight on it. He remembered that it hadn't hurt, for those few magical minutes last night after he and Hayley had succumbed to the pull of the matebond…but it was definitely back to its normal state of wrongness now. His knee joint felt as though someone had been hammering rusty nails through it.

Oh well. It's not like I'm not used to it.

Leaning on the wall for support, he managed to limp his way to the kitchen. He halted in the doorway, startled by the shards of glass scattered across the tiled floor and the scorch marks on the walls.

"What in God's name happened here?" Griff muttered to himself. His dry voice rasped like sandpaper in his throat.

I am afraid that I did, Ash's calm, quiet telepathic voice said in his mind. *I was in something of a hurry.*

Squinting out the broken window, Griff caught sight of Ash perched at the very top of the tree outside. The Phoenix's fire was dimmed and controlled, but he still burned brighter than the sun rising behind him.

"Thank you," Griff said out loud, wishing that he could communicate back telepathically, to show Ash the deep and sincere gratitude in his mind. "So Hayley did manage to contact you?"

Just in time. The Phoenix swooped down to perch on the windowsill, his sweeping tail feathers brushing the ground outside. Griff could feel the heat radiating from the massive, eagle-like form even from six feet away. *Hugh said that a minute later, and there would have been nothing he could do.*

Griff picked his way across the broken glass to the sink. He splashed cold water on his face, then drank from his cupped hand, too parched to waste time finding a cup.

"I owe Hugh an apology," he said, when he emerged again. Catching sight of his cellphone lying discarded in a corner, he bent to pocket it. "That can't have been pleasant for him, having to touch me right after Hayley and I had…ah, well, you know. Must have given him a splitting headache."

Hugh was remarkably tight-lipped about the nature of his shifter animal…but there was no hiding such things from Griff's eagle. He'd long ago worked out exactly what Hugh was, though he respected Hugh's desire to keep it a secret even from the rest of Alpha Team. Griff couldn't blame him for it. Hugh's species was meant to be extinct, every last one hunted down and slaughtered way back in the Middle Ages.

If I was the main ingredient in a potion that's meant to grant eternal youth, I'd be pretty damn secretive about my existence too.

Ash's foot-long talons shifted on the windowsill, leaving scorch marks in the wood. Griff knew that the Fire Commander knew that *he* knew about Hugh, but Ash's cast-iron sense of honor meant he would never openly confirm the paramedic's true nature. *He is tired, but he will recover. Will you?*

Griff shrugged, gesturing with his crooked hand at his bad knee. "Ah, well, I doubt it. But I'll live a while yet, thanks to you all. You can go back home and get some rest now. I'll be fine."

Ash spread his wings…then paused. He turned his head, considering Griff for a long moment with one blazing eye.

I am sorry, Ash said at last. *I understand what it is to taste some-

thing, only to have it snatched away. I share your pain. It is possible to live with it....but you will have to be strong. For your mate's sake.

Before Griff could respond, he was gone. A trail of sparks swirled in his wake, quickly winking out.

He's right. I have to be stronger in future. This was all my fault.

If he hadn't succumbed to temptation and indulged his base, carnal desires, he would never have provoked his inner beasts' jealous rage. He'd selfishly taken advantage of Hayley, and as a result, had nearly left her with a monstrous corpse cooling on her kitchen floor. How would she have explained *that* to Danny?

I can't ever touch her again.

The thought was as cold and bleak as the grey dawn light filtering through the broken window. But it was the truth. He couldn't put Hayley through this again. He *wouldn't*.

I have to leave. Now. Before she wakes up.

Nonetheless, he delayed long enough to sweep up the floor. It wasn't safe to leave broken glass lying around, not when little bare feet would be charging downstairs at any moment.

His heart clenched at the thought of Danny bouncing into the kitchen, how his eyes would shine in delight if he found Griff still there...

No. I have to disappear, completely. It's better for them both.

At the back of his mind, his lion roared, flinging itself futilely against its cage. Griff ignored it. Slipping on his coat and shoes, he limped down the hallway. He didn't dare let himself take one last look at Hayley, for fear his animals would break loose and undo all his good intentions. Very quietly, for the last time, he eased open the front door-

And found himself unexpectedly confronting a man on the doorstep.

The man had obviously just been reaching for the door-knocker. He dropped his outstretched hand, taking a sharp step back in surprise. Griff had never seen him before in his life, yet there was something eerily familiar about his features.

The man's nostrils flared. A low, deep growl ripped through his throat, possessive outrage flaring in his amber eyes.

The stranger's scent hit Griff like a brick. He suddenly knew *exactly* who the man was.

"Who the hell are you?" demanded Danny's father.

CHAPTER 10

Hayley jolted awake to the sound of snarling. Her body flooded with adrenaline in instinctive reaction, her deepest monkey brain screaming at her that there was a dangerous predator nearby.

Oh my God! He's shifting again!

Heart pounding, she scrambled to her feet. "Griff!" Following the snarls, she raced into the hallway—and stopped dead.

Griff was still human, although the sounds ripping from his throat were pure lion. He had his back to her, his hands braced on each side of the doorframe as he squared off against a man outside.

The other man was a little taller than Griff, but much leaner. Nonetheless, he matched Griff snarl for snarl, forcibly trying to push his way into the house. His angular, handsome face was contorted with feral rage.

Even though Hayley hadn't seen that face for five years, she instantly recognized him.

"Reiner?" she gasped.

The sound of her voice broke the two men's stand-off. Griff lurched as he turned, his bad knee buckling. Reiner took advantage of the firefighter's momentary weakness to shove past.

"Where is he?" he demanded in the clipped Danish accent she'd once found so sexy. "Where is my son?"

"He's—what—how-" She felt as unsteady as Griff, her legs threatening to give way with sheer shock. "Reiner, what are you *doing* here?"

"I was in London on business. I came as soon as I got your email." Reiner took a step toward her, his fists clenching. Hayley couldn't help shrinking back from the raw, animal power emanating from him. "Now, *where is my son?*"

"Don't. Move." Griff caught Reiner's arm, jerking the other lion shifter back. Even though Griff could barely stand upright, his golden eyes still blazed with primal fury. "You aren't going anywhere near him until Hayley says you can."

"He is *my* son!" Reiner knocked Griff's hand away. "Stand in my way again and I'll rip out your throat."

"No!" Hayley thrust herself between the two men as they started to snarl at each other again. "Reiner, it's okay, he's my…he's a friend."

Reiner's nostrils flared. His withering amber gaze flicked down her body. "It would seem he's rather more than that. Unless you routinely fuck your friends."

Hayley's cheeks heated in humiliation. "That is *none* of your business, Reiner!"

"He's under the same roof as my son. That makes it my business." His muscled chest pressed hard against her shoulder as he leaned forward, glaring across her at Griff. "This is *my* territory. Get out!"

"Mommy?" said a small, sleepy voice from the stairs. "Are Mr. Griff's dragon friends still here?"

All three of them froze.

Danny caught sight of Reiner, and his light brown eyes widened. Hayley had never realized it before, but they were the exact same shade as his father's.

"Oh," Danny said, in a very small voice.

All of the aggression in Reiner's stance instantly vanished, replaced by awestruck wonder. He took three swift steps to the bottom of the stairs. Hayley let him go, unable to stand in the way of such obvious pure, simple joy.

"My son," Reiner said, his voice shaking. He held out his arms. "*My son.*"

"Daddy." Danny practically fell down the stairs into Reiner's embrace. He clung to him with every limb, burying his face in Reiner's chest. His little shoulders shook in wracking sobs. "Daddy. Daddy. Daddy."

Tears sprang into Hayley's eyes. An unbearable, unnamable swirl of emotions choked her throat. She had to turn away before she broke down entirely—and found herself facing Griff. Sheer, overwhelming jealousy was written in every line of his face as he watched Reiner and Danny.

He caught her looking at him, and his expression instantly went blank. "I should go," he said gruffly.

"Wait!" Hayley caught his sleeve as he turned for the door. "You're in no state to go anywhere." She lowered her voice, casting a quick glance over her shoulder at the still-oblivious Reiner. "You nearly died last night, Griff! Stay, let me take care of you. I don't care how much Reiner growls about it-"

"I *have* to go," he interrupted, not looking at her. His shoulders hunched. "I can't stay here. Especially not now."

Anger and upset churned in her stomach as she realized that he already had his jacket and shoes on. "You were just going to leave, weren't you? If Reiner hadn't arrived, you'd have been gone before I even woke up."

"It would have been for the best," he said, very quietly. He met her eyes at last, and the broken agony in his own shattered her heart. "Hayley. Last night…we can't let that happen again. Not ever."

Memories of his contorted, half-animal form flashed through her mind, red-hot and searing.

He nearly died because of me. How can I ask him to risk that again?

She made herself open her fingers, letting his wrist fall from her grip. Even though she knew it was the right thing to do, it felt wrong, deeply wrong, to let him go.

"Will you at least come back to see Danny?" she asked hopelessly, as he limped away.

"No." Griff didn't look back. "He doesn't need me any more."

CHAPTER 11

Danny scowled ferociously down at his drawing. It was so unfair! His daddy had finally, *finally* come to see him, and yet he'd still had to go to school. Danny didn't see why *he* couldn't have stayed home with Daddy, even if Mommy did have to go out to work. Maybe Mommy just didn't want him and Daddy having fun together without her.

We could pretend to go to the bathroom, Simba suggested. Mommy used to call Simba his "imaginary friend," but Danny had always known that he was real. The lion cub bounced with eagerness in his mind, urging him to shift. *We could jump out the window and run away.*

Danny shook his head. Just like Mr. Griff had taught him, he held Simba back, not letting the lion take control of their body. The effort made him feel itchy all over. He took out his frustrations on his drawing, scrubbing so hard with the chunky yellow crayon that he nearly went through the paper.

Simba's ears pricked up. *The woman is talking about us,* he informed Danny.

Danny cocked his own head, concentrating. Simba helped him to hear better, picking out his teacher's voice from the low chatter of the rest of the classroom. Miss Hunter was over at the door, talking to someone Danny couldn't see. He couldn't make out everything she was saying, but he definitely heard his own name.

Are we in trouble? Simba asked anxiously.

"I don't know," Danny whispered as quietly as he could. He tried not to talk to Simba too much at school. He didn't like the way it made the other kids stare and giggle behind his back.

"Danny?" his teacher called. She beckoned him over to her. "Someone's here to see you."

Worried, Danny slid off his chair. Halfway to the door, he caught wind of a familiar scent. "Daddy!" he yelled in joy, leaping up into his arms.

Daddy rumbled, bumping his forehead against Danny's. That was lion for "hello" and "happy to see you." No one had ever had to tell Danny that—he just *knew*, way down deep inside where Simba lived.

"You see?" Daddy said to Miss Hunter. He sounded a little mad, but it wasn't with Danny so it didn't matter. "I told you, this is my son. I have a right to take him."

"You came to get me?" Danny wriggled with excitement. "But Mommy said-"

Hush, Daddy said in his head.

Danny fell silent obediently. It was different from when Mommy told him to be quiet—he could argue with Mommy, but Simba *really* didn't like it if he tried to argue with Daddy. Or Mr. Griff.

Miss Hunter hesitated, fidgeting uncertainly with her long, curly hair. "I'm sorry, but you're not on the list of people authorized to pick Danny up. I'm going to have to call Ms. Parker."

"She's at work, and cannot be interrupted." Daddy glared down at Miss Hunter, his lion looming behind his narrowed eyes. He looked like he was thinking of eating the teacher in one big mouthful—*owp!*—just like the Tiger Who Came To Tea. "You will hand my son over to me. *Now.*"

Miss Hunter flinched, her face going white and funny-looking. "I- I- I suppose we can make an exception. Just this once. Danny, go get your things."

Danny hopped down out of Daddy's arms, racing to collect his bag and coat before his teacher could change her mind. He grabbed his picture too, being careful not to crumple it.

"I made this for you," he said, a little shyly, as they walked out of the school. "It's a present."

Daddy's fierce eyes softened as he took the paper. "This is very good. This is you, here, isn't it? And here's your mother, and here's…" His eyebrows drew together. "Wait. Why have you drawn me with long hair?"

"That's not you. *That's* you." Danny helpfully pointed out the big lion he'd drawn. "That's Mr. Griff, holding Mommy's hand."

We've been bad, Simba whimpered, as Daddy's mouth tightened into a hard, thin line.

"No we haven't," Danny whispered to his lion…though he wasn't entirely sure about that himself. Daddy looked awful mad about something.

"And why," Daddy said, a hint of a snarl in his voice, "is 'Mr. Griff' in this picture?"

"Because it's a picture of our family," Danny said, puzzled. "Mr. Griff's my alpha." He brightened as something occurred to him. "Does that mean he's your alpha too, Daddy?"

He jumped as Daddy ripped the paper in half, crumpling up the piece with Mr. Griff and dropping it on the ground. "He is not your alpha. *I* am your alpha. Now, come on."

He isn't our alpha. Simba's ears flattened. *Why is he saying he is? Has he beaten our alpha?*

"Daddy, you didn't fight Mr. Griff, did you?" Danny asked nervously, having to trot to keep up with Daddy's much longer legs.

"Not yet," Daddy growled. He glanced down at Danny sharply, suddenly looking a little wary. "Why? Do you think he's stronger than me?"

Yes, Simba said, with complete certainty.

"Um…" Somehow, Danny didn't think Daddy would be happy to hear that. "Mommy says it's not nice to fight people, anyway."

Daddy snorted. "'Mommy' isn't a lion." He pointed at a car—a *real* nice car, sleek and low and so shiny Danny could see his own face in the bright red paint. "Here we are."

Danny's eyes widened. "Wow! Is this really yours, Daddy? It's like a real-life racing car!"

"It *is* a real-life racing car." Daddy looked happier, his tight shoulders easing down. "Bet your so-called alpha doesn't have one like it. In you get. We're going for a ride."

Thrilled, Danny climbed into the leather passenger seat—then hesitated. "Daddy, there's no booster seat."

"So?" Daddy slid behind the wheel. "There's a seat belt."

Danny squirmed, torn between his desire to ride in the amazing car and dutiful obedience to Mommy's repeated safety warnings. "I'm not allowed to ride without a booster seat. It's against the law."

"Human law." Daddy snorted again. "We're *lions*. We make our own laws. Now buckle up."

Simba nudged him, wordlessly urging him to obey the bigger lion. Danny didn't need much persuasion. He happily clicked his seat belt shut. "Where are we going, Daddy?"

The car roared like an animal as Daddy started the engine. "It's a surprise."

CHAPTER 12

"You have been pining all day," John announced without preamble, barging into Griff's room without knocking first. "You need to eat."

"I'm not pining," Griff said, without looking round. He lay on his back on the bed, staring up at the ceiling. "I'm resting."

"'Resting' involves taking care of your body, oath-brother. *You* are pining." John thumped a tray down onto Griff's bedside table. "I have made you nourishing soup. By boiling things."

From the smell that hit Griff's nostrils, John had made soup by boiling *all* the things. "Thanks. But I'm not hungry."

John hummed, ominously. Griff rolled over to see the sea dragon glaring at him with narrowed eyes, the mysterious soup rising up out of the bowl like a cobra.

You will feed yourself, John said telepathically, as tendrils of soup wove around his outstretched hand. *Or I will feed you.*

Faced with the prospect of having terrible soup magically forced into his bodily orifices, Griff sat up quickly. "Ah…on second thought, I'm starving. Need more than soup. Would you be offended if I made myself a sandwich?"

I would be delighted if you made yourself a sandwich. John didn't stop humming as he followed Griff to the kitchen, the soup coiling around his wrist like a monstrous snake. *I will keep the soup ready, though. Just in case you lose your appetite.*

Griff shot him a level look as he started slicing bread. "John. Did you make terrible soup on purpose?"

I do not follow your meaning, John sent, his blue eyes as wide and tranquil as a tropical lagoon. *I am just a simple sea dragon who does not understand your strange land ways. Eat your sandwich.*

Griff shook his head ruefully, but complied. John waited until he'd swallowed the last bite before letting the reeking soup slide off his hand and down the drain.

"There," the sea dragon shifter said, sounding pleased. "Now you have fortified yourself. Restored in body, you are prepared to steel your soul and face your destiny."

"What destiny?" Griff said suspiciously.

John slid Griff's cellphone across the kitchen table.

Griff looked at it. "My destiny involves the phone."

"Your *destiny* involves your mate." John pointed at the phone. "Call her."

Griff groaned, rubbing his palms over his face. "John…"

"More terrible soup," John rumbled, "could be made."

"I don't care if you force feed me cream-of-pickled-herring-and-peanut-butter," Griff snapped, crossing his arms over his chest and glaring at the sea dragon. "I am *not* calling Hayley. For a start, I don't even know her number."

His forbidding expression never changing, John handed him a scrap of paper. "Now you do."

Griff's lion and eagle stirred, hackles rising with suspicious jealousy. He thrust them back down again. "Why do *you* have Hayley's number?"

"Because I asked her for it, last night." John shrugged one massive shoulder, his stern face softening a little. "I know you, my oath-brother. I knew that you would choose to tear out your heart rather than risk causing your mate future pain. But there is some pain that can only be embraced. Your sacrifice is noble, but misguided. You are being too honorable."

Griff let out a short, ironic huff of breath. "Says the literal *Knight*?"

"Honor is not a shield to hide behind." John nudged the phone closer to him. "It is a sword, to give you the strength to face your demons. You must face what frightens you, oath-brother. You must not flee from it."

Griff slammed his fist down onto the table, making his empty plate jump. "For God's sake, I'm not *frightened* of Reiner! It's just that he's Danny's father. He's the one that Danny wants, the one he needs. Not me. I can't get in the way."

"I did not mean Reiner. I meant what *truly* frightens you." John met his eyes, his own deep and dark. "Living."

Griff was saved from having to try to unravel *that* one by his phone ringing. He caught it as it vibrated off the table. *Unknown Caller*, read the display, followed by a number. He glanced from the screen to the note. It was the same number.

Hayley's number.

"Your mate cries out for you," John said, as Griff's thumb hesitated over the *End Call* button. "Will you truly ignore her plea?"

His eagle and lion both leaned against his mind, from opposite directions, until Griff felt like he would be crushed flat between them. A warning, prickling energy ran over his skin. Griff clenched his jaw, but had no choice but to submit to his animals' desires. He didn't have the strength to resist another uncontrolled shift.

He put the phone to his ear, silently cursing his own weakness. "Hayley?"

"Griff!" Adrenaline surged through Griff's blood at the sheer panic in his mate's voice. "Reiner took Danny. They're gone."

CHAPTER 13

Hayley clung to Chase's long black mane, the wind whipping her own hair across her face. At any other time, soaring through the sky on the back of a pegasus would have been a magical experience. But right now, she was too sick with dread to think of anything other than her missing son.

"Reiner hasn't taken him to the airport, at least," Griff shouted into her ear. His powerful body pressed reassuringly against her back, his strong arms holding her steady. "He can't be more than a few miles away. Chase says that he can sense Danny clearly."

At least that means he's alive. Hayley held onto that thought as tightly as she gripped the pegasus. It was cold comfort. Alive wasn't the same as unharmed.

"Hayley." Griff's arm tightened around her waist. "I'm Danny's alpha. I'd sense if he was in trouble."

Please let that be true, Hayley prayed.

Chase curved his neck, looking back at Griff with one black, intelligent eye. Hayley felt Griff nod as if in response to something the pegasus shifter had said. "Chase says they're down there, in those woods up ahead. Hang on."

Despite the warning, Hayley still lurched as Chase banked hard.

Only Griff's grip kept her from sliding off the pegasus's slick back as they spiraled down.

Griff leaned over, his intent eyes scanning the trees below. "There, Chase! I saw them. Put us down in that clearing over there."

Chase obligingly swooped down to the clearing, beating his wings hard to settle gracefully to the ground. Griff slid off his back first, with a brief grimace as he landed on his bad leg. Nonetheless, he lifted Hayley down easily, setting her on her feet.

"They saw us landing," he said, pointing into the woods. "They're coming to meet us."

"Danny!" Hayley cried out, unable to keep the shrill note of panic out of her voice. She stumbled across the clearing, tufts of dry brown grass catching at her feet. *"Danny!"*

An excited *mrrrr-row!* answered her. Hayley fell to her knees, sobbing in relief as Danny bounded out from between the trees. He was in lion form, his spotted, tawny coat perfectly blending with the autumn leaves. There was something more confident, bolder, about his movements as he bounced toward her. He no longer tripped over his own paws, or let his tail trail forgotten behind him. He had the fluid, beautiful grace of an animal. A *real* animal.

He's not a little boy dressed up as a lion, Hayley realized, properly, for the first time. *He is a lion.*

She was knocked flat on her back by the power of his pounce. He bumped his forehead enthusiastically against her own, clearly delighted with himself—and then paused. He sniffed her, an anxious-sounding *mrrr?* rumbling in his throat.

"Your ma was worried sick about you," Griff told him. He didn't raise his voice or look at all angry—just stern, and serious. "We all were. We didn't know where you'd gone."

"It's all right now," Hayley said quickly, feeling Danny cringe under Griff's obvious disapproval. She hugged him tight, rubbing her face against his soft fur. "Everything's okay, baby. I'm just glad you're safe."

Danny's rough pink tongue licked gently at her tear-streaked cheek. He whimpered, looking up at Griff.

"You weren't to know," Griff said. His gaze moved to the tree line, and his jaw set in a hard, tight line. "But he *didn't* tell us."

Hayley's pulse leaped as she caught sight of an enormous, golden form slinking through the undergrowth. Every instinct in her body screamed at her to grab her child and run, *run*, away from the dangerous predator.

It's only Reiner, she tried to tell herself...but there was no "only" about it.

She'd only ever seen lions lazing around in zoos before, safely behind bars. She'd never realized before just how *big* they were. Reiner's massive jaws could have comfortably engulfed her entire head. His paws were bigger than dinner plates. She couldn't move, couldn't take her eyes off that powerful, terrifying form as he stalked toward her.

Griff's hand fell on her shoulder, protective and comforting. There was more than a hint of snarl in his voice as he addressed Reiner. "That's enough. Stop trying to intimidate her."

Reiner halted, though his lip wrinkled back a little, exposing a fang. He sank to his hindquarters, curling his tail over his front paws. His entire attitude was insouciant, just daring them to object to his behavior.

Maybe it was Griff's solid presence at her back, or maybe just anger sparked by Reiner's arrogant, entitled air, but Hayley found her courage at last. Danny jumped off her as she surged to her feet.

Striding up to Reiner, she poked him right in his big pink nose. "You do *not* take Danny anywhere without telling me first! *Ever!*"

Reiner glared right back at her. His tawny form shimmered, turning back into a man. "I am his father," he said haughtily, apparently completely unselfconscious about being stark naked. "I have the right to be with my son."

Reiner might be entirely unabashed by his lack of clothing, but Hayley wasn't. She jerked her eyes back upward, her cheeks heating. He was just as athletically muscular as she remembered. She didn't find him at all sexually attractive anymore, but she had to admit he was still, objectively speaking, a beautiful man.

Once, that sculpted, powerful body had completely addled her mind, blinding her to the flaws hidden under the attractive surface. She didn't regret the relationship—she'd gotten Danny out of it, after all—but she couldn't believe she'd been so stupid.

From Reiner's sudden smirk, he'd caught the involuntary drift of her attention. "Thinking of old times, Hayley?" He flexed a little, his abs tightening. "If you're feeling a pang of regret, I might be persuaded to give you a second chance."

"*You* left *me*, Reiner!" Hayley jabbed him again with her finger, this time in the middle of his hard chest. "You do not get to just waltz in here and claim full parental rights. You haven't even *acknowledged* Danny before now!"

"Hayley," Griff said warningly. He turned to Danny. "Lad, me and your ma and da need to have one of those boring grown-up conversations now. Why don't you go play with my friend Chase over there? Practice your pouncing."

Chase stomped one back hoof, shooting Griff a look that was clearly the equine equivalent of *I will get you for this*. Nonetheless, he pranced away, swishing his long black tail invitingly at Danny. The lion cub didn't need any further encouragement. With the enthusiasm of a kitten spotting a laser pointer, he bounded after the pegasus.

"I thought this was something you'd probably prefer he didn't hear," Griff murmured to Hayley apologetically. His voice hardened as he turned to Reiner. "You only became interested in Danny once you learned he was a shifter, didn't you?"

"Of course," Reiner said, as if this was not only understandable but admirable. "What on earth would I want with a human child? I kept track of him, naturally, just in case it turned out the shifter genes bred true."

"If he'd never shifted, you would never have gotten in touch?" Hayley said, unable to comprehend how anyone could be so cold. "He's your son, Reiner, regardless of whether he turns into a lion or not!"

"If he was not a shifter, he would be no son of mine." Reiner looked across the clearing at Danny, who had managed to leap onto

Chase's back. Reiner's expression softened as he watched Danny cling onto the pegasus with all four paws, his milk-teeth nipping playfully at Chase's neck. "But he is. And he is a son to be proud of. Look at him! So bold and fearless. He will be a true alpha one day."

Hayley couldn't deny that there was genuine affection in Reiner's voice. "Well...I'm glad you've at least decided to take an interest now. But Reiner, you have to see things from my perspective. I know you're trying to make up for lost time, but I nearly died of terror when I went to pick Danny up from school and discovered that he wasn't there. You *can't* do that again."

Reiner glared back at her, his customary arrogance sliding back in place like a mask. "I will do what is best for my son. He needs to learn shifter ways, not to be locked up in some useless human school. Why did you worry? You knew he was with me."

"Yes, but I don't *know* you, Reiner! You wanted me to kill Danny before he was even born!" Angry tears sprang into Hayley's eyes as she remembered his horrible parting words, years ago. "How was I supposed to know you didn't just come back to finish the job?"

Reiner's muscles bunched with outrage. "How *dare* you imply that I would ever harm my son!"

"Both of you, that's enough." Griff spoke quietly, but his voice rang with that odd, iron-hard note of utter command. "He'll hear you if you start shouting at each other."

Hayley had indeed been about to yell at Reiner, but she found that her mouth had snapped shut of its own accord. Reiner too subsided, though he didn't look at all happy about it.

"*I* am Danny's alpha," Griff said to Reiner, that ominous, forceful growl still edging his words. "He is a member of my pride, and I am bound to protect him. I can tell that you would indeed never hurt him, but that does not mean I trust your judgment. Until I am satisfied that he is safe in your care, you *will not* take him anywhere without my permission."

Reiner held Griff's stare. His lips pulled back from his teeth, like a lion baring its fangs. "I could challenge you for him."

Griff's eyes flared yellow, as bright and fierce as the heart of the sun. "Try. It."

Reiner flinched back a little. He scowled down at the ground, breaking eye contact. "What if Danny *wants* me as his alpha?" he muttered.

"Then I would release him to you," Griff said coolly. "If you can win his heart and trust, I'll not stand in your way. But until then, I am his alpha, and you will respect my decisions for him. *Is that clear?*"

Reiner's eyes blazed with frustrated resentment, but he grudgingly nodded.

I'm his mother! Hayley wanted to scream at both of them. *Don't I get a say?*

But she didn't dare interrupt. Whatever was going on was clearly a shifter thing. She couldn't risk destabilizing the fragile peace agreement that Griff seemed to have negotiated with Reiner.

She knew that Griff could tell what she was thinking from the swift, apologetic glance he shot her. "Hayley, do you want Reiner to take you and Danny back home? Or would you rather that Chase take you and Danny, and I'll go with Reiner?"

From the look Reiner was giving Griff, if the firefighter got into a car with him, only one of them would be coming out again. "We'll go with Reiner," Hayley said hastily. She hesitated, eying the glowering lion shifter.

He always hated not getting his own way. I have to be the bigger person, give him a way to save face. If he is going to be a real father to Danny, I'm going to have to learn how to compromise with him.

"We don't have to go straight away, Reiner," she said to him, forcing herself to speak respectfully. "If you want more time with Danny, that is."

Any hope that he'd accept this peace offering died in the withering glare he gave her. "Thank you so much for offering me a few paltry hours with the son I haven't seen in *five years*," he said sarcastically. "It's *so* generous of you."

"I'll just go say goodbye to Danny, then Chase and I will be on our way." Griff took Hayley's arm—to all appearances casually, but she could feel the tension in his strong grip. "Quick word, Hayley?"

"What is it?" she asked under her breath, as he led her away from Reiner.

He shook his head at her, very slightly. He didn't speak again until they were at the other end of the clearing, where Chase and Danny were playing tag. Danny broke off his pursuit of Chase, bouncing happily up to Griff. The firefighter ruffled the cub's fur, then looked at Chase.

"If you want to go say hello to Reiner," Griff said to the pegasus, very quietly, "now would be a very good time."

Chase's ears flicked back and forth in apparent confusion. Then he snorted, tossing his head. He trotted toward the lion shifter.

Halfway across the clearing, he shimmered, turning human. Hayley was relieved to see that *he* at least kept his clothes on when he transformed.

"That should keep Reiner occupied for a few minutes," Griff said, as Chase loudly hailed a somewhat bemused-looking Reiner. "No one can pay attention to anything else when they're being subjected to Chase in full flow."

"What's going on?" Hayley was starting to feel very nervous by the level of secrecy. "What don't you want him to overhear?"

"This." Griff went down on one knee, so he could look Danny straight in the eyes. "Danny, this is very, very important. You must not tell your da that I can't shift."

Danny tilted his head quizzically. He must have said something telepathically, because Griff shook his head.

"No, he doesn't." Glancing up at Hayley, he added, "And we're *bloody* lucky that's true. He'd have challenged me in a heartbeat, otherwise."

Hayley went cold as she realized the implication. "A challenge is a physical fight? He'd attack you in lion form?"

Danny's tail lashed back and forth. He let out an indignant hiss.

"Shifter law isn't always fair," Griff said grimly. "Danny, if your da challenges me and wins, he'd become your alpha. And then he'd be able to order you never to see me again. He doesn't like me."

Danny's eyes widened in distress. He made a plaintive mewling sound, which even Hayley could tell was the lion equivalent of *why?*

"Because he loves *you* so much. He wants to have you all to himself. He doesn't want to share, not with me, not with your-" Griff stopped, abruptly, but Hayley knew what he'd nearly said.

Not with your mother.

"Griff," Hayley whispered, her mouth dry with fear. "Reiner's going to find out eventually."

"I know," Griff said grimly. "We're on borrowed time. Let's hope it's long enough."

"To do what?" she asked him, hoping against hope that he had a plan.

Griff straightened, his expression hard as stone. "To get you a really, really good lawyer."

CHAPTER 14

"What do you mean, we can't take Reiner to court?" Unable to keep still, Griff paced across the lawyer's office. Frustration and anger boiled under the surface of his skin. "You're a bloody fae hound, Michael! Since when do the Wild Hunt sit on their arses and let wrongdoers go unpunished?"

Michael's professionally neutral expression didn't alter, but his dark eyes flashed blood red for second. "We don't," the shifter lawyer said coolly. "But in the eyes of the law, Reiner Ljonsson isn't a wrongdoer. Much as I'd like to pull him down for you, I can't. And as your lawyer, I have to warn you that if you take Reiner to court over custody of Danny now…you're going to lose."

"But I'm Danny's mother," Hayley protested. Her brown eyes were huge in her frightened face. "Children always stay with their mother, don't they?"

Michael shook his close-shaven, elegant head. "Not shifter children. That's why we have our own court, to handle these cases. Our laws are designed to protect our children from being kept away from their birthright. Except in very, *very* exceptional circumstances, the shifter parent always gets custody."

Hayley swallowed. "But…Reiner lives in Valtyra. Surely the law can't really force Danny and me to move to a country where we don't even speak the language."

"Not both of you," Michael said grimly, and Hayley went stark white. "Just Danny. I've looked into Valtyran law. As a non-shifter, you can't even enter the country without a Valtyran sponsor. And from what you tell me of Reiner, he's not exactly likely to be willing to do that. Griff, if you're going to punch something, use that wall over there, please."

Griff, who had indeed just been about to smash his fist into the nearest wall, caught himself. The one the lawyer was pointing at was covered in dents and scratches, some of them alarmingly deep.

His lion eyed the marks warily, its rage abruptly dimming. *Territorial marks? They are very large. Very, very large. Are we trespassing?*

"What in God's name did that?" Griff asked, staring up at a particularly impressive crater near the ceiling.

"Wooly mammoth," the lawyer said. He shrugged one shoulder. "Very touchy people, mammoths."

Stupid cat, Griff's eagle taunted his lion. *Frightened of marks on a wall. And you think* you *can protect our fledgling?*

Griff pressed his fist to his forehead, pain splitting his skull like an axe as his two beasts went for each other. He clenched his teeth. *I don't have time for this!*

Deliberately, he thought of Reiner. His lion checked itself in midspring, while his eagle aborted its plunging dive, both diverted by the mental image of their common enemy. Griff took advantage of his beasts' distraction to grab them both by the scruffs of their necks, forcing them back into their separate areas of his mind.

"Griff?" Hayley touched his hand, hesitantly. "Are you okay?"

Griff's headache faded, washed away by the exquisite fire sparked by the lightest brush of her skin against his. His lion and eagle leaned forward in unison, yearning for more.

All her problems...and she's still worried about me. I'm just another burden on her.

He took a step back, thrusting his hand into the pocket of his jacket. "I'm fine now. Michael, tell me there's something you can do.

Or the next time you see me, you'll be prosecuting me on murder charges."

"I'm a fae hound of the Wild Hunt, Griff." Michael's eyes flashed red again. "Don't even joke about that sort of thing in front of me."

Griff matched his stare, not backing down. "Who said I was joking?"

"Griff, you can't," Hayley said. She rubbed her hands over her face, emerging looking wan but determined. "Reiner's rich, but even he hasn't got the funds to search all of America. I'll take Danny and disappear, if I have to."

Michael glanced up at the ceiling, a wince crossing his handsome face. "As someone who has to uphold child welfare even before client confidentiality, I did not just hear that." He sighed, looking back across at them both. "Look, neither of you do anything rash. I said you would lose if you took Reiner to court *now*. I didn't say ever."

Hope rose in Hayley's face. "You mean, there's something we can do to help win a favorable judgment?"

"Possibly." Michael steepled his long fingers, leaning his elbows on his polished desk. "It depends how far you're willing to go. For example, if you were to marry a shifter-"

Hayley didn't even wait for him to finish. "Griff, will you marry me?"

YES! Griff's lion and eagle roared as one.

"No," he said, roughly. He had to look away from the shocked hurt in her eyes. "That won't work. Tell her, Michael."

"Legally, he's not a shifter," Michael said to Hayley, apologetically. "By definition, a shifter has to be able to shift. Otherwise any human criminal could claim to be one of us, and demand to be judged according to our laws. It doesn't matter how you, or me, or anyone may personally view Griff...according to the law, he's just a regular human being."

Hayley stared at the lawyer. "Are you seriously advising me to marry any old random shifter? What do you expect me to do, get one out of a mail-order catalogue?"

Griff let out a brief, humorless bark of laughter. "No need for that.

John Doe owes me a life-debt." He pinched the bridge of his nose, fighting down a migraine as his animals howled with rage at the mere *idea* of giving their mate away to someone else. "Bet he never expected me to call it in like this."

"I am *not* marrying John!" Hayley said hotly. "Not even for pretend!"

Michael coughed, looking a little embarrassed. "Ah, it would have to be for real. The court would see through a fake marriage."

"Well, there you go." Hayley folded her arms, glaring at the lawyer. "Do you have any *practical* suggestions?"

Michael spread his hands. "If this comes to court, your only chance of winning custody is to demonstrate that you can provide Danny with a supportive shifter role model. If you can't do that through your mate, the next best thing is to have multiple close shifter friends. You need to get yourself—and him—integrated into the local shifter community. As quickly as possible. Fortunately, you shouldn't have any problems there. Griff's very well-connected."

Hayley bit her lip, glancing up at Griff. He could read her expression as clearly as if her thoughts were printed above her head in glowing neon letters: *But that means we'll have to spend a lot of time together...*

His eagle keened a high, piercing cry of loneliness. *She fears we will plummet out of the sky, leaving her alone in the storm. She does not want us at her wingtip. She knows she cannot rely on us.*

"It'll be all right," Griff told Hayley, forcing the words past the ache in his chest. "I just have to make the initial introductions for you. You'll be able to take it from there by yourself."

She looked down at her hands, her hair swinging forward to shadow her face. "Okay," she said, very quietly.

Michael cleared his throat, breaking the uncomfortable silence. "The longer you can keep Reiner in the dark, the better. I have to reiterate, it's best if you can keep this out of court entirely. If he does find out, I strongly recommend that you settle with him privately, if you can. Persuade him that it's in Danny's best interests to stay with his mother."

"That would require Reiner to become an actual alpha, rather than an insecure beta spoiling for a fight," Griff said darkly. "We've probably got a better chance of *me* learning to shift."

"What a good idea. Please do that." Michael shuffled through papers on his desk. "It would make my life immeasurably easier. Now, about the other matter-"

Griff held up his hand, forestalling him. "Hayley, would you mind waiting in the car? I've got some…private business I need to discuss. This will only take a moment."

Hurt flashed across Hayley's face, but she left without argument. Griff waited until he'd heard the office door swing shut behind her downstairs before turning back to Michael. "You have it ready for me to sign?"

"All in order." Michael slid the paper across the desk, along with a pen. "I can witness it now, if you like."

"Good." Griff flipped through the pages, quickly checking that everything was as he'd specified. "I appreciate the rush job. How much do I owe you?"

"Oh, call it a few bottles of your mother's best Scotch. It doesn't take long to draw up a will when there's only one beneficiary." Michael cocked a curious eyebrow at Griff. "Why don't you want her to know?"

"Because she'd probably argue." Griff scrawled an awkward, left-handed signature. "It's easier this way."

Michael's gaze flicked to Griff's crooked, frozen right hand. "That's new," he observed, quietly.

Griff made a noncommittal noise. He pushed the will back to Michael. "Thanks for this. It's a weight off my mind to know that at least Hayley will be taken care of financially when something happens to me."

Michael cast him a level look as he countersigned the document. "You mean *if* something happens to you."

"No," Griff said simply. "I don't."

CHAPTER 15

Grown-ups, Danny had decided, were just plain *weird*.

He couldn't understand it. Everything was wonderful, yet Mommy, Daddy, and Mr. Griff seemed determined not to be happy. They all pretended that they were, but Danny could tell the difference.

Daddy came round nearly every day to take him out into the woods to be lions together. When Mommy hugged Danny goodbye, it was always a little too hard and long, as if she was still worried about Daddy picking him up. Danny couldn't work out why. Daddy had gotten a booster seat for the amazing car, after all.

Danny loved being lions. Daddy was always much happier on four paws than he was when he was a person. When he was a person, he talked too much about how Mommy and Mr. Griff were doing things wrong and how much better everything would be if *he* was Danny's alpha.

It made Danny feel strange and nervous when Daddy talked like that. It was better when they were just being lions. Everything was simpler as lions.

Mr. Griff was around a lot, but somehow it felt like he wasn't. It was like whenever he played with Danny, his lion was a very long way away, keeping a wary distance. And he never, ever touched Mommy. That was wrong, Danny knew, though he wasn't quite sure why. It was something to do with needing to have both a mommy alpha *and* a daddy alpha in a pride, otherwise there wouldn't be any new little lions. Simba worried about it a lot, anyway.

Mommy worried a lot too. Danny could hear her crying sometimes, late at night, when she thought he was asleep. She didn't know that Simba let him hear her. Sometimes he really, really wanted to climb out of his bed and into hers, to give her a big hug and tell her everything was going to be okay.

But he didn't dare. Mommy always thought that she had to fix things all by herself. If she knew Danny's big plan, she might ruin the whole thing.

The problem, Danny had decided after careful thought and a lot of discussion with Simba, was that Mommy and Daddy hadn't properly understood their places in the pride. Mommy was supposed to be Mr. Griff's mate—which was like being married, but more so, according to Simba—but for some reason she didn't seem to want to be. And Daddy was supposed to be beta, helping defend the territory and raise the cubs, but for some reason *he* didn't want to be.

It was all very strange. Why didn't Mommy and Daddy want to be in Mr. Griff's pride? Couldn't they *see* that Mr. Griff was the biggest, bestest alpha ever?

Danny had tried to explain all this to Daddy, but he just got all grumbly and snarly and wouldn't listen. It was like he was jealous of Mr. Griff, which was silly because being an alpha or not wasn't something anyone could help. It didn't make Mr. Griff *better* than Daddy, any more than Daddy having a nice car meant he was better than Mr. Griff. It just meant that they had different jobs.

Danny had learned a lot about alphas and being a shifter from Mr. Griff and his friends. Mr. Griff had *amazing* friends.

That was what had given Danny his idea. Mr. Griff had introduced him and Mommy to some of his friends who were mated, and that had made it clear to Danny that Mommy and Mr. Griff just weren't doing it right. They needed someone to help them out.

Danny and Simba had a plan. They were going to make sure that Mommy and Mr. Griff became a proper alpha pair. They were going to make sure that Daddy *realized* that Mommy and Mr. Griff were a proper, mated alpha pair. Then everyone would be in the right place, and everyone would be happy.

And they had the perfect opportunity to carry out their plan, because soon it was going to be a very special day. A day when nobody, not even Daddy or Mommy or Mr. Griff, could possibly be sad. The very best time of year, apart from Christmas! Danny could hardly wait.

At Halloween, he was going to fix *everything*.

CHAPTER 16

"It's Halloween!" Danny shrieked at the top of his lungs, the cape of his Mike the Knight costume flying behind him as he ran in excited circles around Hayley. "It's finally Halloween! Hurry, Mommy, hurry!"

He hasn't even eaten any of his candy yet, Hayley thought in amused dismay. *What's he going to be like* after *the sugar hits?*

"Okay you, calm down," she said, trying to keep him in the beam of her flashlight as they walked down the street. "Mr. Griff isn't going to want to take us to the party if you're screeching like a crazed monkey."

Danny instantly took her hand, his brown eyes wide with concern. "I'm being good. I really am. Promise, promise, *promise* we can go, Mommy?"

Hayley couldn't help laughing at his over-the-top look of cherubic innocence. "I promise. I know how much this means to you."

He's so excited about this party. I guess he just can't get enough of being around other shifters

The thought gave her a pang in her chest. Over the past few weeks, she'd seen Danny blossom as he explored this new, secret world. She'd come to realize just how cruel it would be to keep him apart from his birthright. And Reiner was part of that. No matter how uncomfortable Hayley found it, Danny *needed* his father. He had to have someone who fully understood what it meant to be a shifter.

Griff isn't enough, whispered a small, traitorous voice in her mind. *Maybe even Griff's friends aren't enough. Maybe the law is right. Maybe I can't ever give Danny what he truly needs.*

Hayley banished the sickening thought. She wasn't going to let any of her worries taint Danny's enjoyment of this special night. Resolutely, she straightened her rabbit-ear headband, trying to get into the Halloween spirit.

How many chances do you get to go to a Halloween party with real, actual shapeshifters? This'll be fun. Halloween is meant to be a break from reality, a chance to pretend to be someone else. I could do with being someone else, for a bit.

I certainly look like someone else, at least.

The costume shop hadn't had a lot of options for larger ladies. She'd been going to go as a ghost, but Danny had pitched a fit at the prospect. In the end she'd had to relent and allow *him* to pick out her costume…though she'd drawn the line at the donning the fuzzy bikini. After a bit of a battle, Danny had grudgingly allowed her to wear the ears and fluffy tail paired with a soft but figure-hugging knitted black dress. The overall effect, she feared, was still rather closer to Playboy bunny than was entirely appropriate.

I shouldn't have let Danny talk me into this outfit. It's not fair to Griff.

Or me, for that matter.

Hayley breath sighed out. Ever since *that* night, Griff had treated her with meticulous, painful courtesy, as if he just saw her as Danny's mother and not a woman at all. In return, she did her very best to pretend that *he* was just some odd kind of sports coach for Danny.

But she couldn't forget the fire of his touch, or the heat of his mouth between her legs. When he was playing with Danny, she couldn't stop herself from avidly watching the flex of his biceps or the powerful curve of his back. And, just a few times, she'd caught Griff looking at her too, with a feral, exciting intensity that made her core clench in longing.

But then…he'd look away, taking a deep breath, and when he met her eyes again the burning desire in his own would be tamped down again, fiercely repressed. She knew that he didn't dare risk another uncontrolled shift. She knew that they couldn't ever touch again.

That would be Hayley's cue to find some excuse to leave the room, hiding away until she too could contain the feelings threatening to overspill in her heart. Though sometimes her body yearned for his so badly that she physically shook with longing, she would *not* give in to her selfish desires.

If he could suppress his deep, animal instincts, then so could she. She'd sworn she wouldn't make it any harder on him than it already was.

Hayley looked down at her costume. *Why, why,* why *didn't I just drape a sheet over my head?*

"There's Mr. Griff's house!" Danny yelled, forgetting in his excitement that he was being good. "Come on, Mommy!"

Shaking her head to dispel her gloomy thoughts, Hayley let him tow her up Griff's driveway. Small, hand-carved pumpkin lanterns lit the way. Hayley was privately pleased by the subdued, minimal decorations. She knew some people liked to go all-out with spooky graveyards and bloody zombie hands nailed to the door, but she personally didn't think they were suitable for little kids.

This is nice. Tasteful. Nothing scary at-

The door opened. Danny shrieked in terror, cowering behind Hayley as a towering apparition in demonic spiked armor loomed ominously over them both.

"Why do small children keep doing that?" said John Doe's deep voice from behind the draconic helmet, sounding bewildered.

Heart still hammering, Hayley blinked at his outfit. Curving, oddly organic-looking plates of some opalescent material armored John's massive shoulders and arms, leaving most of his impressive torso bare. Thick, scaled leggings protected his legs. He had a sword longer than Hayley was tall strapped to his back, a fist-sized pearl gleaming on the pommel.

"That...is quite some costume, John," Hayley said weakly.

"I am not wearing a costume," John said, flipping up his visor.

"This is the formal armor of the Order of the First Water, sworn defenders of the Pearl Throne."

Danny peeked round Hayley's legs. "You mean that's *real* knight armor, Sir John?"

"Yes. I do not get many opportunities to wear it, these days." The sea dragon shifter let out a deep, heartfelt sigh. "I am beginning to regret my decision to do so tonight. By my count, I have now made thirty-seven small children cry."

"Yes, but you've also inspired at least that many teenage crushes," Griff's amused voice floated around John's shoulder. "I swear there's one group of girls who keep swapping costumes and coming back. Hello, Danny."

"Mr. Griff!" Danny frowned, looking Griff up and down. "Why are you wearing a skirt?"

"It's a kilt, lad," Griff said, spreading his arms to display his plaid. He let out a rich chuckle. "I'm cheating too. This is just the way my clan traditionally dresses on formal occasions. But you Sassenachs find it exotic, so I thought it would do for a costume. Do you like it?"

"I told you to wear something awesome. Like a Batman suit. Not a *skirt*." Danny turned to Hayley, looking doubtfully up at her. "Mommy, do you like Mr. Griff's costume?"

"Guh," Hayley managed to say.

And I was worried about my *costume being too sexy.*

She tore her eyes away from Griff's muscular calves, moistening her dry lips. "Y-yes," she said weakly. "I think it's very…nice."

"Mph." Danny did not sound convinced. He pushed Hayley forward, his tone brightening. "Mr. Griff, look at Mommy's costume!"

Griff's golden eyes heated, and she knew that he could see her arousal. His hungry gaze swept down her own figure-hugging outfit.

Oh, I really, really, really *should have come as a ghost.*

"He picked it," she said hastily, cheeks hot with mortification. "Um, I mean, I'm meant be a bunny. Like, a *real* bunny."

"That's right," Danny said happily. "Because lions and eagles *both* like bunnies."

Oh dear Lord, was that his logic?

"Aye. We do," Griff said, his voice a deep growl. He cleared his throat, looking back down at Danny. "Well, lad, ready to get going?"

"Yes!" Danny shouted, seizing Griff's hand. "Are you coming too, Sir John?"

"I must stay and guard the door." John flipped his visor shut again. "Though I must admit, I am not accustomed to stopping assailants by offering them lollipops."

"All right if we stop off at a couple of my friends' places along the way?" Griff asked Danny as they started up the road. "They're two you haven't met yet, but I think you'd like them."

Danny looked a little worried. "We won't be late for the party, will we?"

"I promise, we'll get there in plenty of time." Griff looked over Danny's head at Hayley, smiling. The sight made her heart leap—he hadn't smiled properly like that since, well, Reiner. "I've never known a boy to be so excited about a party. I only hope it lives up to his expectations."

"I'm sure it will," Hayley said, smiling back. *Just friends,* she reminded herself sternly. *Friends on a nice fun night out. As friends.* "He's been obsessed ever since you mentioned it. So, who are you taking us to visit?"

"Hugh, for one." Griff turned off the main street. "He won't come to the party—too many people—but he secretly loves getting trick-or-treaters. Most people don't realize it, but he's got a hidden soft spot for children, our Hugh. But first, I wanted to drop by on someone else. I want to have one last try at convincing her to join us."

The street got narrow, and darker, as Griff led them deeper into the maze of alleyways. There weren't many pumpkins in *this* neighborhood. Hayley wouldn't have felt safe on her own, but she trusted Griff to know what he was doing.

"Here we go," Griff said, stopping outside a dented door with peeling paint. Someone had carefully cut *Happy Halloween!* out of newspaper print, sticking the letters to the inside of the window. "You want to knock, Danny?"

Danny gave Griff a slightly dubious look, but dutifully knocked.

The door opened instant, as if someone had been waiting right on the other side.

"Trick or treat!" announced a beaming teenage girl in a home-made fairy princess costume and a wheelchair. Pink glittering ribbons were woven through the spokes.

Danny frowned. "That's what *I'm* supposed to say!"

"Sorry," the girl said cheerfully. "I just like saying it too. I never get to go out myself. Hi, Big G! And you're Hayley, right? I'm Hope."

"Nice to meet you," Hayley said, carefully shaking the offered hand. Hope's bones were as delicate as a bird's, her fingers barely able to grip Hayley's. "Are you a...?"

"Shifter?" Hope wheeled her chair back a little, letting them into the narrow hallway. "Nope, that's my sister. Unfortunately. You're wasting your time, G. She won't come. She won't even let *me* come."

"Hmm." Griff's mouth tightened. "Well, let me see what I can do."

"Good luck." Hope did not sound hopeful. Her thin shoulders heaved in a tragic sigh. "I cannot *wait* until I'm eighteen, and can finally do what I want."

Griff patted her on the shoulder as he edged round her wheelchair. "She's just trying to look out for you, you know."

"Yeah, well, I wish she wouldn't." Hope turned her attention back to Danny, brightening again. "Hey, I hope you like candy, because I've got a *ton*. Turns out most kids around here prefer throwing eggs to getting treats."

Hayley left Danny rummaging enthusiastically in the offered bucket of candy, following Griff down the short, dark hallway. "What sort of shifter is her sister?" she asked in an undertone.

Griff shot her a swift, strangely guarded glance. "Wyvern."

Wyvern? Where have I heard that before...?

Hayley grabbed Griff's wrist as he raised his hand to knock on a closed door. It was the first time she'd touched him for weeks. She made herself ignore the rush of desire that shot through her blood.

"Wyvern as in wyvern venom?" she hissed. "As in the poison you made me inject you with? The poison that nearly *killed* you?"

"That wasn't her fault." Shaking her off, Griff firmly knocked on the door. "Ivy? I know you're in there. You can't hide from me."

The door opened a crack, revealing one green eye and a sliver of sulky expression. "You should listen to your friend, G. Just go away."

"I can't do that, Ivy." Griff put his shoulder to the door, shoving it open. "Please come out."

Hayley wasn't entirely sure what she'd expected a wyvern shifter to look like, but she had to admit Ivy wasn't it. The young woman was soft and curvy, with a round, pretty face despite her ferocious scowl. She was dressed head-to-toe in layers of leather and denim, every inch of her skin below the chin covered.

She folded her gloved hands under her armpits, glaring at Griff. "You come back for some more poison? One heart attack wasn't enough for you?"

"Ivy, I told you, I don't blame you for anything," Griff said patiently. "It was entirely my own idea, and you tried to talk me out of it, and in any event, you probably saved my life. Now, are you going to stop hiding yourself away and come out to meet everyone?"

"Yeah, because all your friends would just *love* to hang out with me." Ivy snorted. "I'm sure ponyboy will even buy me a drink."

"I'll handle Chase," Griff coaxed. "Come on, Ivy. For Hope's sake, if not your own."

Ivy's green eyes narrowed. "Tell you what, G. I *will* come. If you just let me do one thing first." She stepped toward Hayley, stretching out her hand. "After all, if you want me to go to a big, crowded party, then you must be okay with me doing *this*…"

Hayley, who'd automatically started to take Ivy's offered hand, yelped as Griff knocked her own arm aside. His broad form was abruptly between the her and the wyvern shifter, every muscle tense.

Ivy's lip curled. "Yeah. Didn't think so."

Griff sighed, raking his fingers through his hair. "I'm sorry, Ivy. I didn't mean to do that. Just instincts. You know how it is."

"Yeah, well." Ivy stepped back, closing the door again. "If you really want to help me, G…you know what you can do."

"What was that all about?" Hayley asked Griff, after they'd collected Danny and said goodbye to Hope.

"Ivy's touch is poisonous," he said quietly, so that Danny—running excitedly on ahead waving a glow stick—didn't overhear. "Even in human form. She's fairly safe when she's wearing gloves, but…well, 'fairly safe' isn't good enough for my inner beasts."

"Poor kid." Ivy's wary defensiveness took on a whole new meaning. Having seen how much a community of fellow shifters meant to Danny, Hayley felt sorry for the isolated wyvern shifter. "What did she mean, you could help her?"

"Not me, really." Griff let out his breath in a long sigh. "Ash could, but he won't. Ivy wants me to try to persuade him-"

"Griff?" Hayley found that she was walking by herself. She turned to see that he'd frozen in mid-step. "What is it?"

All the blood had drained from his face. "Distract me."

"Huh? Danny!" Hayley shouted over her shoulder as she hurried back to Griff. Her blood ran cold as she realized that he was fighting his inner beasts. "Griff! What set them off?"

"I thought of—something." His left fist clenched, shaking. Sweat beaded on his forehead. "But I can't—let them know—*distract me!*"

She could only think of one thing to do. Stretching up on tip-toe, she kissed him.

She'd meant it to be short, just to shock his animals out of their anger. But once she'd started, she couldn't stop. She laced her fingers round the back of his neck, pulling him down further, his mouth as hungry and demanding as hers. He made a low, desperate sound deep in his throat, crushing her against his strong body. It was like they were two magnets, drawn together by some unstoppable, cosmic force.

"Mommy? Mr. Griff?"

They leaped apart guiltily.

Brow furrowed, Danny looked between them, first at Hayley, then up at Griff. His small shoulders heaved in a huge, relieved sigh.

"*Finally,*" he said in satisfaction.

CHAPTER 17

Griff very carefully concentrated on the feel of Hayley's fingers wound through his. He focused on the exquisite softness of her skin, the intoxicating heat of her body next to his. He let his overwhelming desire for her surge...covering up the idea that Ivy had sparked in his mind.

He could feel his eagle's stare boring into the inside of his skull, trying to see what he was concealing from it. His lion was less suspicious. It rolled in delight, luxuriating in their mate's presence like a kitten in a bed of catnip.

Hayley stole a sidelong glimpse of his profile as they passed under a streetlamp. "Have they settled down again?" she asked.

"Aye. All's well. For the moment, at least." *Which means that I should really let go now...*

As if reading his mind, Hayley's fingers tightened on his hand. "You know," she said softly, "I was thinking earlier about how Halloween lets you pretend to be someone else, just for one night. I was thinking how much fun that would be."

"That does sound like a grand time." He looked down into her upturned face. "Who would you like to be?"

"Just a woman." Tentatively, as if doubting her welcome, she leaned into his side. "Just a woman, out with her son. And her man."

Griff drew in a short, sharp breath, longing piercing his heart like an arrow. He was fiercely aware of every point of contact between her body and his.

I shouldn't. It'll only make it harder to stop.

"Aye," he said, his voice as soft as hers had been, as if reality couldn't notice them as long as they were whispering. "I'd like to pretend that too. Just for one night."

He felt Hayley's tense muscles relax. She leaned her head against his shoulder. "Just for one night."

"Why are you slowing down, Mr. Griff? Hurry!" Danny pulled at Griff's other hand, straining ahead like an eager puppy on a leash. "I can hear music! We're nearly at the party!"

A couple of betas from the local wolf pack were hanging casually around the entrance to an alleyway, ready to politely—or not so politely—turn back any too-curious mundanes. Recognizing Griff, they waved the three of them through without challenge.

Griff hadn't taken Hayley and Danny to the Full Moon before. Normally, the shifter-only pub was also an adult-only establishment. Not that it was a rowdy drinking den—Rose Swanmay, the proprietor, made sure of that. But it *was* a place for shifters of all types to relax and enjoy the company of their own kind, which meant it sometimes got a little boisterous. Children were not exactly banned, but they were usually discouraged.

But not tonight. Tonight, strings of tiny orange lights crisscrossed the narrow alleyway, turning it into a magical, glittering tunnel. The outside of the old, whitewashed pub had been transformed into a witch's cottage from a fairytale, with fake cobwebs under the eaves and a mysterious, glowing cauldron bubbling next to the door. Jack o' lanterns grinned cheerfully, candles flickering in the dark.

"*Wow*," breathed Danny and Hayley together.

Griff smiled, enjoying the astonishment and delight shining from both their faces. "Halloween's a bit of a special time for shifters," he said as he led them toward the pub. "Traditionally, it used to be the night we let our animal sides run wild. Most of us don't go out looking for some poor soul to chase down anymore, but we do still like to let our hair down a bit."

"There's Chase!" Danny waved excitedly at the pegasus shifter, who was standing near the door of the pub with a giggling pack of children gathered around him. "Hello, Mr. Chase!"

"Danny! Excellent, another child!" Chase hurried over, his entourage of kids following him like a line of ducklings. "Listen, I have a big favor to ask you. Also, completely coincidentally, I just so happen to have a great deal of chocolate."

Griff blinked at Chase as light from the open pub door illuminated the pegasus shifter's face. "*What* have you done to yourself?"

Chase spread his arms wide, beaming. "I, my friend, have *outdone* myself."

Chase's previously black hair was now almost every color of the rainbow, dyed in thick stripes from red to violet—every color, that is, except blue. *That* seemed to have been reserved for the rest of him.

His flight suit was blue. His boots were blue. His hands, face, and every single inch of exposed skin: Blue.

Griff shook his head. "I haven't the faintest idea how you did that. Or, more importantly, why. What are you meant to be, a Smurf?"

"Your cultural references are sadly outdated," Chase informed him haughtily. "If you were as down with the kids as *I* am, you would instantly recognize who I am."

"Oh my." Hayley giggled. "You haven't. You're actually...?"

Chase shimmered. Kids screamed in joy as the powder-blue pegasus pranced on the spot, his rainbow-striped mane and tail rippling.

"RAINBOW DASH!" Danny collapsed with laughter.

"What on earth is a Rainbow Dash?" Griff said, bewildered.

"Don't ask," said Chase's mate Connie, coming up beside him. She rolled her eyes at her mate, who was now shamelessly posing for his delighted audience. "If you'd told me this time last year that I'd be spending the night before Halloween painting a horse blue, I'd have laughed in your face."

"I didn't even know you *could* paint horses." Griff's sharp eyes noticed that none of the dye was coming off on the hands of the small girls enthusiastically stroking Chase's fur. "Ah...that stuff isn't permanent, is it?"

"It wasn't meant to be. I think Chase may have accidentally embedded it into his skin and hair, though, when he shifted back to human." Connie smirked. "You should see where the rainbow stripes on his tail ended up."

Hayley came back from admiring Chase, wiping away tears of laughter. "Hi Connie." She gave Chase's mate a brief, warm hug. The two had become fast friends since Griff had introduced them. "So, you weren't tempted to go for a matching outfit? You'd make a *wonderful* Twilight Sparkle."

Connie shot her a mock-glare. She was dressed as a WWII fighter pilot—though Griff strongly suspected that it was a real vintage uniform, not a costume. She did own a genuine, original Spitfire, after all. "Maybe next year." She gave Hayley a long, speculative look. "That's quite some costume you've got on yourself."

Hayley blushed a little. "Danny picked it," she mumbled. "He just thought it was a bunny costume, and I couldn't really explain to him... well, you know."

"Hmm." Connie's gaze flicked from Hayley to Griff and back again. She wound her arm firmly through Hayley's. "Can I steal you for a little while? Girl talk, Griff. Would bore you silly."

Hayley raised an eyebrow at him, and he shrugged back. He was no more able than she was to guess what was on Connie's mind. "Have fun. You want me to look after Danny while you're chatting?"

"No need," Chase said grandly, shifting back into human form. "*I* shall watch him. I am watching *all* the children tonight. I am the official designated babysitter, so that all the hard-working parents can enjoy themselves safe in the knowledge that their precious darlings are in safe hands. Or hooves."

"Chase," Griff said suspiciously. "Did you kidnap these kids?"

"Why do people keep asking me that?" Chase looked wounded. "Is it so hard to believe that parents would voluntarily hand over the fruits of their loins to me? I *am* extraordinarily good with children, after all."

Griff stared at him. "Since when?"

Chase shot him a glare. "Since always."

"Since his biological clock started ticking," Connie corrected, dryly. "Even though I've told him he doesn't have one."

"*We* have one. We only have so many fertile years available to us," Chase said to her earnestly. "If we don't get started soon, we'll have difficulty fitting in all fourteen children."

Connie jabbed him in the stomach. "*You* can have fourteen children. Just as soon as you work out how to become a seahorse shifter and gestate them yourself. *I'm* drawing the line at three."

Chase beamed round at Griff and Hayley. "Last week she was drawing the line at two. I'm winning."

Connie threw Hayley a pleading look. "You see why I need to talk to you?" She dragged her off toward the pub. "Please, please, *please* tell me many horrible stories about spending months throwing up constantly and waddling around like an elephant with a thyroid problem. Bring me back to my senses."

Griff chuckled as they disappeared inside. "Fourteen kids?" he said to Chase. "Really?"

"I'm actually going for four," Chase confessed. "Always start negotiations high." He elbowed Griff in the side, giving him a sly grin. "So, you and Hayley were looking awfully cozy. Walking hand-in-hand, I noticed."

"No comment. Did you happen to notice whether Ash is here, or were you too busy stealing children?"

"I am not *stealing* children. I plan to give them back." Chase shrugged. "And he's inside. Though you'd better catch him quick, you know he only ever puts in a token appearance at this sort of thing."

"Good point." Griff cocked an eyebrow at Danny. "Well, lad? You want to play out here with Chase for a while, or stay with me?"

No matter how much Griff might enjoy pulling Chase's leg, he didn't actually have any hesitation in leaving Danny in the pegasus shifter's care. He knew that Chase's playful exuberance concealed a protective streak a mile wide. Danny would be safe with him.

"I want to hang out with Chase," Danny said promptly. His decision may have been slightly influenced by the fistful of candy bars Chase had just produced out of one of his many pockets. "Can I come and find you later, though?"

Griff ruffled his hair. "Anytime. Just ask Chase when you want me. He can find anyone, you know."

Leaving Chase organizing the kids into teams for some sort of game, he ducked into the pub. The main room was packed with shifters of all sorts, laughing and talking. Behind the long wooden bar, Rose was handing out drinks and smiles. She wore an extravagant feathered carnival mask, the glossy blue-black plumes perfectly complimenting her flawless ebony skin.

Griff caught a glimpse of Hayley and Connie perched on stools at one end of the bar, along with Virginia, Dai's mate. Hayley seemed to be in the middle of explaining something that required a great deal of hand gestures. From the somewhat horrified yet fascinated expressions on the other two women's faces, Griff strongly suspected that the conversation had turned rather gynecological in nature.

Definitely not going to interrupt that.

He picked his way through the crowd, exchanging brief nods and greetings as he went. It was so crowded and busy, even his eagle wasn't immediately able to spot Ash. He did see Dai, half a head taller than anyone else and wearing a glittering gold helmet and flowing red cape, but it was too noisy for Griff to catch his attention. Griff cursed his own inability to mindspeak to his teammates. *That* would have made finding Ash much easier.

The back of the pub had been cleared for dancing, with a tiny stage erected for a local all-shifter ceilidh band. The lead fiddle player struck an eerie, keening note across his strings, like an alpha wolf calling to his pack. The other members joined in, flute and guitar and accordion howling back in answer. The drum pounded like a heartbeat, and the band launched into a wild, racing tune. Shifters cheered, surging onto the dance floor.

With the crowd thinning, Griff finally managed to spot Ash, alone in a quiet, shadowed corner booth. Griff was amused to note that, once again, Ash had come as a firefighter.

"You know, Halloween is meant to be for dressing up," Griff teased, sliding into the seat opposite the Fire Commander. "Pretending to be someone else."

"I am dressed up," Ash said, mildly. He made a small, brief gesture, indicating his dark blue suit with its gold rank insignia. "This is a dress uniform. In any event, you are also just wearing formal attire, I note."

"Ah, well, you have me there." Griff straightened the plaid draped over his shoulder, smiling. "Though…my outfit choice *may* have something to do with the fact that I happened to notice that Hayley has a complete collection of Outlander novels. In hardback."

The Fire Commander tilted his head a degree, acknowledging the point. "You are in a good mood tonight."

Griff's smile twisted, just a little. "I'm pretending to be someone else."

"Ah." Ash's dark eyes studied him for a long moment. Even to Griff's eagle-sharp senses, the Fire Commander was a completely unreadable book—not just closed, but bound in chains and locked away in a deep vault. "So the situation is unchanged. I am sorry to hear that."

Griff leaned his elbows on the table, folding his arms. "I went to see Ivy this evening."

Ash didn't so much as blink at the apparent topic jump. "And is her situation also unchanged?"

"Aye. She still wants you to burn away her wyvern."

"No," Ash said flatly, without even a second of hesitation.

Griff let out his breath. "She just wants to be able to touch people, Ash. Even if that means becoming a mundane human instead of a shifter."

Ash was respected in the shifter community for who he was…but he was feared for *what* he was. It was widely known that the Phoenix could burn anything. Not just physical materials like stone and steel, but metaphysical things as well.

Memories. Personality traits. Even a shifter's inner animal. Griff knew that he'd only done it a handful of times, in situations of dire need, but it was the reason most shifters kept as far away from the Fire Commander as they could.

Ash shook his head. "She does not know what she is asking. If the Parliament of Shifters had not demanded that I use my power to punish arsonists, I would not do it to any shifter under any circumstances. Not even to my worst enemy."

Griff looked out at the cheerful crowd without speaking for a long, long moment. "How about to a friend?"

"I will not burn away Ivy's wyvern. Not even for you."

"To a friend, Ash," Griff said, very quietly. "Not for a friend."

Out of the corner of his eye, he saw Ash go very, very still.

"Is this a conversation which it is safe to have?" Ash said at last, just as softly. "I would have thought your beasts would…object."

Griff's eagle was motionless, staring intently into his soul as though his thoughts were prey scurrying through long grass. His lion stirred a little, disturbed by the eagle's focus but unable itself to understand what had caused it.

"If we speak elliptically, we should be fine." Neither of his animals were good at abstract thought, or following a metaphor. Nonetheless, Griff kept a tight rein on his emotions, erecting a firm mental wall between himself and them. "I'll let you know if there's a problem."

Ash nodded in understanding. "Do you remember Bertram Russell?"

Well, I did tell him to speak elliptically. Griff had no idea where this was going. "The dragon shifter who attacked Dai and Virginia?"

Griff had never met him in person, but all of Alpha Team had been involved in helping Dai protect his mate from the arrogant, ruthless dragon shifter. Ash, however, had been the one to finally stop Bertram. The Phoenix had burned away his dragon, permanently removing his ability to shift.

Ash toyed with his glass of water. "Do you know what happened to him, afterwards?"

Griff shook his head. "No idea. Didn't really care, as long as he didn't bother us again."

"He is a tour guide at a small Roman heritage site," Ash said quietly. "He helps visiting schoolchildren dress up in costumes and color in pictures of the mosaics. He answers their questions, as much as he can. By all accounts, he is happy."

Ice ran down Griff's spine. Bertram had been fiercely competitive, a brilliant academic with an ego the size of his dragon.

And now he's content in some little backwater local museum...

"Our animals are woven through our souls," Ash said, when Griff didn't speak. "Even I cannot tell where the fire will race, once I light the spark. I took a dragon, and ended up also taking a man's pride, his ambition. I once had to take a man's wolf, and it left him unable to work in a team ever again. What else could I end up inadvertently destroying? A man's courage? His astuteness?" He looked straight at Griff. "Everything that made him who he was?"

Griff moistened his dry lips. "A man might be willing to destroy anything, in order to protect his mate."

Something flared behind Ash's eyes, a black fire like a dying sun. "I understand that well." The crack in his calm lasted barely a heartbeat, sealed over so quickly that Griff almost doubted he'd ever seen that brief moment of anguish at all. "It is…possible, that I could burn away just enough, and no more. It is possible that I could take one thing, and leave another. But I do not know for certain."

"I understand that. And I appreciate that you'd rather not be having this conversation at all. But…it might be the only way. If Hayley married a shifter, Reiner wouldn't be able to claim Danny. And she has, ah, very firm opinions on which shifters she might be willing to marry."

"I imagine that it is a very short list." It was the closest Griff had every heard Ash come to making an actual joke. The Phoenix *was* rattled, underneath that rigidly controlled exterior. "Griffin, I must tell you something. To my…perception, you are indeed different to other shifters. I can sense the divide in your soul. But I cannot tell which half is which."

"That's all right. In a way, I'm glad." Griff smiled with black humor. "You know the old moral dilemma about only having one space in a lifeboat, and having to choose which family member to save? Better not to have to make that choice. Better to leave it to random chance."

Ash took a sip of his water. "Best not to be at sea at all."

"That ship sailed a long time ago, alas." Griff leaned back with a sigh. "Ash, I promise, I won't rush into anything. I won't ask this of you unless there is no other choice. But…it is good to know that I *do* have at least one choice. If it comes to it."

Whatever Ash said in response was drowned out by Chase's agitated mental voice abruptly crashing into Griff's head. *Griff, we've got a problem. Reiner's here.*

CHAPTER 18

"Let me get this straight." Connie held up her hands, counting items off on her fingers. "Bloating. Vomiting. Swollen ankles. Heartburn. Mood swings. Weird food cravings."

"You forgot hemorrhoids," Hayley said helpfully.

"I'm *trying* to forget the hemorrhoids." Connie shuddered. "And on top of this, you spend the last few months unable to so much as get out of a chair without a fork lift truck. And, just to cap it all off, you then get to experience absolutely the worst pain of your entire life."

Hayley sipped her cocktail, hiding her grin. "That's about the size of it."

Connie threw up her hands in despair. "Why would anyone *do* this voluntarily?"

"I'm beginning to wonder that myself," Virginia murmured.

Hayley had only met Virginia once before, and she was still a little in awe of her. She *was* a world-famous archaeologist, after all. As if that wasn't bad enough, she was also drop-dead gorgeous. Hayley had caught more than a few men wistfully eying Virginia's stunning curves, accentuated by the skin-tight shorts and cropped vest of her Lara Croft costume. She was the perfect match to her mate Dai, as beautiful and strong as his dragon, and intimidatingly self-possessed.

Now, however, there was the tiniest crack in Virginia's confident air. One of her hands had crept to rest on her rounded belly. Hayley put two and two together.

"Oh my God!" she gasped, her hands flying to her mouth. "Virginia, are you...?"

A hint of a blush darkened Virginia's warm ochre cheeks. "We weren't going to tell anyone yet, because it's still so early. But yes."

"I can't believe it!" Connie threw her arms around the taller woman, hugging her. "Congratulations! When are you due?"

"Around May." Virginia's full lips curved in a wry smile. "From what Hayley's been telling us, I'm now really glad I'm not going to be heavily pregnant in mid-summer, and wallowing in my own sweat like a hippo."

"I wouldn't have said all those things if I'd known!" Hayley exclaimed, feeling mortified. "I was exaggerating. Honest. It's really not so bad."

Virginia raised one eyebrow at her.

"Okay, it kind of is," Hayley confessed. "But seriously, all the discomfort and everything...it's worth it. You forget it all, the instant you have your baby in your arms."

"Truly?" Virginia didn't sound her usual polished, self-confident self. Her brown eyes begged for reassurance. "You aren't just saying that?"

Hayley put her hand over Virginia's, squeezing a little. "Let's put it this way. When I had Danny, I was on my own, flat broke, having to take any temp work I could get just to keep a roof over our heads. I had no sleep, no money, no partner, and no support at all. And if I could go back in time...I would do it all again. In a *heartbeat.*"

Virginia squeezed back, the calm strength returning to her face. "Thank you," she said sincerely.

"Now I feel like a complete wuss." Connie folded her arms, glaring down into her drink. "I wish I was as brave you two."

As brave as you two? Hayley couldn't imagine being thought of in the same category as brilliant, bold Virginia. "Hey, you fly vintage fighter planes for a living. I teach little kids. Which one of us is the brave one again?"

"You," Connie said promptly. "I'd rather face a tornado than a class of thirty children. I'm terrified of having to cope with even one kid. Let alone the whole herd that Chase wants."

"Well, fourteen does sound a little excessive." Hayley grinned at her.

"Oh, he really wants four. It's just more fun to pretend that I don't know that. He can be very inventive when he's trying to get his own way." Connie bit her lip. "I do want kids, I think. It's just…my mom passed away when I was little, and my dad isn't exactly the best parental role model. I'm so scared that I might turn out to be a terrible mother."

"*I'm* still terrified that I'm a terrible mother," Hayley said ruefully. "You aren't alone in that. And I think you'd be a great mom. Chase will make a great dad, too. Danny likes both of you a lot."

"He's such a sweet kid." Connie sighed. "If I could be certain that mine would turn out half as well, I wouldn't be nearly so worried. Rose," she turned to the woman tending the bar, who was cleaning glasses nearby, "what do *you* think?"

Hayley was a little startled by this unexpected appeal to the pub owner…but then Rose glanced up, and she understood. Even half-concealed behind the feathery carnival mask, Rose had the kindest, wisest face she'd ever seen. She could only have been in her mid-forties, but she possessed a sort of deep, unhurried calm that made her seem ageless. In a strange way, she reminded Hayley of Ash—the same sense of hidden power, tightly leashed.

"I think that you should never let fear stand in the way of your heart's desire," Rose said to Connie…but her eyes flicked briefly to Hayley. She had an odd sense that Rose was aiming the statement at *her*, just as much as Connie.

"That's the problem, I don't know if it *is* my heart's desire." Connie looked hopefully across the bar at Rose. "Can you tell for me, Rose? I mean, you can see mate bonds, after all. Can you see other sorts of things in people's hearts too? Like, how maternal someone is?"

Rose laughed. "I can see some things, true, but not that. But I don't need special powers to know that you're going to make a fine mother. You have enough love in your heart to nurture an entire brood of children." She dropped her voice a little. "Your own mother made sure of that."

Connie blinked rapidly, as if having to fight to hold back sudden tears. "Thanks, Rose," she whispered. "That...that means a lot."

"You can see mate bonds?" Hayley said to Rose, partly to give Connie a chance to recover her composure, but mainly just out of interest. "Really?"

Rose nodded in assent, her hands still busy cleaning glasses. "It's one of the reasons shifters come here. I can instantly tell if I've met someone's mate before, even if *they've* never met. I've matched up more than a few of my customers by now."

"I wish you'd find your mate, Rose," Virginia said. "It doesn't seem fair that you're still alone, when you've helped so many of us."

"Ah, well. Just fate, I suppose." Rose smiled, a little sadly. "I travelled the world when I was younger, searching, but never found him. Maybe he'll walk through my door one of these days."

Hayley bit back the question on the tip of her tongue, unsure whether it would be rude to ask what Rose's animal was. She didn't yet know enough about shifter ways to have a firm grasp on their unspoken rules of etiquette.

She *had* learned enough, though, to know that a shifter's power came from their inner beast. Griff's perceptiveness came from his eagle, while his innate ability to command came from his lion. But what on earth could give Rose the sort of power that she had?

Rose glanced at her sidelong, a teasing smile tugging at her lips. "I can feel your curiosity from here. Go on. Guess."

From Virginia and Connie's grins, they already knew. Hayley narrowed her eyes, scrutinizing the bartender. Rose might look soft and round, but the elegance in the way she held herself would have made a prima ballerina green with envy. Even just polishing glasses, there was a breathtaking grace to every movement of her delicate hands.

Something strong, but not dangerous. Not a predator. Something calm and graceful. And...something that symbolizes devotion? Something that mates for life, and pines away if that love is lost...

The graceful curve of Rose's neck and the long, shimmering black feathers on her mask gave her away. "You're a swan!"

"Not many get that right. You've got good eyes." Rose tilted her head a little, her expression enigmatic behind her mask. "Sharp eyes are a good match to an eagle. But you need courage if you're going to match a lion. Especially when his own courage falters."

"Griff, falter?" Hayley wasn't sure whether to laugh or take offence at the idea. "I don't think Griff's ever been afraid of anything in his entire life."

"Up until recently, I'd have agreed with you." Rose looked at something over Hayley's shoulder. "But not anymore. You might want to ask him about that."

"Hayley." She spun round at Griff's voice, right behind her. He was looking grim. "We've got a potential problem. Reiner's here."

"Reiner? *Here?*" Hayley couldn't imagine Reiner voluntarily coming to a Halloween party. He'd always looked down his nose at the holiday, calling it a 'vulgar American perversion of ancient traditions.' "Why?"

"I don't know, but we have to try to head him off." Griff took her hand, helping her down from the bar stool. "There are too many people who know me here."

She gasped as she realized the danger. "Someone could let your secret slip."

Connie cocked her head to one side, lips moving soundlessly for a moment. "Chase is improvising a very, very long joke outside," she said, and Hayley realized that she'd been communicating telepathically with her mate. "But he says to hurry, because Reiner doesn't look like he's going to wait for the punchline."

Virginia's expression went a little unfocussed as well. A moment later, Dai's tall form cut through the crowd toward them.

"Virginia says you might need some backup," the dragon shifter said to Griff. In his Anglo-Saxon warrior costume, he looked more than ready to step onto a battlefield.

"No fighting on my premises, boys," Rose said warningly. "All shifters are welcome, as long as they behave themselves. I won't have anyone acting like this is their personal territory. Not even Alpha Team."

"I'm sorry, Rose, but I can't just let Reiner come in here and start chatting," Griff growled. "You don't understand. I *can't* let him find out what I really am."

"You're trying to wear too many masks. It might do you good for some of them to slip." Rose gave him a level look. "I mean it, Griff. My house, my rules. You do *not* have the right to decide who enters here."

"You will respect Ms. Swanmay," said Ash, making Hayley jump. She hadn't even noticed him standing quietly behind Griff. For such a powerful shifter, the Phoenix had a remarkable ability to make himself blend into the background.

Frustrated growls rumbled in both Griff and Dai's chests, but they didn't try to argue with their Commander. "Let's see if we can *peacefully* persuade Reiner to go somewhere else, then," Griff said, not sounding optimistic. "Otherwise we're going to have to somehow ride herd on him all night."

"Or just get Chase to annoy him so much that *he* throws the first punch," Dai murmured. He briefly touched Virginia's bare arm, love and worry clear even in just that small gesture. "Stay here. Just in case."

With a quick, apologetic wave of farewell to Virginia and Connie, Hayley followed the two men out of the pub. Gooseflesh pimpled on her arms as she stepped out into the night. It felt much colder after the warmth inside.

Reiner was looking both bewildered and besieged, with Danny clinging onto one of his hands and Chase onto his other sleeve. The trio were encircled by the pack of shifter kids, all apparently hanging onto Chase's every word as he rattled nonsense at top speed.

"So then the actress says to the Bishop-" Chase broke off as Griff and Dai strode up. He let go of Reiner with a relieved sigh. "Oh, thank

God. I really wasn't sure how I was going to finish that in a way suitable for young, eavesdropping ears. Come on kids, who wants to go get something to drink?"

Griff set his feet, facing the lion shifter head on as Chase herded the kids safely into the pub. Dai took up position at his shoulder, green eyes narrowed behind his helmet.

"What are you doing here, Reiner?" Griff said bluntly. His fists were bunched, muscles tense and ready despite Rose's warning. "I'm not having you spoil Danny's Halloween. If you're looking to start trouble, do it some other time."

Reiner's hand tightened on Danny's. "I'm here because *my son* wants me here."

"I told Daddy to come," Danny piped up cheerfully. Hayley was relieved that he didn't seem to have picked up on the hostile undercurrents. "I want him to share Halloween too."

Hayley's heart broke at his innocence, even as she wanted to throttle him for setting this up without running it past her first. "That's very sweet of you, honey, but, um…I don't think Daddy likes dancing and dressing up and all that kind of thing."

Reiner bristled. "If my son wants me to dance, then I will dance," he announced grimly. He looked like he'd have much preferred it if Danny had asked him to eat a nice heaping plate of worms.

"It's okay, Daddy. I know you don't like dancing." Danny beamed up at Reiner. "I don't, either. But Mommy does, so I thought maybe she and Mr. Griff could do that while you and me could go be lions instead. Because you said that *your* Daddy always took you out hunting at Halloween, so I want to do that with you too. Would that be okay, Mr. Griff?"

Griff blinked at him, looking as taken aback by this speech as Hayley was. "Ah…I think you'd better ask your ma."

"Um…" Hayley remembered something that Griff had mentioned about traditional shifter Halloween customs. "Exactly what kind of hunting, Reiner?"

Reiner's shoulders stiffened in offense. "I'm not going to take him hunting humans, if that's what you're asking. Deer or rabbits will have to do." His gaze slid down her costume. "*Real* rabbits."

Hayley wasn't desperately thrilled by the prospect of her gentle boy sinking his teeth into some poor little bunny, but there was no denying that Danny *was*. He hopped up and down with eagerness, his face alight with anticipation.

"Please, Mommy?" he begged. "Pleeeeeease? I promise I'll eat it all up, every last bit."

Is that supposed to help? Shuddering with revulsion, Hayley shot a pleading look at Griff. He shrugged apologetically.

"We *are* lions, at heart," he murmured into her ear. "Let him go. It will mean a lot to both of them, and I think we can trust Reiner this much, at least. In any case, I'll know through the pride-bond if Danny gets upset for any reason, and Chase can always take us straight to them."

Hayley sighed, giving in. "All right," she said reluctantly. "You can go."

"Yaaaaay!" Danny flung his arms around her. "You're the best mommy ever!"

Hayley hugged him back, wishing that she never had to let him go. "Just make sure you stay away from roads and, and people and everything, okay?"

Reiner put a possessive hand on Danny's shoulder. "*I* will make sure *my son* stays safe."

"See that you do," growled Griff, with a flex of alpha power in his voice. Reiner gave him a resentful glare, but jerked his chin in a nod.

"Mommy," Danny said thoughtfully, letting go of her and taking Reiner's hand instead. "We're probably going to be up *real* late. Maybe I should sleep over at Daddy's. Is that okay?"

Absolutely not! Hayley wanted to yell. But Reiner was staring down at Danny with such a thunderstruck look, like a man who'd just been given a present he hadn't even known he'd wanted, that the words died on her tongue. "Well…but you haven't got pajamas or a toothbrush or anything."

"Lions don't *need* pajamas or toothbrushes," Danny said confidently. "Do they, Daddy?"

"They do if they want to keep their fangs, lad," Griff rumbled before Reiner could speak. "Real lions don't eat chocolate, but from the look of your face the same isn't true of you."

"I know an all-night store near my place," Reiner said to Griff. For once, he didn't sound arrogant. His expression was more vulnerable than she'd ever seen before, still half-dazed with wonder. "I could pick up the basics, just for tonight. And I'll drop him back off by nine tomorrow morning. I swear on my family name."

Hayley would have preferred it if Reiner had acted as though *she* had the final say, rather than Griff, but maybe that would have been one miracle too many. She nodded at Griff, very slightly.

"Very well." He gave Reiner a stern—but not aggressive—look. "Don't make me regret this."

"Oh, Mr. Griff," Danny said, turning back as Reiner started to lead him away. His brown eyes were wide and guileless. "Make sure Mommy isn't lonely, okay? She's never had to sleep without me there. She might get scared of the dark without a lion around."

Hayley's mouth hung open. So did Griff's.

"And to think you told me *I* was incompetent in matters of romance," Dai murmured as Danny skipped off. The dragon shifter clapped a hand on Griff's shoulder, a broad smirk spreading across his face. "Congratulations, my friend. You've just been set up by a five-year-old."

CHAPTER 19

"Are you really sure Danny's still all right?" Hayley asked anxiously as they turned into her driveway.

"Aye, truly," Griff replied, for the tenth time on the long, otherwise silent walk back to her house. He could feel the cub's excitement through the pride-bond, like a small sparkling firework at the back of his mind. "He's having a grand time. Probably the best Halloween of his entire life."

Bitter jealousy gnawed at his bones. *He* was Danny's alpha. *He* should be taking Danny on his first hunt. Griff would have given his right arm to be able to do that for him.

But would you give up your eagle? whispered a tiny, private thought, so deep even his animals couldn't hear. *For just the* chance *of being able to be a true alpha lion for Danny? Would you truly burn away half your heritage?*

He still didn't know if, at the bitter end, he'd be able to force himself to do it. If it was just the choice between that or death, he wouldn't even have considered it. But if it was the choice between Ash's fire, or Reiner taking Danny…

"I'm so sorry for spoiling your Halloween, Griff." Hayley fumbled in her purse for her house keys. "I just wasn't in the mood to stay at the party. I'll be okay now, if you want to head back to rejoin your friends."

"To tell the truth, I'm not really in the mood for a party myself." Griff tried to muster a casual smile. "I think I'll just head home too."

No, rumbled his lion. Its eyes gleamed in his mind, hot and predatory. *The pride is happy on the hunt, occupied elsewhere. Now it is time to stalk and claim our prize.*

The moon is full and the winds are wild, his eagle murmured. *It is not a night to be alone in the nest.*

Griff clenched his jaw, trying to ignore his beasts' whispers. He noticed that Hayley had hesitated at the open door, biting her lip as she stared into the dark corridor. "Something wrong?"

"The house is just so…quiet," she said, softly. "So empty."

Before Griff could respond, she squared her shoulders. Light blazed as she flicked the switch, turning on the hall lamp. She turned back to him with a wan, forced smile. "Just being silly. I haven't spent a night on my own since Danny was born. It'll, it'll be nice to have some time to myself."

Her bottom lip was trembling, ever so slightly. "Hayley," Griff said gently. "Do you want me to stay?"

"No, no, no!" Her head swung in emphatic arcs of denial, even as every line of her body screamed *yes!* "I wouldn't—that wouldn't be fair to you. I couldn't ask you to do that."

"It's no trouble." Griff forestalled any further argument by stepping in and closing the door behind himself. "This way, if you wake up in the night and are at all worried about Danny, you can just ask me to check the pride-bond for you."

Yes, purred his lion. *We will be right at her back, all night…*

No we won't. Out loud, Griff said, "It's not like I haven't spent a night on your sofa before, after all."

"Oh, you don't have to sleep on the sofa!" He could tell just how relieved Hayley was by the way that she didn't try to talk him out of staying. "You can sleep in my bed, if you want."

Griff cleared his throat, fighting down a surge of lust at the idea. "Ah. Now that *would* be trouble."

Hayley went a delightful shade of pink. "I meant, I can sleep in Danny's! I'd fit into it better than you."

Griff was fairly certain he'd be able to get much more rest wedged into a kid-sized bed than he would trying to sleep surrounded by Hayley's intoxicating scent. "If it's all the same to you, I'd rather take Danny's room." He tried to make a joke of it, smiling at her. "I always *did* want dinosaur wallpaper when I was little."

Hayley giggled, rather more loudly than the feeble jest deserved. "Well, I'll get you some clean sheets, at least."

Hayley started up the stairs, the white puff of the rabbit tail on her rear bobbing enticingly. Without conscious decision, Griff found that he was following her, as intently as a stalking lion. He wrenched his gaze upward, forcing himself to fix on the back of her head instead of the luscious curves of her backside.

Unfortunately, that just meant that when she turned around to say something, he inadvertently locked eyes with her.

"Oh," Hayley gasped.

He quickly looked away, but he knew she'd already seen the hunger burning in his soul. "I'm fine. It's just—I'll be fine. Give me a moment."

"Is it your beasts?" She stepped closer, putting a hand on his arm. Just that simple touch nearly broke his resolve. Only iron control kept him from crushing her up against the nearest wall and taking her there and then. "Are they fighting again?"

He let out his breath, shakily. "My beasts and I all want the same thing right now. That's rather the problem."

A flush crept up her neck. He could see her nipples stiffening through the soft clinging fabric of her dress, and his cock surged in answer. He knew he had to step back, put some distance between them, but he couldn't force himself to move away.

"Rose said something strange to me tonight." Hayley hadn't moved back either. "She said I should ask you what you're afraid of." She hesitated, her eyes searching his face. "Is it...Griff, are you afraid it might happen again?"

He knew she meant his uncontrolled shift, after they'd made love.

Her expression was open, vulnerable, demanding that he tell her the truth.

"No," he said, honestly. "That doesn't frighten me. Hayley, even if I knew for absolute certain, without a shadow of a doubt, that I'd die if I touched you again…I would do it, in a heartbeat. I would rather live for a single hour in your arms than another fifty years apart. I'm not afraid of dying."

A tear overspilled, tracking down her cheek, but her eyes were steady, uncompromising. "So what *are* you afraid of?"

"Hurting you," he whispered. He drew in a deep breath, bracing himself. "I can't stand the thought of leaving you alone. It's not only Reiner, and what it would mean for Danny. Even setting aside all those complications…Hayley, when I die, at least I won't be in pain anymore. But I'm frightened that I'll leave *you* in pain. I'm terrified that I'll break your heart."

"Isn't that my risk to take?" Hayley looked fierce as a lioness, even through her tears. "Griff, your life is yours to risk or not, but it's *my* choice what I do with my heart. Rose said I needed to have courage, if I was to be a lion's match. I'm tired of wearing a mask, pretending that there's nothing between us. Whether we ever touch again or not, nothing will change that fact that I love you. I'm not afraid of that. I'm not afraid of what that might mean, in future. I love you *now*. That's all that matters."

He pulled her into his arms, unable to hold back any longer. He kissed her fiercely, his hands coming up to cup her face. His heart swelled with joy and terror, until he felt like it might break in his chest from the sweet pain of it.

He pulled back a little, leaned his forehead against hers. "You have courage enough for both of us," he said, his voice rough. "I'm the one who has to match *you*."

He bent to claim her lips again. She melted into him, her mouth sweet and tender under his. Succumbing to his desire, he pushed her up against the wall, pressing the whole length of his body against her soft curves. His cock was a rigid bar between them. He craved to sink into her warmth, to be utterly enfolded by her.

"Griff," she gasped, as he left her mouth to start kissing his way down her neck. Her hips thrust a little, helplessly, and he very nearly came in his kilt there and then. "Wait. Are you sure this is safe?"

It felt as hard as hauling his animals apart when they fought, but he managed to pull back from her. "You did say my life was mine to risk."

"Yes, but…" Flushed pink with mingled desire and embarrassment, she bit her lip. "I'm going to sound like a complete hypocrite, but *I'm* scared of causing another one of your uncontrolled shifts."

She had a point. He braced his hands against the wall on either side of her head, trying to control his ragged breathing. "Give me a second. I was caught by surprise last time. I'll see if I can take some precautions."

Closing his eyes, he forced himself to take stock of his soul. His lion and eagle were too blind with lust to even notice each other at the moment, but after last time, he knew that could change in an instant. Gritting his teeth, he repressed his beasts, using the discipline of long practice to lock them away. He strengthened their mental cages, building high, thick walls to keep them apart from both each other, and himself.

It was rather like putting on a full-body condom. He had a nagging, uncomfortable sense of a barrier between himself and the world, dimming all sensation. Still, it was better than risking an uncontrolled shift.

"There. That should be safer now." He opened his eyes again, and Hayley made a small, startled sound. "What is it?"

"All the gold's gone." She traced the corner of his eye lightly with her fingertip. "You look…human."

He wished that he could interpret her expression, but with his eagle chained, his perception was a tenth of its usual level. "I hope you're not too disappointed. I *am* just a normal human at the moment, when my beasts are caged like this. But that's the way it has to be."

This is the way it might have to permanently *be…*He shoved the chilling thought back down.

"I'm not disappointed!" As if to prove it, Hayley slid her hands around his chest, drawing him back close again. "It's you I love, not your powers. I'd love you even if you were only human."

A shiver ran down his back at her unwittingly ominous words. He stopped her from saying anything more by kissing her, more slowly this time. It was different without his beasts' urgency snarling through his blood, but she was still Hayley, his Hayley. She was still his mate.

"There *is* one advantage to keeping my beasts chained, you know," he murmured, his lips brushing hers. He straightened, drawing her with him into her bedroom. "It means I can take my time."

Slowly, he eased down the zipper of her dress. Her breath caught as he ran his hands up her exposed back, tracing the gentle dip of her spine. He worked the soft, clinging fabric of the dress down, uncovering first her plump, enticing shoulders, then the delicious swells of her breasts. He couldn't resist nuzzling between them, nipping gently at her creamy skin as he pushed her dress off completely, letting it puddle on the floor around her feet.

"Hayley," he breathed, tasting her, inhaling her, trying to memorize every glorious inch of her body. "Mine."

He wanted to kneel to unpeel her tights from her gorgeous thighs, but pain screamed through his bad leg when he tried to bend it. The long walk back to the house from the pub had made the joint seize up.

Evidently noticing his wince, Hayley stretched up on her toes to kiss him. "I'll do it." Peeking up at him a little shyly through her lowered eyelashes, she slipped the tights off, leaving her standing in only a lacy bra and matching panties.

At the sight of her, all the breath left his lungs, as if he'd been punched in the stomach. His cock strained, desperate for her. "I've changed my mind. I *can't* take my time."

Her lips curved in a naughty smile. "Tough, because now I want to take *my* time." She ran her fingers under the looped fabric of his plaid, tracing the lines of his chest. "I've never seen you naked. And I've always wondered what a Scotsman wears under his kilt..."

Griff couldn't help chuckling as she tried to slide the plaid off his shoulder, only to be baffled by the way it was tied. A traditional great kilt really wasn't something a novice could dismantle. "Ah, you do realize that I'm wearing eighteen feet of fabric?"

She cast him a half-exasperated, half-amused glare, still wrestling with the mysteries of the garment. "Then I guess I'll *really* be taking my time."

"Here." He undid the outer belt, then guided her hands to the thinner, hidden belt that held the kilt pleated. He grinned at her as the heavy folds of fabric fell away. "Fortunately, my ancestors were very impatient men."

"Well *you* can just be patient a bit longer," Hayley retorted tartly. With teasing slowness, she started to undo the buttons of his shirt.

A growl rose in his throat as she worked her way down. Even with his beasts tightly restrained, every slight brush of her fingertips against his bare skin made his cock throb with need.

"Okay, now I am a little disappointed." Hayley had encountered his briefs. "So the rumors aren't true?"

"Actually, they are," he gasped as she knelt to slide them down over his hips. The cool air was almost agonizing on his freed cock. "Don't tell anyone I was bringing shame on my forefathers."

Still on her knees as she stripped him of his last few garments, Hayley's eyes gleamed slyly up at him. "My lips," she murmured, sliding her hands up the backs of his legs, "are sealed."

He groaned as her warm, soft lips enfolded the head of his cock. He wound his fingers into her silky hair, fighting for control as she took him deeper. Her tongue curled around the underside, flicking exquisitely over his most sensitive areas.

"Hayley," he growled, every muscle in his abdomen tight and rigid as he desperately tried to restrain himself. "Stop. I can't —can't wait."

In answer, she closed her mouth tight around him, sucking hard. His hips bucked as she milked him urgently, her fingers digging into his thighs. He couldn't hold himself back any longer. Hands clenching around her head, he yanked her closer, his thrusting cock entirely filling her welcoming mouth.

White-hot sparks burst in his vision as he came hard, emptying himself into her. She took every drop, her tongue teasing and flicking in encouragement until he was utterly, completely spent.

Shuddering with the aftershocks of pleasure, he relaxed his grip on her head. She came up gasping for air, but with an expression of intense, smug satisfaction. She gave his cock one last parting kiss—it burned like a brand on his oversensitive, still-engorged head—before allowing him to lift her to her feet again.

"I don't have condoms," she admitted. "And I was fairly certain you wouldn't have restocked either."

He kissed her, deep and lingering, tasting the faint traces of his own salt on her tongue. At the back of his mind, his lion and eagle flung themselves against the walls of his control, intensely aroused by that intoxicating mingling of their scents. Walled off from his consciousness, his beasts hadn't partaken of his own release. From the ominous pain gathering inside his skull, he knew he wouldn't be able to hold them much longer.

"Lion or eagle?" he murmured against her lips. "I have to let them one of them out now, or risk them both breaking free of their own accord."

Hayley leaned back a little to look at him curiously. "Does it make a difference? Which one you release, I mean."

"Very much so." He trailed his finger over the curve of her breast, savoring her sharp intake of breath. "And since you're right—I *don't* have condoms—it had best be my eagle. My lion can be a bit...dominant."

From the way her pupils went wide and dark, he thought she rather liked the sound of that. His senses sharpened as he allowed his eagle to soar free, and he abruptly knew just how *much* she would like that. He knew other things too—how the nape of her neck begged to be seized in his teeth, how her thighs trembled to feel his caress, exactly where he should be gentle and where he should be rough...

"Oh," she gasped, as he started to put his observations into practice. "I—I think I'm going to like your eagle. The lion will have to wait for another time." She looked up at him with sudden fierceness, her determined expression at odds with the obedience of her body as he pushed her down onto the bed. "Because there *are* going to be other times, Griff. Lots and lots of them. Promise me that."

"Aye," he said softly, before he covered her mouth with his own. "I promise."

And in that moment, he made his decision. He knew that he would do whatever was necessary to keep that promise.

Tonight for the eagle. Griff kept the thought hidden away in the most private depths of his mind, out of sight of his beasts. *And tomorrow, a night for the lion. I can give them both one night with our mate, at least.*

Before I submit us all to Ash's fire...and we see how much survives the inferno.

CHAPTER 20

"That was the best Halloween ever." Danny bounced on Reiner's guest bed, his borrowed T-shirt flapping around his knees. It was the smallest shirt Reiner owned, but it still drowned the boy. "I liked it best when you pounced right on that deer, Daddy, pow! You knocked him right down flat!"

Reiner caught Danny in mid-jump, making him shriek in delight. "I'll knock *you* down flat if you don't get yourself into bed. I can't believe you're still so full of energy."

Pride swelled in Reiner's chest as Danny wriggled and giggled, trying to free himself. Not even six years old, on his first hunt, and the boy had still managed to achieve a throat-lock on a fully-grown deer. If he'd been just a little older and bigger, Reiner was certain that he'd have throttled the animal all by himself.

Wouldn't that just wipe the smugness off my dear brother's face? When none of his own ever-so-perfect pure-bred offspring have managed to lay paw on so much as a rabbit yet...

"You know, I was only able to pounce on that deer because you were holding him for me," Reiner said to Danny. "Really, the credit is half yours."

Danny's eyes widened. Reiner still got a little thrill every time he gazed into those amber eyes—so similar to his own that it was like looking at his reflection in a mirror. "Really, Daddy? You mean *I* killed the deer too?"

"Absolutely." Reiner smiled, triumphant. "When we tell everyone back home, that's exactly what we'll say."

Let's see how my dear alpha brother likes that. *I can't wait to see the moment he realizes that his sons are going to be beta to* mine.

His lion flicked its tail in mild irritation. *We have our own place, as our cub will have his. We are no less valuable to the pride than any other. Not even the alpha.*

Reiner's jaw tightened a little at his lion's unquestioning acceptance of the pride hierarchy. Why, why couldn't *he* have had an alpha lion, fiercely proud and ravenous for power? No matter how he fought to win the place and respect he deserved, he'd always been hampered by his inner lion's instinctive submissiveness. It wasn't fair.

But at least life would be better for his son.

No asshole alpha is ever going to push you *around*, Reiner silently promised Danny as he tucked him into bed. *I'll teach you to be so strong and dominant, you'll just have to stare at another lion to have them whimpering and showing you their belly. I'll make sure you can have anything you want. I swear it.*

Danny stretched out like a starfish, his arms and legs not even coming close to reaching the edges of the double bed. "This is the biggest bed ever, Daddy! And the biggest bedroom. Why's your house so huge?"

Reiner blinked at him, taken aback. "This, huge? This is just a hovel, compared to my real house back home."

"What's a hovel?" Danny asked.

Reiner waved dismissively around at the bedroom, with its sleek, minimalist furniture and views out over the fishing lake. "This is. You just wait until you see the Ljonsson estates back home. Then you'll understand."

When Reiner had learned that Danny was his true son, he'd immediately rented out the best house he could find near Brighton—an old hunting lodge set in fifteen acres of private woodland, half an hour away from the city. Even so, it was barely adequate for a real lion's needs. He couldn't comprehend how any shifter could possibly stand to live in built-up Brighton itself.

My poor son has been utterly deprived if he considers this *to be a huge house.* A prickle of anger ran through his blood. *I trusted Hayley to provide at least a minimum level of care. How can she have failed so badly? It's a good thing I stepped in when I did.*

"Wait until I take you to Valtyra," he said to Danny. "You'll love it. Everyone knows about shifters back home. We'll be able to be lions whenever we want, without having to worry about frightening stupid humans."

Danny looked suitably excited at the prospect. "Are there more deers there? Can we hunt them?"

"There are deer, and boar, and even elk. We'll hunt them all. I promise."

A stab of homesickness twisted his guts. He wished that he could just take Danny back on the next flight.

If only that asshole alpha didn't have his claws in my son!

"I wish we could go there tomorrow," Danny said wistfully, and Reiner's heart melted at the unwitting echo of his own thoughts. "But I've got to go to school and Mommy has to go to work. Maybe we can go during summer vacation." He frowned a little. "We'll have to ask Mr. Griff. Daddy, do firefighters get to take summer vacation?"

Reiner clenched his jaw. *Can I not have* one *conversation with my son without that damned alpha coming up?*

"I don't think they do," he said, trying not to sound too curt. "So your alpha won't come. Anyway, wouldn't you like to take a trip together? Just the two of us?"

"Without Mommy?" Danny pulled the covers up to his chin, as if hiding from a monster in the dark. "But I've never been away without Mommy. Can't she come too?"

"She wouldn't want to come. She and your alpha would jump at the chance to have private time alone together. They were eager enough for you to come with me tonight, weren't they?"

A twinge of jealousy shot through him at the mental image of that arrogant alpha in Hayley's bed. Even if she was a bit fatter and more tired-looking than when he'd known her, she was still an extremely attractive woman. Reiner wouldn't have said no to a second round... but of course there was no chance of that, now that she only had eyes for her oh-so-alpha mate.

Reiner consoled himself with the thought that at least *he'd* had her first. And she'd been younger and riper then, too. If only she'd been a shifter! But there was simply no way he could ever have taken a mundane human home to his family. Not when his perfect older brother had already mated a perfect alpha lioness and started producing perfect pure-bred cubs...

Our cub is perfect, his lion said, its mental voice a soft purr.

So he is. Reiner shook off his dark thoughts, focusing on the shining promise of the better future ahead.

"Your mother and her mate don't want a cub like you getting in the way all the time," he said to Danny. "They'd be happy if you stayed with me for longer. They just don't want to hurt your feelings by telling you so."

"Oh," Danny said quietly. His little face was shadowed in the moonlight. "I didn't think of that."

"Don't worry. *I* always want to have you around." He stroked Danny's golden hair back from his forehead. "You go to sleep now, my son. I'll be right next door if you need me."

"Okay, Daddy." Danny yawned hugely, his expression relaxing again as he snuggled down. "I did really like hunting tonight. Can we do that again? Here, I mean. Not back at your proper home."

"You'll have to ask your alpha." He couldn't resist adding, "Make sure you tell him you want *me* to take you hunting, not him."

"Oh, Mr. Griff won't mind." Danny's voice had gone soft and sleepy. "He doesn't hunt."

"He doesn't?" Reiner's hand paused. Some traditionalists—Reiner's own grandfather among them—still held that hunting was women's work. Was that bastard Griff laughing at him even now? "Why? Does he think it's something only lionesses should do?"

Danny giggled. "That's silly. Who would think that?"

"Never mind. It's not important." Reiner relaxed a little. At least that asshole alpha wasn't filling his son's head with ridiculous old-fashioned nonsense. "But why doesn't Griff like hunting?"

"I think he'd *like* to," Danny mumbled, his eyes drifting shut. "But he can't. He wouldn't be able to bite the deer, after all. Not with person teeth."

...Person teeth?

"Why would he try to hunt without shifting?" Reiner asked, bewildered.

"Ummm." Danny's eyes popped open. He suddenly looked as guilty as if Reiner had just caught him eating his entire stash of Halloween candy. "Never mind." He rolled over, squeezing his eyes tight shut again. "Night-night, Daddy."

Reiner switched the bedside light back on.

"Hey!" Danny flung his arm over his face. "I was sleeping!"

Reiner ignored the protest, leaning over him intently. Inside, his lion crouched, every muscle tense, tail lashing. Normally, it was the voice of caution, holding him back…but not this time.

If the alpha cannot even catch a deer, his lion snarled, *he cannot protect the pride. He cannot protect our cub. If the alpha is unfit...*

"Danny." Reiner let his lion rise, let its force show in his voice and eyes, despite the way it made Danny cower. "Tell me *exactly* why Griff can't hunt."

CHAPTER 21

As soon as I get off work, I'm going straight to the store, Hayley thought as she watched Griff move around the kitchen. *And I'm buying condoms. Lots and lots of condoms.*

Lacking other options, Griff had put his Halloween outfit back on again this morning—though the unselfconscious ease with which he'd donned the kilt had made it clear it really wasn't just a costume for him. Hayley wondered how often he wore it. She wondered how often she could *persuade* him to wear it.

"As often as you like," Griff said, without looking up from buttering toast.

Hayley made a face at his broad back. "Okay, clearly we're going to have to lay some ground rules about using your eagle powers."

Griff threw her a teasing glance. "I thought you rather liked my eagle."

"What I like in the bedroom and what I like in the kitchen are two entirely separate things," Hayley informed him grandly.

As one, they looked at the kitchen table, then at each other. They both burst out laughing.

The doorbell chimed. "That'll be Reiner and Danny," Hayley said, trying to bring her giggles under control. She really, really didn't want either of them asking what the joke was. "Right on time, too. You were right, we *could* trust Reiner. Maybe we can make sleepovers at Daddy's a regular event."

Griff caught her for a kiss as she went past. "I certainly hope so."

Still glowing from the brief embrace, Hayley beamed as she opened the front door. "Hi-"

"*Where is he?*" The door slammed back as Reiner thrust his way inside. Hayley gasped as he barged past, knocking her into a wall.

"What on earth-?" Griff appeared in the door of the kitchen, still holding a butter knife. His eyes abruptly blazed gold, and his voice cracked like a whip. "Reiner! Stop!"

Reiner shrugged off Griff's alpha command, never pausing. He had a wild, triumphant expression, his teeth bared. Towing a struggling Danny by one wrist in his wake, he strode right up to the firefighter.

"You have no power over me," he snarled, right into Griff's face. "Griffin MacCormick, *I challenge you!*"

"I'm sorry, Mr. Griff," Danny babbled. His face was stricken with guilt. "I didn't mean to tell. I'm sorry, I'm *sorry!*"

"It's not your fault, lad." Griff kept his eyes locked with Reiner's. He hadn't backed down so much as an inch. "Reiner, let the cub go. Now."

"You have no power over me," Reiner repeated, but he opened his hand. Danny flew straight into Hayley's arms.

"It's all right, baby, it's all right," Hayley whispered futilely to him. His entire body shook as though he had his fingers in an electrical socket.

"Hayley, take Danny upstairs." Griff's voice was very calm, betraying none of the tension in his body. "This isn't something he should watch."

"Go up to your room, baby." She pushed Danny in the direction of the stairs, but didn't follow him herself. "The grown-ups need to talk for a minute. It'll be ok."

When Danny had disappeared into his bedroom, Hayley swung round to confront Reiner. "You. Get out of my house."

Reiner laughed scornfully, glancing at her with a sneer. "*You* have even less power over me than he-"

Without a hint of warning, Griff punched him straight in the face. Reiner staggered, and before he could recover Griff had him up against the wall, one forearm shoved across the lion shifter's throat.

"You will respect my mate's territory," he said, still with that deadly calm. "You can challenge me, but you have *no right* to intrude here."

"Then let's take this outside," Reiner spat. His eyes glittered feverishly. "I challenge you for your pride, alpha. Shift and face me like a lion."

"He can't, Reiner, you know he can't!" Hayley tried to pull Griff away, but she might as well have tried to move a mountain. "Griff, just toss him out. He can't make you fight him."

"Oh yes, I can," Reiner said. "And I am. Fight me, alpha. Defend your pride, or lose it."

Very slowly, Griff released Reiner. "There's a dueling arena at the courthouse. We will do this properly, with witnesses."

"Griff, he'll *kill* you!" Hayley whirled on Reiner. "Reiner, I beg you. Just let him go. *Please*. For Danny's sake, don't hurt him."

Reiner straightened a little, his chest swelling as if he was enjoying her pleading. "I suppose I could accept a formal surrender."

"He surrenders, of course he'll surrender," Hayley babbled, before Griff could say anything. She grabbed Griff's arm, his muscles as hard as iron under her fingers. "Griff, *please*. Do it."

A savage snarl tore from Griff's throat. Hayley could see sweat beading on his brow, could tell how hard he was having to fight to keep his animals under control.

If this continues, Reiner won't even have to touch him. His own beasts will rip him apart first.

"Do it for me," Hayley whispered, begging him with every fiber of her soul to listen to her.

Griff swallowed, hard. Gently, he freed himself from her grip. Never breaking eye contact with Reiner, he lowered himself to his knees, tilting his head up to expose his throat.

Reiner's eyes gleamed. "Down further, beta. Down on your belly."

"Reiner-" Hayley started, but Griff shook his head at her, very slightly.

"It'll be all right," he said quietly. "Don't worry."

Then he prostrated himself fully in front of Reiner, lying on his front with his head turned to one side. Smiling savagely, Reiner put his booted foot on the side of Griff's neck. The firefighter didn't so much as move a muscle.

"I accept your submission," Reiner said triumphantly. "*I* am Danny's alpha now." When Griff didn't respond, Reiner glared at him, pressing down on his throat with his full weight. "I've defeated you! Give him to me!"

Hayley didn't see Griff do anything at all, but a sudden piercing, heart-broken shriek came from Danny's room. Whatever had happened between the two lions, Danny had clearly sensed it.

"All right, it's done, let him up!" Hayley shoved at Reiner, as Danny's door banged open upstairs. "Let him go, before Danny sees!"

Reluctantly, Reiner took his foot off Griff's neck. Hayley wanted to help Griff up, but she didn't know whether that would just be one more humiliation. In an agony of indecision, she hovered over him as he stiffly levered himself to his feet.

"Griff, *Griff!*" Danny hurled himself down the stairs and straight into Griff, nearly knocking him over again. "Where are you? Why aren't you in my head anymore? You said you'd never leave me, you *promised!*"

"I'm sorry, lad." Griff hugged him once, briefly, then let him go. "Just remember what I told you about a true alpha."

"Come here, Danny," Reiner ordered. "*I* am your alpha now."

Danny shook his head in incomprehension. "But Mr. Griff-"

"I said, *come here!*" Reiner's voice snapped with that odd, commanding note that Hayley had only ever heard Griff use before.

Danny jerked away from Griff at Reiner's order, like a dog yanked back by its collar. He stared from Griff to Reiner to Hayley in mute betrayal, as though they'd all suddenly turned into strangers.

"It'll be fine," Griff said, as much to Hayley as to Danny. The bitter, shamed set of his shoulders betrayed his lie. "Don't worry. I'll go now."

"No, *he's* going." Hayley confronted Reiner, wishing with all her heart that *she* could turn into a lion. "Get out before I call the cops. And don't you dare come here again."

"I will be back to collect my son," Reiner retorted. "As and when I choose. Or would you prefer to hear from my lawyer?"

Griff's hand fell on her shoulder, squeezing in warning. "There is no need for that." He addressed Reiner's feet, not raising his head. "You are alpha. You have the right to see your cub."

"And you do not." Reiner's tone took on that eerie undercurrent of alpha command again. "Danny, you will not see this man again. You will not be under the same roof as him. If he comes here, you must leave immediately." His voice rose with a sort of giddy malice, like a child waving around a stolen handgun. "You will not meet him, nor speak to him, under any circumstances. *Do you understand?*"

"Yes, Daddy," Danny whispered, his small face still white with shock. Immediately, he started retreating from Griff, his movements forced and jerky. A panicked whimper rose in his throat as his back hit the wall.

"It's all right, lad." Griff circled round Reiner, never turning his back on him. "I'm going. Hayley, I'll call you later. Don't worry. I promise I'll fix this." With a last indecipherable glance at her, he left.

"You- you-" Hayley's hands curled into impotent fists. "*Get out.*"

Reiner backed away, but paused in the doorway. He smirked at her. "You can have your son. Or you can have your mate. But not both. Let's see which one you love more."

CHAPTER 22

He is the alpha, Simba kept insisting. *We have to obey the alpha.*

Danny stared rebelliously at his untouched dinner. He didn't *want* to obey. Not like he'd wanted to obey Mr. Griff.

But Mr. Griff wasn't his alpha anymore. Daddy was.

Daddy's eyebrows drew down. "I *said*, eat your dinner."

Danny could feel Daddy's lion glaring at Simba in his head, just like Daddy was glaring at him across the table. It made Simba flatten against the bottom of Danny's mind, whimpering in submission. No matter how much Danny tried to reassure the cub that it was okay, that Daddy would never, *ever* hurt them, the cub was still scared of the bigger lion.

Just to stop Simba being scared, Danny scooped up a forkful of dinner and put it in his mouth. It was peas. Danny didn't like peas.

He ate them anyway. His alpha wanted him to.

"That's better," Daddy said, back in his normal voice, not the horrible alpha voice that felt like a leash around Danny's neck. "Listen, if you eat up your vegetables, I'll take you out hunting. You'd like that, wouldn't you? Just like last night, remember?"

Danny scowled at him. "I don't wanna go hunting. I want to go back home. I want Mommy."

"Well *I* want you here," Daddy snapped back. "You're going to be staying with me now. And if your mother tries to get you to go anywhere with her, you come and find me and tell me, understand?"

Obey the alpha, Simba whispered. *Alpha is big and we are very small. Obey.*

Daddy's lion made Danny's head jerk down in a nod. But he couldn't make Danny be happy about it. He couldn't even make Danny *pretend* to be happy about it.

An alpha could control every bit of him...but not the bit that made feelings.

Daddy said a very bad word, one that Danny wasn't supposed to know. "Listen, my son." Danny could feel the effort he was making to keep his voice normal, when he really wanted to shout. "I know it's different, but this is the way things are supposed to be. You should be happy! We're a proper pride now. Everything will be better. You'll see."

Danny could feel Daddy's lion pushing at him, like fingers trying to force the corners of his mouth up into a smile. He set his jaw stubbornly.

"This is all *his* fault," Daddy muttered. "You're supposed to follow the strongest lion, without question. Not pine like a dog after some sick cripple. I should have fought him in front of you. Then you'd have seen me defeat him. You'd know I'm the strongest, that I deserve to be alpha."

A very, very tiny growl rumbled in Simba's throat. *He didn't defeat our real alpha. Our real alpha stepped down. We could tell the difference.* The growl shifted up to a whine, Simba's ears flattening in confused misery. *Why did he abandon us? Why didn't he fight for us? Were we bad? Doesn't he want us any more?*

Danny hugged Simba, trying to comfort him. He couldn't explain to his lion that Mr. Griff couldn't fight Daddy, not when he couldn't shift. Simba didn't see Mr. Griff as a person at all—just as the biggest, strongest lion ever.

"It'll be better once we're in Valtyra." Daddy sounded like he was trying to convince himself, as much as Danny. "Living with just humans for so long has you all confused. Once we're back home, you'll soon learn proper ways. I'll teach you. We'll go into the wilderness and live as lions, just the two of us, until we're a true pride."

Just the two of us?

Daddy had said something about going on vacation without Mommy before, but Danny hadn't thought he'd really *meant* it. "What about Mommy?"

Daddy blinked at him, as though he'd almost forgotten Danny was a separate person able to speak for himself. "What?"

"Mommy," Danny repeated. He was starting to get a horrible sick feeling right in the bottom of his stomach. "Mommy has to come too."

"No, she'll stay here. I know this seems hard to you now, but one day you'll realize it was all for your own good. She's just a human. She can't understand you, not like I do."

Simba whimpered, pressing against the inside of Danny's head. The cub wanted him to be quiet, to avoid making the bigger lion angry.

Danny forced words out anyway, through his tightening throat. "I'm not going anywhere without Mommy! Not ever!"

"You will go where I tell you to, when I tell you to!" Daddy's burning eyes filled Danny's whole head, trying to drive out all his own thoughts. "I am your alpha! You will do as I say!"

A true alpha never forces anyone, said Mr. Griff's voice in his memory. *You remember that, always.*

"No." He met Daddy's eyes, and the surprise in them gave him the courage to stand up, clenching his fists. "No! I won't go, and you can't make me!"

Daddy shot to his feet, looming over him. "I am your alpha! You *will* obey me!"

No! Simba was on his feet too, fangs bared at the presence at the back of their mind. *You are not worthy to be alpha! We challenge you!*

Simba leaped, claws bared. Daddy's lion had to retreat in the face of Simba's fearless attack. With a *snap*, the pride-bond went dead.

"I don't want you as my alpha!" Danny yelled, right into Daddy's shocked face. "You hurt Mr. Griff, when it wasn't even fair! I wish *he* was still my alpha! I wish *he* was my daddy! I don't want you! *Go away!*"

Daddy snarled, his hands clenching. Danny's skin prickled as Simba surged forward—but Daddy stopped dead. He stared at his own fists, then down at Danny. His face went white.

"No," Daddy whispered in horror. "I nearly—no!"

Daddy whirled, his own form shimmering. His clothes tore away as he shifted. On four paws, he charged blindly out the door. Danny heard him crashing through the trees. His enraged, agonized roars faded away as he disappeared into the woods.

Simba wanted to run too, all the way home to Mommy, but Danny held his lion back. "It's too far," he said to the cub out loud. "And we don't know the way."

We can't stay here. Simba's tail lashed in agitation. *What if he comes back?*

Danny made himself a deep breath, focusing on staying calm, just like Mr. Griff had taught him. Frowning, he tried to think with his human head instead of his lion's heart. "We need a plan."

The front door was nice and thick. It made a big bang when Danny pushed it shut. He found a big metal key in the lock, and turned it with a reassuring click. Then he went through all the rooms downstairs, checking that all the windows were closed too.

"There," he said to Simba, when he was satisfied that Daddy wouldn't be able to get back in. "Now we just need to call for help."

Simba looked mournfully at the dark, cold place where the pridebond—the *real* pride-bond, not Daddy's fake one—had been. *How?*

There was a phone in one of the bedrooms upstairs—a funny old-fashioned phone that was plugged in, not like a proper phone that you could put in your pocket. It took Danny a little puzzling how to work it, since it didn't have a screen to touch, but in the end he figured out which buttons to press.

He didn't know Mommy's number, but there was one number he *did* know. It was a different number from the one in America, he remembered. Mommy had made sure that he learned it by heart. She'd told him to call it if he was ever hurt or scared or needed help.

He definitely needed help now.

"999," said a stranger's voice in his ear. "What is the nature of your emergency?"

"Can I talk to the firefighters?" Danny remembered to add, "Please?"

There were a few clicks, then a different man said, "East Sussex Fire and Rescue Service. Where is your emergency?"

Danny thought this was a very strange way of saying hello. "Is Mr. Griff there?"

There was a pause. "What do you think this is, the damn Yellow Pages? I'm a fire dispatcher, not an operator. Is there a fire near you? Do you need a fire engine?"

"No, thank you," Danny said politely. "I just need Mr. Griff. He's a firefighter, so I know he works here. Could you get him for me? Please?"

"Oh, for the love of-" The man sighed heavily. "Kid, unless you've actually got a fire—a *big* fire—don't call the fire department. Got it?"

"Um…okay," Danny said, dubiously. "But-"

The phone made a funny beeping sound in his ear. The man had hung up.

Now what? Simba wanted to know.

Danny hopped down off the bed. "Now I guess we look for some matches."

CHAPTER 23

Griff had never felt less like going in to work.

He'd spent half the day waiting impatiently for Ash to come off duty. But when Griff had finally managed to accost him at the fire station, the Phoenix had flatly refused to try to burn away one of his shifter animals right away.

"You are not in a fit state of mind to make this decision now," Ash had told him. The Fire Commander hadn't even had a chance to change out of his turnout gear, the scent of smoke still heavy around him. "And in any event, I am not in a fit state physically to attempt it. I must rest, and you must reflect. You must be absolutely certain that this is the only way forward. Think. If you have me do this, it cannot be undone."

The best Griff had been able to do was to force Ash to reluctantly promise to make the attempt tomorrow, if Griff didn't change his mind before then. He knew that he wouldn't. Now that Reiner was Danny's alpha as well as father, he had a double claim to the boy. His legal position was practically unassailable.

Griff knew that Hayley had hidden Danny's passport, but that wouldn't delay Reiner for long. All he had to do was get a Valtyran passport for Danny, and he'd be able to take him out of the country any time he liked. There would be nothing standing in his way.

I have to stop him. I have to be able to shift.

If Ash burned away his eagle, leaving him a lion shifter, then he'd be able to challenge Reiner directly. If his eagle was the one to survive…well, the situation would be less straightforward, but at least he'd legally be a shifter. Hayley would have a strong case for retaining custody of Danny.

If neither of his animals survived…Griff refused to even contemplate that possibility. Which left him with nothing to do except watch the minutes crawl past, agonizingly slowly. If it hadn't been for his bad leg, he would have been pacing like a caged lion.

His own lion *was* pacing, endlessly circling in his mind, its rage and humiliation boiling under his skin. His eagle's accusing eyes tracked the lion's every move. It blamed the lion for losing Danny to Reiner, and it took all of Griff's control to keep its fury leashed. Its talons clenched on his bones, trying to twist them into its own shape. He could feel his body vibrating, ever so slightly, right on the edge of an uncontrolled shift.

Normally, he would have called in sick—he couldn't risk having a seizure in the middle of the control room. But he was scheduled to cover the evening shift, which was always short-handed thanks to the unsociable hours required. If he didn't turn up, he'd be leaving the fire department dangerously short-staffed. He couldn't put the city at risk just for his own personal crisis.

Plus, of course, I'd probably get fired, Griff thought with bleak humor as he rode the elevator up to the control room. *Pun intended.*

He was already on probation, thanks to his frozen hand. Unfortunately, being a fire dispatcher involved a *lot* of typing. Another black mark on his record would cost him his job. And *that* would cost him his life insurance…which would in turn cost Hayley a lot of money.

At least there's one advantage to having a terminal condition that doctors don't believe in. The insurance industry doesn't believe in it either.

At the moment, he was worth a lot more to Hayley dead than alive.

He could only pray that after Ash finished with him tomorrow, that would no longer be true.

"You look like hammered shit," Kevin greeted him as he entered the control room.

"Good to see you too," Griff replied, stiffly folding himself into his chair. He looked around at the otherwise deserted office. "Where's Claire? I thought she was on duty tonight with you."

"Guess you weren't the only one spending Halloween getting wasted. She called in sick." Kevin scowled in irritation, pulling his headset off his ears. "You have no idea how glad I am to see you, even if you do look like dog vomit. I have been bursting to piss for bloody hours."

"I'm logged in," Griff said, slipping his own headset on. He cast a quick, practiced glance at the status of the department, noting that all the fire engines were already out attending to incidents. "Busy night, I see."

"Like you wouldn't believe. I've even been having to route calls to our backup control centers to handle." Kevin was already heading for the door. "Hey, got a funny story about a prank call earlier, actually. I'll tell you when I get back."

Griff frowned at his screen as Kevin left. He didn't like how backup control had been allocating resources, keeping nothing in reserve. Every single crew was stacked up already. If a new call came in-

As if on cue, his headset beeped at him. With a practiced flick, he hit the answer button. "East Sussex Fire and Rescue Service. Where is your emergency?"

"Mr. Griff!"

His heart stopped at the familiar voice. *"Danny?"*

"I tried to call earlier but you weren't there. The other man told me not to call again unless there was a big fire." Danny stopped, coughing. "I think the fire's big enough now."

GO! roared his lion. Griff lost valuable seconds to a full-body spasm, the lion's frantic claws ripping across his mind. His eagle was a storm of wings and talons, beating against the inside of his skull. *Our cub is in danger! GO!*

"Danny, where are you?" he managed to gasp out through the pain.

"Daddy's house. Daddy's not here. I, um, yelled at him a lot, then he ran into the woods and I locked him out." Danny coughed again, the sound of it like a saw blade across Griff's own throat. "Mr. Griff, the fire's getting *really* big now."

"I'm sending help to you, Danny." His good hand flew across the keyboard, steady despite the agony wracking his bones. He briefly muted Danny's line, switching instead to the all-crew broadcast. "Code red, code red, all crews respond! I've got a kid trapped in a burning building! I need a team, *now!*"

Without waiting for a verbal response, he switched back to Danny. He kept his voice soft and calm, no matter how his inner beasts screamed at him. "Okay, Danny. I need you to tell me exactly where you are in the house."

"Upstairs in the bedroom, where the phone is."

"That's good," he said encouragingly, though it wasn't. Upstairs was very, very bad indeed. "And where's the fire?"

"Downstairs." Danny's voice went high and wobbly. "*All* downstairs. I'm sorry, Mr. Griff, I didn't mean to!"

"It's okay, Danny." Griff snarled soundlessly at the ETAs popping up on his screen as crews responded to the alert. *Too slow, too slow!* "Is the bedroom door closed?"

"Yes, I closed it to stop the smoke but it's still coming in real fast." Danny gulped down a sob. "I tried to open the window but it's stuck. Please, please, come get me."

Griff had to grab at the desk, bracing himself as a seizure shook his body. His beasts were single-minded with the need to reach their cub. His muscles writhed against each other, trying to twist into wings and paws. Every fiber of his being cried out to run to the boy's aid.

But Danny needed his human mind now, not his animals' instincts.

"Help is coming, Danny." Griff's hand shook on the control board as he frantically re-prioritized tasks, dispatching every fire engine he could to Reiner's house. "Just stay down low, out of the smoke."

His fingers cracked and bent halfway through dialing Ash's emergency contact number. He scrabbled futilely at the keys, his paw-hands unable to press single buttons. His control board flung up a dozen errors as the system tried to process the gibberish commands.

ASH! he tried to send telepathically—but he could feel the mental shout just bounce off the inside of his own skull. He'd never been able to contact other shifters that way.

He just had enough dexterity left to jab the mute button on his headset. "KEVIN!" he roared. "GET IN HERE!"

"Jesus Christ! Can't a guy even take a piss around-" Kevin stopped dead in the doorway.

"Take over!" Griff fell out of his chair, forced to all fours as his spine twisted. "Call Ash!"

Kevin shook his head in mute incomprehension. Face white with shock, he started backing away.

Griff didn't have time to explain, or to cajole. He locked eyes with the other dispatcher, unleashing his full alpha dominance. "*Stop.*"

Kevin froze like a deer caught in car headlights.

"Go to the control board." Griff fought to keep his throat and tongue human. "Call Fire Commander Ash."

Moving as stiffly as a robot, Kevin did so.

A rush of relief shot through Griff as he heard Ash pick up the call. "Ash, get the team to Danny," Griff ordered, not waiting for Ash to speak. "He's trapped in a fire. *Go!*"

The phone line instantly went dead, Ash not wasting even a second to respond. Nonetheless, Griff could feel the Phoenix's acknowledgement in his mind, a brief, blazing telepathic communication like a rescue beacon flaring in the night.

I can sense him, Chase's mental voice crashed through his head, as swift and unstoppable as the pegasus himself. *We're on our way, Griff.*

I'm already in the air, Dai sent too, a second later. *I'm bringing John and Hugh.*

We will not fail you, oath-brother. John's telepathic tone was fierce and focused. Griff could feel him calling clouds across the sky, shaping them into a torrent strong enough to drown any inferno. *Tell your son that we come!*

Griff let out his breath. He relaxed his alpha hold over the shaking Kevin. "Sorry. Now, I need you to-"

Kevin bolted like a rabbit. Griff didn't have a chance to reestablish his dominance before the other dispatcher had fled out of sight.

Griff snarled, cursing himself, but it was too late to do anything about it now. His erratic heartbeat lurched as he realized he hadn't heard anything from Danny for at least a minute. His headset was still on, askew over his lengthening skull. He managed to get his talons round the microphone, unmuting it again. "Danny? Can you hear me?"

"Please come, Mr. Griff, please!"

The panic in Danny's voice hurt worse than his twisting bones. "My friends are on their way now. I'm going to stay right here with you until they arrive. It won't be long. Chase can find anyone, remember?"

Got to keep him calm. Give him something to focus on. Just a little longer...

"Danny, I've got a very important job for you," Griff managed to get out through gritted fangs. He closed his eyes, focusing on the sound of Danny's scratchy, labored breathing in his ear. "I need you to check the door for me. Crawl over on your belly, like a snake. Don't open the door, just touch it and see if it's hot. Can you do that for me? Now?"

He heard shuffling, then a yelp of pain. "It burned me!"

That meant there was no escape that way—and if Danny opened the door, the fire would be sucked into the room. "Danny, do *not* open the door. Can you see any blankets or pillows?"

Danny went into a long coughing fit. When he finally answered, his voice was hoarse and raspy. "Yes. There's lots."

"I want you to stuff as many as you can under the door. Block it up so the smoke can't get in. Make sure you stay down low, understand?"

"Okay," Danny whispered, sounding very small and scared. "I have to put the phone down. You won't go away, will you?"

"I promise, I'll be here. I'll won't leave you, ever."

Distantly, he was aware of curling into a ball, fur and feathers ripping from his skin, joints snapping and contorting. But as long as he could still speak, everything else was irrelevant. He ignored the pain, ignored his beasts, ignored whatever was happening to his tortured body. Nothing mattered except Danny.

Even though Reiner had broken their pride-bond, he could still feel an echo of it, like a phantom limb. Griff focused on it fiercely, blocking out everything except that faint, tenuous link. He sent all his own strength, all his pride, all his courage down that slender connection.

We can see the house. Ash's mental voice sounded faintly in his head. *We are nearly there, Griff. Tell him to hold on just a few moments longer.*

"I did it!" Danny's voice came back, much stronger than before. "The smoke's not coming in so fast any more."

"Well done, lad," Griff gasped. "My friends are nearly there. Just hold on."

"Mr. Griff, are you okay? You sound funny."

"Don't worry about me." A primal fire was roaring through his blood, devouring his consciousness. He fought for just a few more seconds of lucidity. "Crawl over to the window. Can you see my friends yet?"

"Umm...no. Just—" Without warning, Danny shrieked.

"Danny?" The line had gone dead. *"Danny!"*

I've got him! Dai's triumphant telepathic roar echoed around Griff's shattering mind. *We've got him, Griff. He's safe.*

That was all Griff needed to hear.

Danny's safe. I can let go now.

His beasts rose up, and devoured him.

CHAPTER 24

No one was listening to Danny.

He tried again. "Please, Dr. Hugh. I just want-"

"Don't try to talk yet." Dr. Hugh's white hair kept changing color, red-blue-red-blue, in the whirling lights of the fire engines. His hands felt nice on Danny's neck, a tingly sort of warmth driving away all the soreness. "You've breathed in a lot of smoke. Just hold still while I fix it."

"He needs to get to hospital!" Daddy snarled at Dr. Hugh. "Where's the damn ambulance?"

"How should I know?" Mr. Hugh snapped, glaring right back as if he wasn't scared of Daddy's lion at all. "For the last time, move *away*. You're giving me a migraine, hovering so close. I can't work with you breathing down the back of my neck."

Daddy didn't budge one bit. He'd run out of the woods right as Mr. Dai was putting Danny back down on the ground, and he hadn't let go of Danny's hand ever since. Danny didn't mind, not now that Daddy was back to being just Daddy again. Daddy was much nicer when he wasn't pretending to be an alpha. He didn't even seem mad about Danny burning up his house.

Danny hoped he wouldn't be mad about Mr. Dai knocking down the wall, either. Turned out that dragons were *real* strong.

Danny kicked his feet impatiently, willing Dr. Hugh to hurry so that he could talk. He stared out the back door of the fire engine, watching all the firefighters run around through the smoke and rain. Danny wasn't quite sure why so many of them had decided to turn up, when Mr. Griff's friends had already rescued him.

He also didn't understand why they were all rushing around so excitedly. Mr. Ash and Sir John were doing all the *real* work, after all. They weren't making any fuss about it, either. Well, Sir John was singing, but that was a nice noise, not like all the yelling the other firefighters were doing.

Danny wished they would all quiet down so that he could hear Sir John better. Maybe if he could learn the words, *he'd* be able to make it rain by singing to the clouds too. He'd have to ask Sir John to teach him, some other time.

"Danny!"

Danny's stomach flipped over at Mommy's scream. She sounded as scared as if *she* was trapped in a fire.

"Mommy!" He tried to wriggle free of Daddy and Dr. Hugh, but they both held him tight, stopping him from jumping out of the fire engine. "Let me go! *Mommy!*"

"You can't run out there, it's not safe." Dr. Hugh jerked his chin at the flickering red glow of the still-burning house. "Don't worry. Chase is bringing her straight here."

Sure enough, a second later Mommy scrambled up into the back of the fire engine too. At the sight of her, Danny wrenched himself free from Daddy and Dr. Hugh. A *hundred* dragons couldn't have kept him out of Mommy's arms.

"My baby, my baby," she sobbed, squeezing him so tight he couldn't breathe.

Danny didn't care. He buried his face in her neck, smelling her, smelling home. Dr. Hugh's hands might be able to heal, but Mommy's touch was stronger magic. The aching tightness in his chest finally vanished.

"Are you okay?" she said, thrusting him away so that her anxious eyes could inspect every inch of him. "Are you hurt?"

"He's going to be fine," Dr. Hugh answered for him. "Just a little smoke inhalation. I've fixed all the damage."

"He should still go to the hospital," Daddy said stubbornly. "I want him to be checked over properly."

"I don't care what you want! You get no say in anything, ever again!" Mommy clutched at Danny as if she thought Daddy might try to snatch him away. "How could you let this happen? *Where were you?*"

Daddy's eyes slid away from Mommy's accusing ones. "I only went outside for a moment."

Danny stared at him. It was *bad* to tell fibs. "But-"

Daddy's lion flashed behind his eyes, and Danny fell silent. He didn't want to start another fight. It was better when members of the pride weren't mad at each other.

"It was only for a moment," Daddy repeated, as though he could make it true if he said it enough times. "Danny was having a tantrum. I had to give him space to calm down, so I went outside."

"Without any clothes on," Dr. Hugh murmured.

Daddy glared at him, clutching the shiny silver blanket he'd borrowed tighter around his waist. "I was shifted! How was I supposed to know he'd lock me out! Let alone decide to set the place on fire!" He turned his glare on Mommy. "This is all your fault! He could never have come up with such an evil idea on his own. You've been poisoning him against me!"

Mommy bared her teeth at him, just like a lion. "How *dare* you!"

"No fighting!" Danny yelled at the top of his lungs. His voice was still all scratchy from the smoke, but it was loud enough to make all the grown-ups stop and stare at him. "You can't fight now. We have to go find Mr. Griff."

Daddy made a small, disgusted sound at the back of his throat. "Indeed I do. The other half of this scheme. I won't let him surrender to me *this* time. I'm going to-"

"You will be silent." Mr. Ash appeared at the back of the fire engine, outside in the rain. He didn't yell or look mad or anything, but Daddy's mouth still snapped shut.

Nobody talked back to Mr. Ash.

Ask the Alpha-of-Alphas about our *alpha,* Simba urged Danny, as Mr. Ash started telling Mommy and Daddy something too complicated for Danny to follow. *Our alpha belongs to him. He must know where he is. Hurry!*

Despite his lion cub's urgency, Danny hesitated. Mr. Ash wasn't *scary*, exactly, but he made Danny's tongue stick to the roof of his mouth. He wasn't an easy person to talk to at the best of times, and now was definitely not a good time.

Mr. Ash wasn't wearing safety gear like the other firefighters. His regular clothes were covered in little holes where sparks from the burning house had blown on him. He wasn't wet at all, despite Sir John's rain. Danny could hear the faint hiss of raindrops sizzling into nothing just before they hit his skin.

Danny swallowed hard, gathering up his courage. "Mr. Ash?"

Mr. Ash, who had been in the middle of talking about reports and procedures and boring grown-up stuff with Mommy and Daddy, stopped mid-word. Danny flinched a little as that dark, deep gaze fell on him. "Yes, Daniel?"

"Where's Mr. Griff? Is he coming too?"

"I am afraid he cannot. He is needed back in the control room, where he can monitor what is happening and tell us all what needs to be done."

"Can I talk to him? Please?"

"He'll be very busy right now, honey," Mommy said to him. "We'll go see him as soon as we can. You can thank him then." She gave Daddy a hard stare. "We can *all* thank him."

"I need to talk to him *now*," Danny said stubbornly. "Please, Mr. Ash. Can you talk to him in your head? I can't find him and I want to know if he's okay."

"I have been attempting to keep him updated as to what is happening here, but I do not know if he is listening. He is unable to respond to me telepathically." Mr. Ash considered him for a moment, his eyebrows drawing down a little. "Daniel, do you still have a pride-bond to Griffin?"

"Sort of. I think. I could feel him earlier, when he was talking to me on the phone, but he's gone again now." Something about that eerie silence at the back of his head made Danny's stomach churn, like he needed to throw up. "Please, Mr. Ash. Something's wrong."

Mr. Ash leaned back, flagging down a passing firefighter. "Excuse me. I need to talk to the control room, please."

"I'll fetch the radio, but it won't do you any good, sir." The firefighter shook her head, looking annoyed under her helmet. "They've got absolutely no clue what's going on down here. Or up there, for that matter."

Mr. Ash frowned. "Is Griffin MacCormick not still handling this incident?"

"I wish. We can't raise anybody at our control room. We've had to switch to backup control from the next area, and *those* muppets can't tell their arses from their elbows."

Mr. Ash went very still.

"Sir?" The firefighter waved her gloved hand in front of his face. "Do you still want the radio, sir?"

"No," said Mr. Ash, as Dr. Hugh started frantically flinging things back into his doctor's bag. "Thank you. Please ask the second-in-command to take over here. Alpha Team must attend to another emergency."

CHAPTER 25

According to the hospital floorplan, Ward S officially didn't exist. According to the signs above the door to the small annex, it was the Highly Contagious Diseases Research Centre (Access Strictly Restricted).

What it actually was, past the triple-locked doors and hulking security guards, was the shifter ward.

After six hours curled up in an uncomfortable plastic chair in the tiny waiting room, Hayley was desperately hungry and longing for a coffee, but she didn't dare leave to find a vending machine. She was scared that she'd never manage to get back in again. She'd only managed to enter in the first place because she'd been personally escorted by Fire Commander Ash.

The Phoenix had been allowed through to Griff's private room, but Hayley had been firmly stopped at the door. Apparently Griff was still in critical condition. No matter how much she begged passing nurses and doctors for any more information, that was all anyone would tell her.

Why's Ash allowed in, but not me? What's taking them so long? Why won't anyone tell me what's happening?

All Hayley could do was clutch her phone, exchanging comfort-ingly banal texts with Connie about when Danny was likely to wake up and what he was allowed for breakfast. She and Chase had agreed to stay over at Hayley's house, so that she could head to the hospital to be with Griff. Hayley was deeply grateful to them both. There was no way in *hell* she was letting Reiner take Danny. Not ever again.

I'll flee the country first. I'll disappear. He is never, ever going to have sole responsibility for Danny. Not after this.

"Hayley?" She jumped, her dozing head jerking up at Hugh's voice. The paramedic looked ten times as shattered as Hayley felt, his pale skin ashen in the harsh fluorescent lights. "You're still here?"

"Of course I'm still here." Hayley jumped to her feet. "How is he? Is he going to be okay?"

"He's stable." Hugh swayed on his feet. "For now."

Hayley instinctively reached out to support him, but he recoiled from her hand so violently that his back slammed into the wall. She'd forgotten that the paramedic hated to be touched.

"Sorry," he muttered, staying as far away from her as it was physically possible to get. "Too tired to keep my psychic walls up. Hayley, I've done everything I can for him. He's conscious and lucid, and I don't think he's in immediate danger."

The unspoken *but*...hung in the air between them.

Hayley swallowed. "But?"

Hugh sighed, raking a hand through his disheveled silver hair. "He's half-shifted. His body is a horrendous mismatch of parts, and it's putting extreme stress on his internal organs. His heart and lungs are barely functional, but his digestive system...well. You get the picture. It's a bloody mess."

"He was stuck halfway before." Hayley remembered how she'd watched Griff's twisted, half-beast form gradually ease back to human, during that long vigil weeks ago. "He came back then. He can come back now, can't he?"

"I don't think he can. I've never seen anything like this before." Hugh scrubbed his hands over his face, rubbing at his bloodshot eyes. "Ash was trying to burn out one of Griff's animals and get him unstuck that way…but Griff and his lion and eagle are too intertwined now. Even Ash can't distinguish between the three of them."

Hayley stared at him. "Ash has been trying to do *what?*"

Hugh shook his head. "The details aren't important now. It didn't work. Ash can't do anything. I can't do anything. Hayley, he's got weeks left at best. Possibly days."

No.

Hayley's knees wanted to buckle. She made herself stand up straight and tall, spine rigid. "I want to see him."

Hugh hesitated. "He's…he doesn't want you to see him. Not like this."

"I don't give a damn. I am his mate and I *will* see him. *Now.*"

Wisely, Hugh didn't try to argue. Without a further word, he escorted her down the corridor, flashing his hospital ID pass as they passed yet another security checkpoint.

Hugh opened a plain, unmarked door, revealing a small private room. A couple of beeping machines lined the foot of a hospital bed, wires trailing off under the covers. Most of the bed was blocked from view by a privacy screen.

"I told you not to let her in here, Hugh," said a low, pained voice. The words were so badly distorted, Hayley could barely understand them. "Ash. Take her away."

Ash emerged from behind the screen. The Phoenix did not look quite so collected as usual. He was still wearing the same clothes he'd been earlier, at the fire. The smell of smoke hung around him, and something else too—a hot, scorching scent like desert winds and burnt metal.

"Ms. Parker," he said, nodding at her.

Hayley braced herself for an argument, but Ash just touched Hugh's elbow, drawing him away. The pair left, and the door clicked softly shut behind them.

"Bastards." A deep growl drifted out from behind the screen. "Hayley, *please.* I don't want you to remember me like this."

Hayley's heart hammered, but her hand was steady. She pushed back the privacy curtain.

"Like what?" She met his mismatched eyes without flinching. "Like the man I love? Like my mate?"

All the breath sighed out of him. His muzzle wrinkled a little, like he was trying to smile. "I love you."

"I love you too." Hayley threaded her fingers through his left paw, careful of the claws. "Don't ever try to keep me away again. I thought we'd agreed you weren't going to do that anymore."

"I won't." The sheets stirred oddly, next to his bent legs. It took Hayley a moment to realize that it was a tail, flicking under the covers. "Where's Danny? I can feel he's sleeping, and that he's safe and happy, but not more than that."

"He's back home, with Chase and Connie. He wanted to come to the hospital too, but I wouldn't let him."

"Good," Griff said, simply. "Don't."

"Griff-"

"*Don't.*" His right arm—no, his right *wing*—flexed in agitation, the gleaming feathers unfurling and closing again like a massive golden fan. "Promise me."

"All right, I promise. I won't bring him unless you say it's okay." She tightened her hand on his, feeling the roughness of his thick, feline pads. "But he wants to say thank you. And he'll want to say, to say…"

She couldn't finish the sentence, words jamming up in her tightening throat.

"To say goodbye," Griff finished for her. He leaned his head back against the pillows with another deep sigh, closing his eyes. "I'll think about it. Turns out I'm a lot more vain than I care to admit."

Even under the fur, she could see the pain in the drawn tightness of his distorted face. "You're tired. You should rest."

"I've got all of eternity to rest." He opened his eyes again, though she knew the effort it cost him. "We need to talk about you. And Danny. And Reiner."

"Later. You need to concentrate on regaining your strength." She stroked his feathery mane back from his forehead. "Don't worry about any of that now."

"I *have* to worry about it now," Griff said fiercely. "I'm not going to be able to worry about it later. And I am *not* going to die and leave you at the mercy of that, that-"

One of the machines connected to him let out a shrill whistle.

"Hugh!" Hayley shrieked, as Griff convulsed.

The door banged back. It wasn't Hugh who rushed in, though, but a whole pack of white-coated nurses. They swept Hayley aside, one of them grabbing her arm as the rest converged on Griff's thrashing form. She caught a brief glimpse of two of the nurses struggling to hold down his powerful, mismatched limbs while a third plunged a syringe into the side of his neck, before she was hustled out the door.

"Let me go!" Hayley twisted futilely against the nurse's grip, but he was clearly a shifter. He held her captive with inhuman ease. "I want to stay with him!"

"I don't care what you want," the nurse snapped as he dragged her back along the corridor. "I don't have time to deal with hysterical humans. How did you even get in here in the first place?"

"I have a right to be here." Hayley looked around wildly for Ash or Hugh, but they were nowhere to be seen. "You can't throw me out. I'm his mate!"

"I have no idea what that freak is, but he's certainly no shifter." The nurse dumped her unceremoniously outside the ward doors. "And that means he can't have a mate. You have no rights here. Get out, and stay out."

∼

There was a police car parked outside her house. Hayley stared blankly at it as she paid her taxi driver, her numb mind struggling to process its presence.

Police car. Here.

Why would Connie call the police? Has Reiner been trying to get in?

"Connie? Chase?" she called softly as she let herself into the house. She could tell immediately from the stillness that Danny was still asleep, even though it was nearly ten in the morning.

He must be exhausted after everything last night. We'll both need lots of rest today. I'll have to call school, and work...

Her brain stalled out. She was simply too tired to think of what else needed to be done. At least she could count on Griff's friends—*her* friends—to help out.

"Connie?" she said again, heading for the front room. "Why's there a police car-?"

She stopped dead.

There wasn't just a police car outside.

There were police officers in her house.

"Hayley!" Connie leaped up from a chair, taking her hands. The curvy pilot's face was pale and worried. "I'm so sorry. I couldn't to tell you over the phone. I didn't want you to feel like you had to rush back."

"She *should* have rushed back," muttered a man sitting on her sofa. He was wearing a sharp suit and an extremely pissed-off expression. "She's kept us waiting over an hour."

If looks could kill, Chase would have *buried* the man over an hour ago. The pegasus shifter radiated menace as he glared at both the man, and a woman seated next to him. Every muscle in his shoulders and chest was tense and ready.

"I'm sorry too, Hayley," he said. "We couldn't keep them out. But just give me the word, and I swear I will *kick* them out. One way or another."

The two police officers flanking the sofa growled, low in their throats. With a jolt, Hayley realized that they possessed the subtle but unmistakable feral aura of shifters.

"There's no need for that," said the woman, rising. Her pink twinset had clearly been chosen to appear friendly and approachable, but there was a certain firmness to the set of her jaw that meant the overall effect was of a Rottweiler wearing a fuzzy cardigan. "Let's not have any unpleasantness."

"What is this?" Hayley looked around at them all, unable to comprehend why there were so many strangers in her house. "What's going on?"

"Me first," the man on the sofa interrupted as the woman opened her mouth. "I've wasted enough time here today already." He got up, unceremoniously thrusting a folder of papers into Hayley's hand. "Ms. Hayley Dana Parker, on behalf of my client, Mr. Reiner Hans Ljonsson, I am formally notifying you of our intent to sue for full, sole, and immediate custody of Daniel Jamie Parker."

Papers fell out of Hayley's suddenly nerveless hand. *"What?"*

"Due to extreme and urgent concern for his son's safety and welfare, my client has petitioned the court for an extraordinary hearing as per the Juvenile Shifter Protection Act of 1968, Section three, paragraph eighteen," the lawyer rattled on in a bored monotone, ignoring her interruption entirely. "You may expect a court summons imminently. Until the case has been settled, you are legally required to keep Danny within Brighton city limits. Should you break these conditions, you will be pursued by the Wild Hunt and, should you survive capture, may face penalties of up to fifteen years' imprisonment. You will find all the details required by your defense team in the provided brief. Any questions? Good. See you in court."

Without waiting so much as a second for a response, the lawyer strode out of the room. Hayley stared after his back in shock, then switched her gaze to the woman. "What?" she repeated.

"I'm sorry, Ms. Parker. I know this must all be rather overwhelming." The woman extended a hand with a smile that didn't reach her hard eyes. "I'm from Shifter Social Services. I'm afraid I'm going to need to ask you some questions."

CHAPTER 26

"Are you certain you are strong enough for this, oath-brother?"

"John, if you ask me that one more time, I swear I'm going to get out of this wheelchair and walk the rest of the way on my own three feet," Griff retorted. "Push me faster, damn it. I'm not made of glass. If we don't hurry, we're going to miss the final verdict."

John sang a soft, worried chord, but sped up his pace. Despite what Griff had told the sea dragon shifter, every tiny rattle of the wheels over the courtroom foyer's tiled floor sent agony spiking through his guts. He gritted his teeth—as best he could, given that his jaw didn't close properly anymore—and endured.

We must be there. We must be at our mate's side, in her hour of need.

Griff didn't know whether the all-consuming, driving thought came from his lion, or his eagle, or his own mind. All three of them were so intertwined that even he couldn't tell them apart anymore. His lion's instincts, his eagle's instincts...they were all just *his* instincts now.

And every instinct compelled him to go to his mate.

If Griff had had his own way, he would have been at Hayley's side for the entire three-day hearing. But the hospital doctors had flatly refused to sign him out. When he'd raged at them, they'd just shot him full of sedatives and restrained him. Apparently any display of anger was just another symptom of his unstable, bestial state.

Of course, when Griff had woken up and tried calmly reasoning with the doctors instead, they'd decided that obviously Hayley couldn't *really* be his mate, as he wasn't showing enough emotional agitation at her predicament. Griff had been very tempted to show them exactly how much agitation he could cause, but that would have just got him tied down to the bed again.

Instead, he'd smiled and nodded. And, as soon as the doctors had left, called John.

Shortly thereafter, the hospital had suffered a severe, sudden, and curiously localized flood. The shifter ward staff had been much too busy panicking over the two feet of seawater sloshing around their break room to even *notice* a patient being quietly wheeled away.

"I do appreciate this, you know," Griff said to John. "You can consider this payment of your life-debt."

John grunted as he picked up the entire wheelchair—Griff included—in order to carry it down a flight of stairs. "This, payment of a life-debt? This is a worthy adventure, oath-brother. *I* am indebted to *you* for allowing me to participate in it."

Griff's breath hissed between his fangs as the wheelchair bumped down to the ground again. "You're going to have to allow me to call the debt quits one day, you know."

"Perhaps." A slight smile tugged at John's stern mouth. "But not this day. Through here?"

"Yes." Griff could hear Michael's refined, measured voice even through the thick closed door. "Quietly. They're making final statements."

We must stay high and hidden. We must scout out the terrain in order to judge how best to join our mate in this hunt. We must stalk softly until we are ready to pounce.

Unfortunately, a seven-foot-tall blue-haired knight pushing a completely shrouded figure in a wheelchair tended to attract people's attention. Especially when someone started shrieking and waving at them the instant they appeared.

"Mr. Griff!" Danny yelled in delight. Only the restraining hand of the social worker seated next to him kept the boy from hurling himself straight at Griff. "You're here, you're *here!*"

Griff grimaced underneath his concealing hood as heads turned all around the large, circular hearing chamber. To Michael's credit, the lawyer barely hesitated a second before smoothly continuing to deliver his closing statements. The judge and court officials also returned to the business at hand, though many of them stared curiously at him for a few moments longer.

"I didn't know you were coming!" Hayley whispered, as John parked his wheelchair next to her seat. Her hand found his, squeezing it in gratitude through the sheets swathing his distorted body. "I didn't even know you were being discharged!"

"Neither did the hospital," Griff murmured back. "Tell you later. How's it going?"

Hayley shook her head. "I thought that Reiner wouldn't have a leg to stand on, not after what happened at his house. But somehow his lawyer twisted all Danny's testimony, made it sound like he's some sort of juvenile delinquent arsonist. Now it all keeps coming back to the question of who can be Danny's alpha. Michael's arguing that it can't be Reiner, since he can't be trusted with Danny's welfare."

The dark circles under her eyes looked like smudges of soot against her ashen skin. Griff knew that the rest of Alpha Team had been looking after her—he'd made sure of *that*—but she still looked like she'd barely eaten or slept for days.

"...Outstanding testimonies from varied, prominent citizens in the local shifter community," Michael was saying. The overhead lights struck blue highlights from the faerie hound's midnight skin as he pointedly held up a thick sheaf of papers. "Not least of which is a personal statement from the Phoenix, known as Ash, testifying that it is his professional opinion that my client holds absolutely no blame for the fire on the evening of November the first. I submit that this utterly refutes and repudiates Mr. Ljonsson's claim that this incident can be used as evidence to deny my client custody. I further counter that as the fire occurred while Mr. Ljonsson had sole responsibility for Daniel Jamie Parker-"

Griff noticed that Reiner's lawyer was staring hard at him. Griff recognized the man—he was a shark shifter of some notoriety, with an excellent track record and a reputation for deviousness. The last time Griff had encountered him had been at an arson trial. Griff had been giving evidence against the shark shifter's client.

On *that* occasion, the lawyer had lost.

The shark touched Reiner's sleeve, leaning over to murmur in his ear. The two fell into an intent, whispered conversation.

Hayley had spotted them too. "What are they up to now?"

"I don't know." To Griff's frustration, he couldn't quite make out the words over Michael's impassioned defense. "But it's something to do with me. And Reiner doesn't look happy about it."

Hayley chewed on her lip. "Let's hope that means it's a good sign for us."

"Thank you, Mr. Cabell," the judge said, as Michael finished his statement. "Do you or your client have anything further to add?"

Michael flashed a quick, inquiring look at Hayley and Griff. They both shook their heads slightly in answer.

"We have no further evidence to present, Your Honor." Michael sat down on Hayley's other side.

The judge turned to Reiner and his lawyer. "Mr. Paucus, your closing statement, please."

The shark shifter stood. "Before proceeding to my closing statement, I would like to submit one further testimony on behalf of my client, Your Honor."

The judge steepled her fingers, casting Paucus a stern look over the tops of her glasses. Griff didn't recognize her. He'd only been involved in criminal court cases before, not family court matters. He could tell from her body language that she was a wolf shifter...and also that she was eager to close the trial. She didn't look pleased by this last-minute disruption.

"You have had three days to present testimonies on behalf of your client, Mr. Paucus," the judge said to the lawyer. "Is there a reason why this one seems to have slipped your mind until now?"

The shark shifter made a courteous little bow. "This witness was previously unavailable. I apologize for the irregularity, but I strongly believe that this testimony should be heard before you reach your final decision."

The judge blew out her breath. Her eyes flicked to the clock, and back to the lawyer. "You may have five minutes. No more, Mr. Paucus. This is not the only hearing scheduled for today."

"Thank you, Your Honor." The shark looked straight across at Griff. "We call Griffin MacCormick to the stand."

CHAPTER 27

"What are they up to?" Hayley whispered to Michael.

Her lawyer shook his head, watching his opposite number with narrowed eyes. "I don't know. I'd have said Paucus was planning to cast doubt on Griff as a reliable witness...except that he *isn't* a witness. I didn't include any testimony from him in our defense case, for exactly this reason. His condition means he's too easy to discredit."

Hayley twisted her hands in the hem of her tunic, her palms sweating as Griff stiffly struggled out of his wheelchair. The hospital sheets wrapped around him like a shroud, hiding even his face from view. Waving off John's assistance, he managed to get himself into witness box on his own two feet, though she could tell the effort it cost him to stand upright.

He shouldn't even be here. What if the stress causes him to have another seizure? Is that Reiner's plan? Is he vindictive enough to hound Griff into a heart attack, just because Griff's twice the lion he'll ever be?

Reiner, however, didn't look like this was all part of some scheme. His jaw was set in a tight, unhappy line, his muscular arms folded across his chest. Paucus said something to him, and Reiner snarled back under his breath, glaring at his lawyer. Hayley was certain that whatever was going on was Paucus's idea, not Reiner's.

That wasn't very comforting. Reiner was petty and arrogant, but not devious. Paucus was another matter.

"Mr. MacCormick, kindly remove your...coverings," the judge said, when the official had finished swearing Griff in. "The court must be able to see your face."

"Mr. McCormick has a severe medical condition," Paucus said smoothly, before Griff could speak. He looked meaningful across the courtroom at Danny. "Some here would find his appearance upsetting. I respectfully beg that the court permit Mr. MacCormick to retain his privacy, Your Honor."

The judge nodded. "Granted. You may proceed with the witness. Five minutes only, Mr. Paucus."

The shark shifter turned to Griff, hands clasped loosely behind his back. "Mr. MacCormick, would you please state your heritage and nature for the benefit of the court?"

"My maternal line are eagle shifters, and my paternal line are lion shifters," Griff said warily. "I possess two inner beasts, both lion and eagle."

"Mr. MacCormick's unusual status is a matter of public record," Paucus said to the room in general, as a small murmur ran round the court. "Mr. MacCormick, you possess the renowned perceptive abilities of the Scottish Highland white-tailed sea eagles, do you not?"

"I do." Even with the sheet hiding his face from view, Hayley could tell from the way he leaned forward that he was focusing those very powers on the lawyer right now, alert for any hint of trickery.

"In layperson's terms, Mr. MacCormick, is it accurate to say that you are able to detect when other people are lying or concealing the truth?"

"Yes." Griff's growl made the word a threat.

"And you have previously been called to use those powers when testifying in criminal court cases, haven't you?"

"Yes," Griff repeated, starting to sound slightly perplexed by the line of questioning.

Hayley was too. She had no idea where Paucus was going with this, and the uncertainty made her heart hammer in her throat.

It's like Paucus is trying to build up *his credibility, not knock it down...*

Paucus addressed the judge. "I have personally been present at trials where Mr. MacCormick's testimony was accepted as proof as to the veracity of other witnesses. I can provide references on request. For now, Your Honor, are you willing to accept that Mr. MacCormick can indeed do what he claims?"

"I am," the judge said, glancing at the clock again. "Time is running out, Mr. Paucus. Is there a point to this?"

"Just a few more questions, Your Honor. Mr. MacCormick, you are romantically involved with Ms. Hayley Parker, and were previously alpha to her son, Daniel Jamie Parker, correct?"

"Yes," Griff said shortly.

"Is it true to say that these facts naturally lead you to be antagonistic toward my client, Mr. Reiner Ljonsson?"

"I don't like him, if that's what you're asking," Griff said dryly. "Though I would dislike him just as intensely if Hayley was *not* my mate. He-"

"Apologies for interrupting," Paucus said, in a tone that was anything but apologetic. "As time is short, please restrict yourself to answering only the questions I ask. In the past, have you physically confronted Mr. Ljonsson?"

"Yes. Several times. He started them all."

"Just the direct question, please, Mr. MacCormick. You also lost a dominance challenge to him, and were forced to relinquish alpha rights over Daniel Parker?"

Griff's assent was more of a snarl than a word. Reiner smirked across the courtroom at him.

"But he-" Danny started. His social worker whispered urgently in his ear, making him quieten down again.

"In summary, Mr. MacCormick, is it fair to state that you violently dislike my client, and personally wish him to lose this case? You have no reason to come to his defense?"

"You're the one who hauled me up here," Griff growled. "Yes. All of those statements are true."

"Thank you. Just one last question. Please answer based on both your eagle powers of observation, and your personal knowledge of my client." The shark shifter bared all his teeth in a cold, predatory smile. "Would Mr. Ljonsson ever knowingly endanger his son?"

Click. Hayley could practically hear the trap springing shut. Her breath froze in her throat.

From Griff's absolute stillness, he'd stopped breathing too. He didn't say anything.

"Your answer, please, Mr. MacCormick," Paucus pressed. "I remind you that you are under oath."

"I…" Griff hesitated. "Reiner's judgment is-"

"It's a simple question, Mr. MacCormick! Would my client ever *knowingly* endanger his son? Yes or no?"

"Objection, Your Honor!" Michael leaped to his feet. "Mr. Paucus is badgering this witness!"

"Overruled." The judge was gazing thoughtfully at Griff, her brow furrowed. "Please answer the question, Mr. MacCormick."

Griff's shrouded head bowed. "No," he said, very softly.

Paucus turned his back on him, smiling sweetly up at the judge. "No further questions, Your Honor."

Michael's eyes were burning red with anger. "Your Honor, I would also like to question this witness."

"You have already made your closing remarks, Mr. Cabell. You had plentiful previous opportunity to gather a statement from Mr. MacCormick if you so wished." The judge checked the time again. "I will take a moment before rendering my verdict. Mr. MacCormick, you may step down."

Hayley jumped up, running to the witness box so quickly she even beat John. Griff's paw clutched at her arm as she helped him back into the wheelchair.

"I'm sorry," he said into her ear, his distorted voice filled with bitter agony. "I shouldn't have come. You should never have met me. I just make everything worse for you."

"Don't say that." Hayley grabbed his shoulder through the sheet, shaking him a little to break him out of his spiral of self-recrimination. "Don't *ever* say that. It wasn't your fault. And it probably won't have made any difference anyway. The judge must have already made up her mind by now, surely."

Griff's concealed face turned in the direction of the judge. She was bent over her notes, her pen tapping thoughtfully on the paper. Hayley couldn't read anything in her professionally blank expression…but Griff made a low, agonized sound deep in his throat.

"She *had* made up her mind," he said. "And now she's changing it."

All Hayley could do was grip his shoulder, trying to comfort him even as she took comfort just from his presence. Minutes crawled by like hours. Across the courtroom, Reiner and his lawyer exchanged triumphant glances.

The judge sat back at last, taking off her glasses. "I am prepared to render my judgment. Ms. Parker, Mr. Ljonsson, please approach with your councils."

Hayley didn't want to leave Griff behind, but she had no choice. Michael took her elbow, escorting her up to the front of the courtroom. The judge's box seemed as high and intimidating as a mountain. Hayley had never felt so scared or so helpless.

"Ms. Parker, Mr. Ljonsson." The judge folded her glasses, placing them neatly before her. "Based on what I have heard, it is clear that it is in Daniel's best interests to have contact with both of you."

Hayley's heart started beating again.

"However," the judge continued, and Hayley's pulse thudded, "this presents logistical difficulties, given Mr. Ljonsson's stated intention to continue to reside in Valtyra. It is clear that we will have to find a way to divide Daniel's time between your two countries."

Reiner scowled. "But-"

The judge gave him a quelling look. "I have not finished, Mr. Ljonsson. It is *also* clear to me that Daniel is in urgent need of a pride. His recent willful and reckless behavior stems from the lack of a true alpha lion to curb his instincts. This situation cannot be allowed to continue. Although it is not ideal to remove Daniel from his school mid-term, I believe that his shifter education must come first. Mr. Ljonsson, for the time being, I am granting you full custody of Daniel, effective immediately."

The bottom dropped out of Hayley's stomach. The room swam in her vision. "No!"

"I know this will be difficult for you to accept, Ms. Parker." The judge's stern gaze softened a little. "You are human, and cannot understand the strength of our instincts. But Daniel *must* have a pride. Mr. Ljonsson can provide him with that. You cannot."

"But, but you said," Hayley stammered out. She wanted to beg, to scream, to grab Danny and run away, *anything* but accept this judgment. "You said he needed to see both of us. He needs *me* too!"

"This is true. He does. At the moment, his need for a pride is greater, but this will change as he masters his lion." The judge turned to Reiner, who was practically glowing with satisfaction. "Mr. Ljonsson, after Daniel has integrated into your pride, you will ensure that he has regular contact with his mother. I will draw up a schedule based around school holidays."

I'm only going to get to see my little boy during school holidays? For just a few weeks, out of months?

"Of course," Reiner said to the judge, surprisingly meekly. His amber eyes gleamed as he glanced at Hayley. "I will be happy to do so…once Danny is firmly established in my pride."

"LYING!" Hayley leaped at Griff's sudden, explosive roar. He surged up from his wheelchair, his concealing sheets slipping away. "He is lying!"

Reiner recoiled in horror from Griff's bestial, snarling features. In that split-second, unguarded moment, Hayley read the truth in Reiner's eyes. He *was* lying. He had no intention of ever returning Danny.

If Danny went to Valtyra, she'd never see him again.

"Your Honor, please, you can't do this." Ignoring the shocked gasps at his appearance, Griff took a step toward the judge. His tail lashed from side to side, the feathered tip sweeping across the floor. "Reiner's lying. Every school holiday, he'll just claim that Danny isn't ready-"

"Your Honor, these are baseless slanders against my client!" Paucus interrupted. "I petition that Mr. MacCormick be removed immediately!"

Griff bared his fangs at the shark, making him flinch. "*You're* the one who made a big song-and-dance of my eagle abilities. You can't pretend not to believe in them now. He is *lying!*"

"Mr. MacCormick!" The judge had visibly paled at Griff's twisted form, but she banged her gavel down decisively. "You are not under oath, and your motivations are suspect."

"Then *put* me under oath-"

"I am not dragging this case out indefinitely, when there is a vulnerable shifter child's welfare at stake! My decision is final. Stand down, or be held in contempt of court."

Hayley rushed to Griff's side as he opened his mouth to say something that would doubtless get him arrested. "Don't," she hissed in his ear. She could feel his arm shaking under her hand, and realized he was perilously close to a full-blown seizure. "Not now. We'll- we'll think of something, we'll find a way to fight this."

His eyes met hers, blazing with intensity. He took a deep breath, and some of the rage left his features...replaced by determination. "Yes. I will."

Then he turned toward Reiner, drawing himself up to his full height as best he could. "Reiner Ljonsson, *I challenge you!*"

CHAPTER 28

Reiner let out a disbelieving bark of laughter. "You cannot possibly be serious. You can barely stand."

"Then you won't have any trouble defeating me, will you?" Griff's muscles were screaming in agony at the effort of standing upright on his backward-bent legs, but he refused to show any sign of weakness. "I challenge you for your pride, Reiner Ljonsson. Face me like a lion."

"Oath-brother, what are you doing?" John's blue eyes were wide with shock. "You are in no condition to attempt this."

Hayley too had gone pale. "Griff, no! He'll kill you!"

Griff ignored them both, focused on Reiner. "Well, Reiner? Answer the challenge."

Reiner hesitated, looking from Griff to the judge as if seeking higher intervention. "This is ridiculous. I'm not debasing myself by acknowledging a challenge from that twisted freak."

The judge banged her gavel down, the sound echoing like a gunshot around the room. "Order! Mr. MacCormick, I will not have you disrupting my courtroom!"

Paucus leaped in to back up his client. "Your Honor, we petition to have Mr. MacCormick removed from court. His condition is clearly causing him to become irrational-"

"Mr. MacCormick's mental state is of no relevance," Michael interrupted. He shot Griff an *I hope you know what you're doing* sort of look. "Alpha challenges are an inviolable right, protected by law and enshrined in lion tradition. With all due respect, Your Honor, you have no power to intervene."

"*Lions,*" the judge muttered under her breath. She fixed Griff with a piercing stare. "Mr. MacCormick, as a wolf shifter myself, I must respect the sacredness of an alpha challenge. Nonetheless, I will ask you to reconsider. Even if you somehow defeat Mr. Ljonsson and become Daniel's legal alpha, I will not change my ruling. Daniel needs the guidance of a true shifter, and a true pride. You cannot provide those things."

He'd been expecting her to say something like that. "I understand, Your Honor."

She narrowed her eyes at him. "Furthermore, in the unlikely event that you kill Mr. Ljonsson during this challenge, I *will* prosecute you to the fullest extent of the law. Accidental deaths during alpha challenges are protected. Deliberate murder is not."

"Is that your plan, cripple?" Reiner clenched his fists, glaring suspiciously at Griff. "What is this, suicide by lion? You think you can entrap me into a murder charge?"

"Your Honor, my client has a valid concern," Mr. Paucus interjected. "In Mr. MacCormick's state, he is highly unlikely to survive the stress of an alpha challenge. Mr. Ljonsson cannot be held responsible for that."

The judge sighed, rubbing her forehead. "Mr. MacCormick, Mr. Paucus is correct. Since you are the challenger, and seem fully cognizant of the risks you are taking, Mr. Ljonsson will not be held liable in the event of your death. For the last time, I ask you to reconsider. Will you withdraw your challenge?"

"I will not. My challenge stands."

Hayley's fingers dug into his arm. "Griff," she whispered, for his ears only. "What are you doing?"

"Buying time," he muttered back. "I'm going to die anyway. Let me make it mean something."

He turned back to Reiner, who was still looking mortally offended by the entire situation. "Reiner, I repeat my challenge. What is your answer?"

"You're deranged." Reiner's lip curled as his scornful gaze swept Griff from head to toe. "You don't stand a chance. I refuse to take part in this mockery of lion tradition."

"I'll happily accept your surrender, if you're too cowardly to fight." Griff smiled at Reiner, aware that his bestial features turning the expression into a mocking snarl. "Get down on your belly. Show me your throat…*beta*."

As Griff had intended, the taunt raised Reiner's hackles. "I'm not frightened of you. I accept your challenge!"

"In which case, court adjourned." The judge rapped her gavel down again. "Gentlemen, you will settle this immediately. I am not having this farce drawn out any longer than necessary. Stewards, please prepare the arena."

"Mr. Griff, Mr. Griff!" Danny broke free of his social worker at last as officials started clearing away chairs. Without the slightest sign of repugnance at Griff's monstrous form, Danny wrapped his arms around his waist, burying his face in Griff's side. "Don't fight Daddy, *please*. He'll hurt you."

"It'll be all right, lad." Griff dropped down to his haunches to embrace the boy. He rubbed his furry cheek against Danny's tear-streaked one in a leonine gesture of love and comfort. "Sometimes this is just the way lions have to settle things."

"He'll hurt you bad," Danny sobbed. "And it will all be my fault."

"*No*." Griff put a flex of alpha power into his emphatic tone. "None of this is your fault. It's mine and your da's fault, because we can't come to an agreement like grown-ups. Don't ever, *ever* feel like this was your fault. Promise me that."

Danny's shoulders shook, but he nodded.

Griff looked over his blond head at the judge. "Your Honor, I don't want him to see this. Permission to let his mother remove him until this is over?"

The judge motioned at the social worker, and at one of the security guards. "Please escort Daniel and Ms. Parker to a waiting area."

"No!" Hayley exclaimed. "I mean, yes, Danny can't see this. But I'm staying. I'm not leaving you to face this alone, Griff."

"He will not be alone," John rumbled. "I shall be here, my lady. Oath-brother, if you cannot be dissuaded from this, then I will be your second."

"No, you won't," Griff said firmly. "You're going with Hayley. I need you to make sure she and Danny are safe."

"But-" John and Hayley started together.

Letting Danny go, Griff grabbed John's arm. Under the pretext of using the sea dragon as support to stand up, he leaned in close to his ear. "I am calling in your debt. On your honor, you *will make sure they are safe*. Do you understand?"

John went absolutely still for an instant. Griff felt his muscles tense as he understood his meaning.

They will be safe. John's telepathic voice was a dirge of grief and loss and utter, unbreakable determination. *I will spirit them away. I will hide them in the wilds where none shall ever find them, and I will lay down my life in their defense. I will repay my debt.*

Unable to respond telepathically, Griff could only embrace him briefly, fiercely. He knew that he could count on the sea dragon to get Hayley and Danny away while everyone else was distracted with his challenge to Reiner.

Hayley was still looking stubborn, unaware of what had passed between John and Griff. "I'm not leaving. John can take Danny, but I'm not leaving."

Letting go of John, Griff turned to her. For the last time, he took her in his arms. For the last time, he breathed in her scent. For the last time, he felt her soft warmth against his body as she clung to him.

"Go with John. He'll explain." He touched her face lightly, hoping that the brief, simple caress could say everything that he didn't have time to put into words. "I love you. Always."

There was no more opportunity for goodbyes or explanations—the stewards had finished clearing away the chairs, and erected the barriers that turned the center of the large, round chamber from a courtroom into an arena. Alpha challenges were not exactly common, but they happened often enough for there to be an established procedure.

To his relief, Hayley reluctantly allowed John to pull her away. Griff waited until the doors had swung shut behind them all before turning to Reiner. "Let's do this, then."

Reiner was already shrugging out of his suit. Quietly, so that the watching witnesses couldn't hear, he snarled, "In a hurry to die, freak?"

Quite the opposite, actually.

Every second he survived was another second Hayley could use to escape. Every second increased the distance between her and the officials who sought to deprive her of her child. Every second increased her chance to save Danny from growing up under Reiner's harsh, misguided influence.

Griff would do whatever he could to buy her those seconds.

He was under no illusions that he would be able to defeat a fully-grown lion with his bare hands. Reiner was going to kill him. The best he could hope for was to make him do it slowly.

Reiner shifted, leaping lithely over the arena barriers in lion form. Taking a deep breath, Griff shrugged off his sheets, though he left his pants on. It wasn't like *he* needed to shift, after all.

Rather less elegantly than Reiner, he struggled over the barrier. It was a relief to drop to all fours, having been upright for so long. Even with his right arm more wing than forepaw, his body worked a lot better this way.

He took a deep breath, ignoring the pain that shot through his chest. His erratic heartbeat steadied as he focused on his opponent.

We will not sell our life cheaply. We will make him tear us apart piece by piece. We will fight to the last drop of blood, to the last breath. We will not fail our mate.

"Begin," said the judge.

CHAPTER 29

"I changed my mind, I can't just leave him." Hayley tried to stop, but John had her wrist engulfed in his huge hand. "John! Let me go. I have to go back."

He shook his head at her, his face set in grim, hard lines. He continued to drag her after the social worker and the security guard. The two had Danny between them, as if they thought Hayley might try to snatch him and run off.

"Here we are," the social worker said in a horribly fake cheerful voice as she opened the door to a small break room. "We can all have a nice little rest in here. Would you like a snack, Danny?"

He glared back up at her, scowling beneath his tousled blond hair. "No. I wanna go back to Mr. Griff."

The security guard rolled his eyes, shoving Danny forward. "Get in, kid. An alpha challenge is no place for you."

John pulled Hayley into the room too, though he had to duck to get through the doorway. Letting go of her arm at last, he shut the door quietly behind the five of them. Catching her eye, he put one finger over his lips.

The social worker and the security guard were still arguing with

Danny. John loomed over them, one enormous hand falling onto each of their shoulders.

"My sincere apologies," he said. With one quick, sharp motion, he banged their heads together.

"John!" Hayley exclaimed in shock, as the social worker and the security guard fell into limp heaps. "What-"

"My oath-brother has charged me with your protection," John interrupted. He opened the door again, casting a quick glance either way down the corridor before motioning them to follow him. "I will get you to safety. Hurry. He cannot buy us much time."

Hayley sucked in her breath as she realized Griff's plan. She grabbed Danny's hand. "Come on, baby. Sir John's taking us on an adventure."

"Is Mr. Griff coming too?" Danny asked hopefully, trotting along at her side. "Is he going to meet us later?"

Hayley couldn't bring herself to answer him. Somewhere behind them, Griff was fighting for his life, for *their* lives. Every step away from him felt like a noose tightening around her throat.

I have to get Danny away. But...I can't leave Griff.

Her head said one thing, and her heart screamed another. She felt as trapped between them as Griff did with his two animals. The conflicting instincts tore at her soul until she couldn't bear it any longer.

"I can't," she burst out, balking in the middle of the street outside the courthouse. "I can't leave him."

John sang a low, agonized chord. "We must. *You* must. He is doing this for you. Do not waste his sacrifice."

"I won't." Dropping to one knee, she took Danny's shoulders, looking him straight in the eye. "Danny, you have to go with Sir John now. Do exactly what he says, understand?"

"Are you going back for Mr. Griff?" At her nod, a smile broke through Danny's worried expression. "Good. The pride is supposed to stick up for the alpha, just like he does for the pride."

Hayley hugged him, hard. "I *will* find you. I promise, I'll find you."

"And I too swear that you shall," John said to her, as she released

Danny. "I will take your son to safety, and then return for you. There is no stone, no wall, no prison ever built that can withstand my kind. I will keep my oath."

Hayley staggered as an abrupt, burning pain lanced through her chest. Somehow she knew, *knew* that it was Griff's pain that she was feeling. He'd been mortally wounded.

He needed her. *Now.*

Without another word, she ran back into the building. She'd dressed up for the trial in her nicest shoes, but now the heels hobbled her. She kicked them off carelessly, her feet slipping on the polished floor as she raced down the corridor.

Another lash of agony twisted her guts. The hallways seemed to stretch endlessly before her, like a bad dream. She charged past a couple of confused security guards, heedless of their shouts. Up ahead, she could hear other noises—bestial snarls and shrieks of rage. The sounds of battle drew her like a magnet.

She didn't know what she could do to help. She didn't know if there *was* anything she could do to help. She just knew that she couldn't leave her mate to die alone.

She burst back into the courtroom, just as an almighty crash rattled the walls. A scene out of a nightmare met her horrified eyes.

The protective barriers that formed the arena had seemed so thick and sturdy, but now two of them were overturned. Griff lay unmoving in the wreckage, broken and bleeding. A wide crimson smear marked his trail, showing where Reiner had thrown him straight through the arena wall.

Witnesses screamed, fleeing higher up the tiered levels of the room as Reiner's massive golden form leaped through the gap in the barriers. The lion had deep scratch marks on the side of his face, and his eyes were alight with savage rage. His tawny coat was splattered with Griff's blood. He left red paw prints behind him as he stalked toward his fallen opponent.

Griff stirred a little, struggling to push himself up on broken limbs. Reiner roared at him, lips wrinkling back from his dripping fangs.

Griff raised his head, meeting Reiner's glare without flinching. Despite his shattered body, he roared back, defiant, undefeated.

Reiner's eyes narrowed. His powerful muscles bunched as he gathered himself for one final pounce.

"NO!" Hayley hurled herself toward them. Her bare feet skidded in Griff's blood as she threw herself between him and Reiner. *"NO!"*

Reiner was either too blind with bloodlust to notice her...or he just didn't care.

Claws extended, he leaped straight for her.

CHAPTER 30

Get up! Get up!

Griff raged at his useless body, struggling to force his broken limbs to obey him. His vision was going black around the edges from blood-loss. But if he could just *move*, he could buy Hayley another five seconds. Those extra five seconds were worth any amount of agony.

It was no use. He couldn't push himself up, couldn't even roll away from Reiner as the lion stalked toward him. All he could do was roar defiance. All he could do was refuse to surrender.

All he could do was hope it would take Reiner at least five more seconds to tear out his throat.

Hayley, Hayley, Hayley.

Her name ran through his mind like a mantra as Reiner gathered himself to spring. Griff held tight to the memory of his wonderful, perfect mate. He wanted his last thoughts to be of her. He filled his mind with her beautiful face and stunning body, picturing her so clearly he could almost see her standing in front of him.

She *was* standing in front of him.

Time froze. With crystal clarity, he saw Reiner leaping toward them, leaping toward *her*. Hayley was right in his path, arms spread, protecting Griff with her own body. The lion's long, powerful form seemed to hang in midair.

NO!

Every atom of his body, every part of his soul, united with the need to protect his mate. Shattered bones reformed, muscles coalescing around them. He surged to his feet. As unstoppable as an avalanche, he leaped to block Reiner's attack, meeting the lion's talons with his own.

Reiner roared in pain as Griff hurled him to one side. The lion hit the ground hard, rolling. He staggered to his paws, snarling—and stopped dead.

Griff spread his wings to protect his mate, his tail lashing. Reiner cowered as Griff screamed at the lion in rage. Griff didn't give him a second to recover. He pounced, sinking his talons into the lion's shoulders, pinning him to the ground. His powerful beak closed around Reiner's throat.

The temptation to bite down was almost overwhelming. But... despite everything, Reiner was still Danny's father. That single fact was the only thing that kept Griff from tearing the lion's head clear off for daring to threaten his mate.

SUBMIT! Griff demanded, hurling the thought like a spear into Reiner's stunned mind. *Submit, or I will kill you!*

Reiner whimpered. *I surrender! I surrender!*

Griff dropped him, backing away. He stayed tense and ready in case it was a trick, but Reiner just fell bonelessly to the ground. The lion rolled, exposing his belly in utter submission.

Alpha. Reiner's telepathic voice shook with terror and awe. *You are Alpha. Forgive me.*

Griff's hackles settled. Satisfied that the lion no longer posed any threat to his mate, he folded his wings-

...*Wait.*

Wings?

CHAPTER 31

One second, Hayley was staring straight down Reiner's throat as he leaped for her. The next thing she knew, she'd been hurled aside, a huge, golden form surging between her and the lion. Vast, gleaming wings spread protectively over her. For a mad moment, Hayley could only think that she'd been saved by an angel.

But it wasn't an angel.

"*Griffin,*" Hayley breathed.

She wasn't sure whether she was saying his name, or naming what he was, or both. But in any event, there was no mistaking that majestic, powerful form.

He could have sprung straight from a heraldic coat-of-arms, or some medieval bestiary. He had the head of an eagle, with fierce golden eyes and an enormous hooked beak, but halfway down his chest the ruff of feathers blended into a lion's tawny coat. His front legs ended in the strong, scaled feet of a bird of prey, but his back legs were entirely lion. His wings spanned the entire width of the arena, every feather shining as if made of pure gold.

He was beautiful, and terrifying, and utterly overwhelming. And he was whole. Finally, he was what he was supposed to be.

He was a griffin. He was *her* Griffin. Her mate.

"Griffin!" she called out again, but he was too fixated on Reiner to notice. She could only stay back, out of the way, as the griffin ruthlessly pinned the lion down.

In a few short moments, it was all over. Reiner lay whimpering and defeated on the ground. And Griff…suddenly stopped and stared down himself, as if he'd only just noticed his new form. His beak dropped open in comic surprise.

"Griff!" Unable to hold back any longer, Hayley flung herself at him. She wound her arms around his soft feathered neck, half-laughing, half-crying. "You're a *griffin*. That's what you've been all along!"

A small, wondering noise rumbled deep in his throat, somewhere between a lion's purr and an eagle's call. The hard side of his beak rubbed against her cheek, tentatively, as if he didn't quite trust his newfound strength.

She hugged him tighter, burying her face in his feathered chest. He was *huge*, at least double the size of even Reiner. He had a clean, wild scent that reminded her of both snowy skies and dry, sunbaked grassland—a strange but beautiful combination, as unique as he was.

"Ah." They both looked up at the judge, who was staring down at them with a completely nonplussed expression. "Yes. Well, that seems to be quite decisive. Mr. MacCormick, it appears that you will be able to be the alpha that Danny requires after all. I shall…I shall have to reconsider my verdict."

"Oh my God, Danny!" Hayley exclaimed, releasing Griff. "John's still-"

She cut herself off, not wanting to spill the secret, illegal plan in front of the judge. Griff understood, though. He cocked his head, his golden eyes going a little unfocussed. Then his beak dropped open in an unmistakable smile. He nudged her shoulder, rumbling.

"You talked to John? Telepathically?" Hayley guessed. "You can do that now?"

He nodded. Spreading his wings in a heraldic pose, he gestured at himself with one front claw.

Delighted laughter bubbled up in her throat. "Of course. *You're a* mythic shifter too. Just like John is. So you can talk to him. Did you tell him to bring Danny back? That everything's okay now?"

He nodded again. The feathers of his ruff raised a little, as if he was starting to get a bit agitated. She could *feel* his delight and awe, glowing in her heart where earlier she'd felt his pain…but she could also sense a growing undercurrent of frustration. And worry.

She stroked his shoulder, a thrill shivering through her at the contrast of the soft fur over the hot, hard muscles beneath. "What's wrong?"

He shuffled his clawed feet, looking a little sheepish. He gestured at himself again.

"I think he's stuck," said Michael, coming up beside her. For once, the polished lawyer had lost his air of ironic detachment. He was grinning from ear to ear. "Trust you, Griff. First you can't shift, and now you can't shift *back*."

Griff rolled his eyes at him. He let out a pained hiss.

"Can you talk to him?" Hayley asked Michael. "You're a mythic shifter too, aren't you?"

The lawyer shook his head. "Fae hound. Similar, but different enough that I can't contact him telepathically."

People were starting to emerge out from behind overturned chairs and benches, creeping back down toward the arena with staring eyes and open mouths. Michael raised his voice, addressing the room at large. "Anyone here a mythic shifter? Charades are only going to get us so far. We need a translator."

Unfortunately, none of the officials turned out to be dragons or anything similar. Hayley thought that Reiner, as a lion, might have been able to talk to Griff, but *he* didn't seem to be able to shift back either. The arrogant lion shifter was nearly catatonic with shock.

In the end, they had to wait until John finally returned with Danny. Hayley spent the time anxiously checking Griff for any wounds, but his transformation seemed to have completely restored him. He was gleaming and flawless, from his powerful beak to his tufted tail. There was no sign that he'd ever been injured at all.

"Oh." When he arrived, Danny didn't seem at all surprised by

Griff's new form. He looked the griffin up and down thoughtfully, and nodded a little, as if something had become clear. "Yep. That explains a *lot*."

"At last, oath-brother. What took you so long?" A joyful melody rippled under John's teasing words. "Come now, shift back. You are an expert in the theory, are you not?"

Griff shot him a dirty look. He growled, low in his throat.

"Can you help him?" Hayley asked the sea dragon shifter. "What's he saying?"

John chuckled under his breath. "That it turns out theory is a lot more difficult than practice."

"Mr. Griff?" Danny tugged on Griff's feathers, his upturned face serious. "Think of cookies, Mr. Griff."

Griff looked down at the boy…and shimmered.

"My boy," he said, gathering Danny up. He turned to Hayley, pulling her into his embrace as well, his face shining with joy and wonder. "My mate."

He held them both in his strong arms, and she knew he would never, ever let go.

EPILOGUE

Three Months Later...

"Mommy, Mommy, Da's here!"

Hayley froze, her pulse spiking with anxiety. By court order, she was required to allow Reiner access to Danny, but until now he'd meekly followed every condition she'd set. His visits with Danny were strictly supervised, either by Griff or one of the other firefighters on Alpha Team. He wasn't allowed to return Danny a minute late...or pick him up a minute early.

So what was he doing turning up a whole *hour* before his scheduled time?

Does he know Griff is still at work? Does he think he can snatch Danny and run before I can call for help? Has he just been biding his time all along, only pretending to be contrite and reformed?

"Da! Da!" Downstairs, Danny's feet charged for the door.

"*Danny!*" Flinging aside her hairbrush, Hayley sprinted for the stairs. "Don't let him in!"

She stopped on the landing, her mouth dropping open.

"I don't have to let him in." Danny paused just long enough to shoot her a single baffled glance. "He's got a *key*, Mommy."

Then he leaped up into Griff's outstretched arms. "Hi Da! Did you have a good day at work?"

From the dumbfounded expression on Griff's face, this was the first *he'd* heard of this new name for himself too.

"What?" Danny looked from him to Hayley and back again, evidently confused by their stunned silence. "You *said* I didn't have to call you Mr. Griff anymore."

"Aye, but…I thought you'd just drop the 'Mr.,'" Griff said, rather weakly.

"I thought he meant *Reiner* was here!" Hayley's heart was still hammering with shock.

"Hmm." Griff cocked an eyebrow at Danny. "Lad, I'm afraid this might get a little confusing."

Danny rolled his eyes at their obtuseness. "Katie at school has a Daddy and a Papa, and no one finds *that* confusing. So Daddy's Daddy, and you're Da. That's okay, isn't it?"

Griff looked up at Hayley, his golden eyes silently echoing Danny's question.

"Of course that's okay," Hayley said, to both of them. Blinking back tears, she came down the stairs to embrace them both. "That's *more* than okay."

"Ugh." Danny wriggled, squished between them. "Let go, Mommy. Da stinks."

A rich chuckle rumbled through Griff's chest. He released Hayley, and let Danny slide to the ground. "I bet I do. Sorry, lad. You're going to have to get used to it, I'm afraid."

Griff did indeed reek of smoke. When he'd left this morning, his firefighter's uniform had still been pristine, but now it was covered in scuffs and smudges. There were streaks of soot at his hairline where he hadn't quite managed to wash up thoroughly before coming home from his shift.

He looked tired, and sweaty…and utterly filled with a deep, quiet joy.

Hayley beamed at him, her heart swelling with pride. "First real fire?"

"Aye." He knelt to undo the laces on his filthy boots. "It's good to be back on the team."

Hayley still wasn't tired of seeing him bend his left knee casually, without even the memory of pain. She also wasn't yet tired of seeing him in his firefighter's uniform. And, she secretly had to admit, it was even sexier when he was all rumpled and disheveled from a hard day saving lives.

Griff glanced at her, grinning as he read her thoughts. "And I was worried that *you* were going to be worried." His sweeping gesture indicated the evidence of the dangerous nature of his work. "When you realized what this job actually involves, I mean."

Hayley ducked down to kiss him, an illicit thrill going through her at the taste of smoke on his lips. "I'm not worried. You *are* the Griffin, after all."

His hand captured the back of her neck, holding her close a moment longer. "Amazing woman," he murmured against her mouth. "My lion-hearted love."

He let her go again, straightening. "I'd better go shower before Reiner gets here. Oh, John volunteered to chaperone him for us this evening. You don't mind, do you?"

"No, of course not." Something about Griff's overly casual tone snagged Hayley's attention. "Why?"

"Just thought it would be nice for us to have an evening to ourselves," Griff said, much too innocently. "I thought we might go out."

She narrowed her eyes at him. "What are you up to, Griff?"

Danny chortled, his small face alight with glee. "It's a secret, Mommy. A *big* secret."

Griff mock-growled at him. Danny slapped both hands over his own mouth, his shoulders shaking with muffled giggles. Before he could spill any more hints, Griff scooped him up under one arm, carrying him firmly off upstairs.

Hayley shook her head in bemusement, watching them go. *What was all that about?*

John, when he arrived, only added to the mystery. The sea dragon turned up with an overnight bag, his sword, and an air of great, secret delight.

"I simply thought it might be wise to bring a few essentials with me, my lady," was all he would say. He held up his bag, which made an odd clinking noise, as if whatever John considered essential for a sleepover was made of solid gold. "So that I could guard your territory and your son overnight, if necessary. Just in case you found yourself...delayed."

Hayley couldn't get anything more out of him. His enigmatic silence just fanned the flames of her curiosity. By the time Reiner finally rang the doorbell, she was practically burning up.

What are *they all up to?*

"Hi," she greeted Reiner. For once, she was too preoccupied to feel her usual flutter of apprehension at the sight of him. "Are you in on this too?"

He stared at her blankly. "In on what?"

"Evidently not," Hayley stood aside to let him in. "Never mind. Griff and I are going out. John is going to stay here with you and Danny, okay?"

He nodded distractedly, as if he barely heard her words. He'd been oddly subdued over the last week, ever since he'd returned from his trip home to Valtyra. Now he too seemed preoccupied with something.

"Hayley," he burst out. He drew himself up, setting his shoulders as if bracing himself for a fight. "I have something I need to say."

Hayley eyed him warily. "Griff!" she called over her shoulder. "Reiner's here. He wants to talk to us."

"What about?" Griff had changed into his kilt, and Hayley momentarily lost her entire train of thought. He moved to stand protectively at her side, fixing Reiner with a piercing stare.

Reiner cleared his throat, fidgeting a little. "It...that is...well. You know how I'm paying maintenance for Danny now?"

"Yes, and don't think you're going to weasel out of it," Hayley snapped. "The judge set a very fair level. Don't tell me you can't afford it."

"No! I mean, that is, I can. It's just…I realized that I should have been paying before. All these years, I mean." He pulled a check out of his pocket. "So…I wanted to give you this."

Hayley blinked at him in complete disbelief. "You *want* to give us *more* money?"

The piece of paper trembled, as if Reiner's hand was shaking. "Yes. Please. If you'll accept."

Then he did something very strange. Keeping his head bowed, he knelt to lay the check at their feet.

What is this? Some sort of trick?

"If you think you can *buy* Danny-" Hayley started.

"Hayley," Griff said, very quietly. He'd gone still as stone, his expression utterly blank. "Do you mind if I handle this?"

Hayley threw up her hands. "Be my guest. I have no idea what's going on tonight. Is everyone drunk? Is there something in the air?"

"Quite possibly," Griff murmured. He looked down at Reiner, who was still crouched on the floor, head bowed. "Why?"

Reiner didn't quite meet his eyes. "Because…Danny says you are a good alpha. I, I think perhaps I do not actually know what that means." His mouth twisted, rather ironically. "But in any event, I *do* know that you are certainly stronger than my brother. Stronger than any lion. *No one* could challenge you. No one could shame me for not being able to."

Griff blew out his breath. "We'll…think about it. I can't give you more answer than that right now."

Reiner nodded submissively. "Thank you." To Hayley's complete confusion, he picked up his check, pocketing it again as he rose. "That's all I ask."

"Okay, spill," she finally demanded, after they'd said goodbye to Danny and gotten in the car. "What on earth was all that about?"

Griff glanced at her sidelong as he drove, his expression still rather thoughtful. "If a lion wants to join a pride, it's traditional to lay a gift at the alpha's feet."

Hayley could barely believe she'd heard him right. "Reiner just asked to join your pride?"

"No, he asked to join *our* pride. He was laying the gift at your feet too. He was acknowledging you as the alpha female." Griff shook his head ruefully. "Believe me, I'm as shocked as you."

Hayley chewed her lip. "Do you think it's a ploy? A way to infiltrate us, and get closer to Danny?"

"No." There was absolute certainty in Griff's tone. "From his body language, he was completely sincere. He genuinely wants to join the pride."

"Something must have happened when he went home to Valtyra," Hayley said slowly, thinking back on Reiner's subdued behavior ever since he'd returned. "Maybe his old pride kicked him out."

"No, I would have been able to tell if that had happened." Griff drove in silence for a long moment. "Reiner used to think that being an alpha meant crushing everyone else down and ruling by fear and intimidation. He got that idea from *somewhere*. I think…I think he went home to his own pride, and compared it to ours. I think, perhaps, his eyes have finally been opened."

"Mmph." Hayley folded her arms over her chest. "Well, I'm not yet ready to start feeling sorry for *Reiner*, of all people. Let alone welcome him into the family with open arms."

Griff's mouth quirked in wry acknowledgement. "That's more than understandable. And as alpha female, you've got the final say in whether he ever joins the pride."

Hayley studied his profile. "But *you'd* let him join, if it was up to you?"

Griff didn't answer for a minute, his eyes on the road. "I can't help imagining a scared little boy with amber eyes, without anyone to teach him what it means to be a real lion. I can't help wondering if that scared little boy is still trapped somewhere inside an angry, scared man."

Hayley put her hand on his, on top of the gearstick. "You'd save everyone in the world if you could, wouldn't you?" she said softly.

The laughter lines around his golden eyes creased as he glanced at her. "Comes with the job, I'm afraid. But enough about Reiner for one night. I'm not having him spoil things even when he doesn't *mean* to."

"Agreed." Hayley noticed that they were heading for Griff's house, rather than into the city center. "Hey, I thought you said we were going out on a date, not just back to your place."

"Oh, we'll go out, I promise." There was an odd undertone in Griff's voice, half-laughter, half...nervousness? He parked the car outside his house. "I just need to pick something up from home first."

Hayley had assumed that meant he would run in while she waited in the car, but he came round and opened her door. She gave him a narrow-eyed look as she took his hand. "What, can't you get this mysterious thing for yourself?"

In the darkness, his eyes glowed with a faint, warm light. "Actually, I need you to carry it for me."

Hayley was starting to have an inkling about what was going on. It therefore wasn't *entirely* a surprise when she walked through the front door and into a heady, perfumed cloud of roses and jasmine.

Fragrant blooms overflowed every surface, transforming Griff's simple house into a glorious bower. Tiny, flickering candles provided a romantic light. Even as her heart started to pound with anticipation, Hayley couldn't help being amused by the fact that they were battery-powered LED tealights, rather than real candles.

Trust a firefighter not to leave flames unattended...

"This is what I needed to get." Griff picked up a tiny box from the coffee table. He went down on one knee, taking her hand. "Hayley Parker, will you-"

"*Yes!*"

Griff burst out laughing. "Will you at least let me finish the question?"

"Sorry." Hayley tried to school her face into an appropriately serious expression, but couldn't suppress her wide, foolish grin. "You've clearly worked hard on this. Go ahead."

"Will you marry me?" Hayley opened her mouth, but Griff quickly held up his free hand, forestalling her. "*And* will you be my mate?"

"Yes! Yes! Of course!" Hayley could barely wait for Griff to slide the stunning diamond solitaire ring onto her finger before she threw her arms around his neck. "Oh, Griff!"

Still on his knees, he caught her, easily supporting her weight as their lips met. Hayley closed her eyes, feeling the familiar sweet fire lance through her. No matter how often they kissed, no matter how often they touched…it was always like the first time.

"Will I be able to hear your thoughts, after we're mated?" she murmured against his lips. "Like Connie and Chase, or Virginia and Dai?"

"Aye." His fingers twined tenderly through her hair. His eyes burned with a deep, contented fire. "We'll be truly joined, mind and soul."

She let out a sigh of longing. "I can barely wait."

The heat in his gaze flared brighter. "Well…the wedding will take a little organizing. My clan is fairly extensive. But the mating…*that* just takes the two of us."

The growl in his voice made her shiver in anticipation. "So we could do it now?"

He grinned at her, looking deliciously feral. "I was hoping you'd say that."

"You mean, you knew I'd say that," Hayley teased, as he swept her up in his arms. "Don't think I've forgotten that John was *planning* on staying overnight."

He laughed softly in her ear, holding her cradled against his chest. "I can't help being observant."

She'd been expecting him to carry her upstairs. But instead, he headed for the back garden, carrying her easily in one arm as he opened the door.

"I did promise to take you out," he said, putting her back on her feet. "And I will. Or rather…*up*."

Hayley's breath caught. She hadn't even *seen* Griff fly yet, though she knew he'd been practicing. His eagle sisters had quite literally taken him under their wings, with much delighted teasing at finally being able to get their own back on their big brother. But he'd refused to let her watch his lessons, claiming that his fledgling attempts were far too embarrassing for her to witness.

"You sure I won't weigh you down too much?" she asked anxiously. "I'm pretty heavy, after all."

His hand slid over her curvy hips and round to her backside, lingering in appreciation. "*You* are perfect. *John* is heavy. He helped me practice this. That's why I waited so long to propose. I wanted to make absolutely certain my flying skills were up to the task."

Hayley raised her eyebrows at him. "You do realize most men don't feel the need to be able to fly before proposing, right?"

"Eagle men do. Flying is part of our mating ritual. And I *am* half-eagle." He shrugged one shoulder. "Though that's the other reason I had to make you wait a while. I needed time to puzzle out how to stitch eagle and lion rituals together."

"So what do lions do?"

He captured her chin in his hand, tilting her head up. "You'll find that out later."

Hayley's toes curled as he bent to kiss her again, slow and lingering...and utterly commanding. Her body instinctively molded itself to his, submitting to his irresistible dominance.

When he released her, she swayed, helplessly yearning for him as he stepped back. The January night raised goosebumps on her skin, but her core still burned with a fierce, hungry fire. She wrapped her arms around herself, shivering with cold and desire as he moved back until he had room to shift.

He met her eyes, and smiled. Then, between one breath and the next, the man was gone. In his place stood the griffin, as fantastical as a statue brought to life.

That's something else I'll never get tired of. Seeing him like this.

She ran her hand down the deadly curve of his massive beak, still barely able to believe that this extraordinary, powerful creature was real. Not only that, he was *hers*.

He was the only one of his kind, utterly unique. And he was hers.

With a whisper like silk, he unfurled one vast, gleaming wing, kneeling down so that she could mount. She scrambled up onto his back, straddling his neck where the feathers blended smoothly into golden fur. She had to grab at his feathers for balance as he crouched, his muscles coiling underneath her.

With feline grace, he leaped straight up into the air. Hayley gasped with delight as the ground fell away beneath them, driven away by the powerful beats of his shining wings. She'd always secretly longed to fly…but never, not even in her wildest dreams, had she'd imagined it would be like this.

There were no walls, no boundaries, no limits. She had no fear whatsoever of falling, not with Griff bearing her up. The wind whipping through her hair was frigid, but his solid warmth between her legs heated every part of her body. She was free, the normal world of rules and restrictions left far behind.

The whole glittering night sky was theirs. He bore her up so high, she felt as though she could stretch out and pluck stars out of the sky as easily as harvesting apples. She reached out a hand in awe, and the diamond on her finger glittered as if a star had indeed fallen into her hand.

When they were so high that the thin air burned like ice in her throat, he paused, stretching his wings out to balance on the wind. She felt his chest swell underneath her. He let out a single high, fierce call, proud and wild. Somehow, she knew that he was proclaiming to all the world that she was his, his mate, now and always.

Tears of joy leaked from the corners of her eyes, whipped away by the wind. "Yes," she whispered. "Yes."

Hold on.

The thought was not quite her own. Hayley caught her breath, a faint, tentative presence tickling the back of her mind, light as a feather.

Hayley. Hold on.

She huddled down against his back, wrapping her arms around his feathered neck. His delight sparkled in her head like a distant firework.

Then he folded his wings, and dove.

Hayley screamed in exhilaration and terror as they plummeted like a stone. The wind snatched at her, trying to tear her from his back. She buried her face in Griff's feathers, clinging on for dear life. Blackness gnawed at the edges of her sight. All she could do was close her eyes, hold on, and trust him.

At the very last moment, he flared his wings. They settled back to the ground as lightly as a falling leaf. The griffin's warm back shivered underneath her, shifting into Griff's strong arms.

"They say that the higher and faster the flight, the stronger the bond," he said in her ear.

She twined her arms around his neck, leaning her whole weight against his hard, muscled bulk. Her legs were still weak from the exhilarating swoop. "Then our bond will be as strong as our love."

He made a low rumble of assent, deep in his chest, as his mouth covered hers again. The hot, hungry length of his cock pressed against her stomach. But more than that, she could *feel* his all-consuming desire for her, a fire burning in the depths of her soul. She could feel how the touch of her tongue against his drove him wild, barely able to restrain himself from pushing her down and taking her there and then.

"Not that I want to wait any longer either," she said, pulling back a little to grin up at him, "but it's pretty cold out. How fast can you get us to the bedroom?"

In answer, he seized her waist in both hands. Hayley giggled as he tossed her over his shoulder in a fireman's hold, striding back into the house. In bare seconds, he'd flipped her down onto his bed.

Scattered rose petals brushed against her cheek. Hayley stretched out her arms, like a child making a snow angel, smiling as the scent of crushed petals rose from the sheets. "You *did* prepare thoroughly."

His mouth quirked in amusement. "I promise, *this* time I have condoms."

She hesitated, looking up at him. "Do we...do we really need them?"

"I'm afraid from your scent you're at the peak of fertility, so-" Griff stopped dead, his face going slack with realization. "Oh. *Oh.*"

She dropped her gaze a little, suddenly feeling too shy to meet his eyes. "Sorry, I shouldn't have said that. It's not the sort of decision you should make in the heat of the-"

That was as far as she got before his body covered hers. His bulk pressed her hard into the bed, laying claim to every inch of her. His hands found the sides of her head, holding her as he kissed her with fierce, desperate intensity, as if she was the air he needed to breathe. She closed her eyes in blissful surrender.

"There's no decision to make," he said, his voice shaking with need. "I want more children with you. The only thing I want more than that is *you*. If you're sure..."

"Completely," Hayley breathed against his lips.

He kissed her again, this time just the lightest butterfly brush of his mouth against hers. Then he pushed himself to his hands and knees, holding himself above her. His eyes burned hotter than she'd ever seen before, swirls of fiery gold.

"Mine," he growled. "My mate."

He straddled her, pinning her hips down underneath him. His hands hooked in the neckline of her dress. With a single, sharp motion, he ripped it apart, exposing her body to his ravenous gaze. His fingers slid up under her bra. Hayley caught her breath, her pussy clenching in response as his fingers dug possessively into the softness of her breasts.

"*Mine.*" Pushing her bra up, he freed her nipples for his hungry mouth. Hayley arched against him, gasping. He took advantage of the motion to unhook her bra, jerking it roughly off. Waves of pleasure pulsed through her core as he sucked hard at first one nipple, then the other.

"Griff!" she cried out, tightening her legs around his waist as her climax surged closer.

Before she peaked, though, he released her, pushing her flat against the bed with one hand. "*Wait.*"

Unbelievably, her body obeyed the flex of alpha power in his voice.

He held her on the very brink of orgasm, every part of her throbbing with frustrated need. She writhed, desperate for release, but was helpless under his strength.

His teeth gleamed in a satisfied smile. Lifting his weight off her, he ran his hand lightly down from her breastbone to the curving swells of her stomach. Trails of fire ignited on her skin. She sobbed at the unbearable pleasure, still held back from climax by his alpha command.

He worked his way lower, spreading her legs. He traced her dripping folds so lightly, she wasn't even sure he was even touching her. Even that faint, barely-there caress echoed through every part of her oversensitive body. She was blinded by need, aware of nothing except him.

"Griff, *please!*" Her fists clenched in the sheets. "Please, please, now!"

He moved away, and she sobbed helplessly, utterly bereft at the loss of his heat against her skin. His eyes still held her, demanding her complete submission. She couldn't reach for him, couldn't move, couldn't do anything except watch as he stood back.

Tantalizingly slowly, he undid the belt of his kilt. The heavy fabric dropped away, revealing his proud, straining cock. He was so erect, the swollen head brushed his rigid abs. A pearl of eager moisture glistened on his tip, showing how hard he was having to hold himself back. Nonetheless, his hands moved leisurely, stripping away his clothes with maddening slowness.

Unhurriedly, he spread her legs wide, kneeling between them. His tip pressed against her opening as he covered her body with his, pinning her wrists above her head with his hands. Hayley wanted to squirm, to slide down and take him inside her throbbing passage, but he held her absolutely motionless.

"*Mine,*" he repeated, one last time.

She exploded around him as at last, *at last*, he thrust into her. That single stroke tipped her into a climax more powerful than any she'd ever known. She wrapped around him, taking him into her soul even as she welcomed him into her body. His pleasure was hers, as hers was his, until she couldn't tell the difference between them. At last, they were one.

When she came back to herself, completely limp and undone by the intensity of the experience, she could still feel him in her head. His deep, utter satisfaction and joy glowed in her soul. It was a fire that she knew would never go out, a secret warmth that would last all the rest of their days.

Oh, she thought in wonder, and knew that he heard her as clearly as if she'd whispered in his ear. *So that's what it's like.*

His chuckle rumbled through her bones. He rolled off her, pulling her to spoon against him, her backside fitting into the curve of his body as if they'd been made for each other. *Aye. We're truly mated now.*

"Mmm." Hayley snuggled back against him, delicious tiredness weighing down her limbs. "Do you think we made a baby?" she asked out loud.

"Too early to tell. But the chances are good." He kissed her shoulder. "And if not this time…well, we'll just have to keep practicing, won't we?"

She giggled, closing her eyes in utter contentment. "I wonder what our children will turn out to be. Griffins, like you? Or will some of them be lions, and some eagles?"

"I know what they will be." His hand traced soft, reverent spirals on her belly. "They'll be loved."

Printed in Great Britain
by Amazon